Praise for Michele Hauf

"Hauf mixes well-developed characters and sparkling dialogue with a paranormal tale and comes out a winner."

—*Romantic Times BOOKreviews* on *Kiss Me Deadly*

Praise for Karen Whiddon

"Effortlessly blending suspense and the paranormal, Karen Whiddon draws readers into the plight of sexy, sensitive Jewel Smith."

—*Romantic Times BOOKreviews* on *Cry of the Wolf*

Praise for Lori Devoti

"*Unbound* delivers a truly unique, fast-paced and sexy adventure."

—*Romantic Times BOOKreviews*

Praise for Anna Leonard

"In *The Night Serpent* (4), a myth based in ancient Egypt and strong characters take readers through a plot that's convincingly realistic."

—*Romantic Times BOOKreviews*

Praise for Vivi Anna

"If you like *CSI*, you'll love this smart, sexy and suspenseful trip through Necropolis."

—Bestselling author Rebecca York on *Blood Secrets*

Praise for Bonnie Vanak

"*Enemy Lover* (4) offers nonstop excitement and great sexual tension."

—*Romantic Times BOOKreviews*

MIDNIGHT CRAVINGS

MICHELE HAUF
KAREN WHIDDON
LORI DEVOTI
ANNA LEONARD
VIVI ANNA
BONNIE VANAK

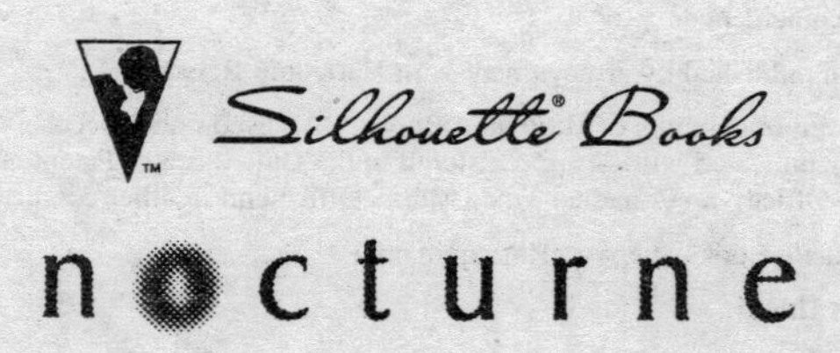

PLEASE RECYCLE · THIS PRODUCT IS RECYCLABLE

Recycling programs for this product may not exist in your area.

MIDNIGHT CRAVINGS

ISBN-13: 978-0-373-25095-0

This edition published by arrangement with Harlequin Books S.A.

Visit Silhouette Books at www.eHarlequin.com

Printed in U.S.A.

CONTENTS

RACING THE MOON

Michele Hauf

To all the regulars who show up at the monthly
Nocturne chats at eHarlequin.com.

MICHELE HAUF

has been writing for over a decade and has published historical, fantasy fiction and paranormal romances. A good strong heroine, action and adventure and a touch of romance make for her favorite kind of story. She lives with her family in Minnesota. You can find out more about her at www.michelehauf.com.

Dear Reader,

I've never been into werewolves. Not sure why. Maybe because vampires fascinate me so much. Then, in *Kiss Me Deadly,* I wrote a small part for the werewolf Severo. He intrigued me enough to want to explore werewolves a little more. Dean Maverick walked into my brain, all sexy and swaggering and desperate to find some sexual healing before the full moon. And what better woman to pair him with than his natural opposite—a cat-shifting familiar. Dean made me fall in love with werewolves. I hope you'll love him, too.

Look for Severo's story this fall in *Moon Kissed!*

Michele

ONE

"Now that is one fine view."

Pulling her tow truck onto the gravel shoulder of Highway 94 behind the stalled Dodge stirred up a whirl of dust. Sunday did a check in the rearview mirror. No lipstick—not her style. At least there were no grease smears on her face.

She hopped out into the evening air thick with the promise of rain and sidled up alongside the stalled truck. The radio blasted an old tune by Honeymoon Suite, and the volume was probably why the fine backside bent over the engine didn't immediately notice her.

Sunday licked her lips as she strolled her gaze over to the tight-fit blue jeans that covered a touch-me-if-you-dare ass. Long legs, slightly bowed, ended at well-scuffed cowboy boots. Standard redneck gear. But there was something different about the guy.

Not like most, her conscience whispered. Ignoring the strange sensation of intuition, she tapped him on the arm.

"Whoa! Didn't see you there. Radio's too loud."

Tall, buff and handsome shot upright from under the hood and flashed a dimpled smile that blinded her. A slight chin cleft and barely there five-o'clock shadow emphasized his square jaw. Short brown hair tufted haphazardly upon his head. Waning sunlight glinted in his gold eyes, and he had a thick lower lip marked with a tiny scar along the bottom right.

Sunday exhaled. Talk about a libido tease.

"Let me turn it down." The music was subdued, and he spun around the front of the hood, dimples intact.

"You figure out the problem?" She bent over the growling engine. Smelled like burned syrup; the engine could be running hot.

"Not yet." He leaned in, brushing her long, bleached hair with a tight, muscled bicep that the black T-shirt strained to encompass. "Engine's still running, but the gas pedal up and gave out."

"Might be the throttle cable."

"Think you can give me a tow to the next town?"

"Steele? That's twelve miles off. My place is just up the road. I can tow it and check it out in the shop."

"You have a shop? Well, this is my lucky day. Gorgeous woman drives up to rescue me, *and* knows a thing or two about cars."

Sunday shrugged and crossed her arms over her chest. The thermometer had hit ninety before ten this morning. Humidity measured on a tropical scale necessitated a tank top, and she never wore a bra. Assuming a shoulder-straight stance, she followed his straying gaze.

He could look all he wanted. She'd reciprocate. It wasn't often fine USDA prime showed up on her stretch of the prairie. The rednecks inhabiting this area were definitely off her radar—as she was off theirs.

It only took a time or two for word to get around when a woman wasn't quite *right* in the sack. The locals avoided her like the proverbial plague.

Catching her gaze on the hug of faded blue jeans low on his hips, she admired the dash of skin that revealed sexy, cut muscles. Her favorite part on a man, that hard, angled ridge that swept from hip to groin.

Bet under the black cotton shirt those abs were rock-hard, too.

Sunday dragged her eyes lower to center stage, and the object of most importance. Nice.

"Wow!" His outburst redirected her attention. "Woman, I don't think I've ever been so thoroughly checked out like you just did. You want me to turn around?" He gestured with his fingers behind his hips.

"Nah, I checked your ass as I was driving up. You'll do." She didn't hide a quirky grin. "Come on, let's get your truck rigged up."

One stranded traveler equaled one much-needed blessing. Business had been poor. Sunday couldn't have given him a ride to town if she'd wanted; the tow truck had just enough gas to make it home.

They'd been listening to the same radio station, which the guy noted as he climbed onto the passenger seat and shoved aside empty root beer bottles on the floor with the side of his boot.

The day had grown long and the sky sepia. Sunday navigated the dusty country roads, edged by four-foot-high cornstalks, to her fifty-acre plot. She lived eight miles out of Steele, and liked her privacy, but necessity demanded she cruise the freeway for broken-down and abandoned vehicles. She certainly wasn't getting any jobs from the locals.

"Drier than a wasteland out there," he commented, holding a palm before the air-conditioning vent. Sunglasses concealed his eyes, but only added to his sexy vibe.

"It's going to rain soon. A lot."

"You think?"

"I know. Can feel it in my bones." She downshifted, but kept her palm on the knob. The smooth steel jiggled in her grip. With tall, dark and dimpled spiking the air with his sensual aura, her imagination was running wild.

Sunday mentally cautioned her libido. Bad things happened when she got so hot.

"You live around here?"

"Nope, headed home to Minnesota," he offered. "I was passing through from Montana. Had to survey some land for a client. I buy up abandoned tracts and auctioned land for environmental-preservation efforts."

"Mighty responsible of you. So what's your name?"

"Ah, sorry. Dean Maverick."

"With a name like that, sounds like you should be riding a mustang through a cigarette ad."

"Yeah? Horses don't like me. I'll stick with the Dodge." An easy charm relaxed his lean frame on the seat, and he tapped his fingers on a knee to the music. "What's your name?"

"Sunday."

"Really? Just Sunday?" Those sexy white teeth could render a woman undone. "Does that come with a cherry on top?"

"Mister, if I had a nickel for every time a guy used that line on me…"

Well, she'd have a nickel. Guys didn't make passes at girls who were more trouble than a tornado on a chicken farm.

But a nickel would get this one a lot more than a tune-up, if he played his cards right.

Dean kicked the snack machine posted at the front of the huge, three-story Quonset garage. The four-car-wide electric door was rolled open, exposing one side of the building to the weird brown sky.

A green-shingled rambler fronted by a faded wood porch sat a hundred yards off. No flowers or yard decorations. Not a single tree for miles. Nor were there visible employees. The chick must live out here alone. She'd explained she took in custom vehicles and anything the boys in the closest town of Steele couldn't handle.

She seemed to like her privacy. Which struck him as odd, because, damn, he'd never met such a gorgeous mechanic in his life. Long and lithe, with a head full of chunky, white-blond locks that twisted haphazardly down her back. The thin blue tank top covered in grease smears made him guess she was about a 36C, and her nipples were constantly hard.

One hand pressed to the snack machine, he glanced over his shoulder. Yep, still hard.

Toeing the base of the machine, he shook his head to clear the licentious thoughts. He so didn't need this right now. He was on a schedule, and hoped like hell she could fix the truck and send him on his way before sundown.

Because the werewolf did not like to be kept at bay.

Pressing the selection button again resulted in no candy bar. He gave the machine one last kick, then strode over to the truck.

"Your machine sucks."

She curled a look up at him from over the engine. Blue eyes surrounded by ribbons of white hair. Mysterious and sexy. And those lips. Dean knew exactly where on his body he'd like to feel that mouth.

"So." He scanned the walls, cringing at the birch-tree wallpaper that decorated the garage interior from floor to ceiling. "You like trees."

"That I do."

"Me, too. Wild, free and forested—that's how I like the world. So if you like trees, why are you here, in the middle of hell knows where, far from any forested land I've seen for hundreds of miles?"

"This is just where I am right now." She stretched forward, groping deep in the engine. The move tugged her shirt high to reveal a taut abdomen. Dean pursed his lips and nodded in appreciation. "I've got a few maples up by the house. Thinking about planting some pines around the garage," she said.

"Good luck with that."

He smoothed a hand over his abs. Should have eaten in Bismarck. But was it hunger for food, or something more visceral? Like flesh on flesh.

She nodded toward the open door. "There's sandwiches up in the house. Why don't you run and grab us a few. Root beer's in the fridge."

"Hospitable of you."

"Just lazy." She chuckled and swiped a hand over her cheek to push back the hair.

And still those nipples called for some dedicated licking. Saliva wet Dean's mouth. "Sandwiches? Right." A necessary distraction. "Unlocked?"

"Yep."

"Boyfriend gonna chase me out?"

She smirked and reached down near the manifold. "That's a chance you'll have to take."

"Can't promise I'll leave him in one piece," Dean said as he strode off.

She called, "Don't get caught in the rain!"

"Don't like rain," he muttered, his boots shuffling over the pea-gravel path up to the house. "And I don't like being stuck alone with Miss Sunday Best when what I really need is to get laid to calm the werewolf."

She had sent him a few *I'm willing* signals. Hadn't been able to drag her eyes from his body when she'd picked him up.

A glance toward the garage spied the shapely figure stretched over the truck engine. Maybe his luck would turn.

She'd spoken true. The only human scent Dean detected upon entering the house was female. No lingering odor from another male. Hell, hers was the only scent he could scavenge, and that was tinted with…something spicy? He couldn't place it, but it would come to him.

There were indeed sandwiches in the fridge. Egg salad. Dean gobbled one down and put back a root beer, then grabbed four more plastic-wrapped sandwich halves and two bottles of pop.

He closed the fridge, and a fifties-style pinup girl winked at him from the calendar taped to the door. He'd seen the same one on the office window in her shop.

"I like a chick into pinups," he decided. "Sunday Best out there can pose over an engine in nothing but high heels and a smile any day. Heck, I'll take her on a Tuesday."

A glance at the clock over the antique gas-burner stove startled him.

"Already seven in the evening? I couldn't have been stalled more than half an hour on the highway. Hell." The sky outside had grown much darker since he'd entered the house ten minutes earlier. "I hope this chick is good. I don't have time to waste."

Arms loaded with sustenance, he pushed open the squeaky screen door with a boot heel—avoiding the built-in cat door—and stepped out onto the warped porch boards.

The sky opened up. Sudden, relentless rain beat down upon his head and shoulders.

Turning back to peer through the screen door, Dean shook his head, sucked it up and made a dash for the garage. He wouldn't tuck his tail between his legs and hide in the house. It wasn't him who hated the rain.

Arms loaded with snacks, Dean sprinted across the yard to the garage. Propping one ankle over the other, Sunday leaned against the Dodge and crossed her arms. She smirked. The fellow had poor timing. She *had* told him it would rain.

Soaking wet, he looked…eatable. The rain-doused shirt clung to impressive pecs, and muscles across his shoulders and arms she hadn't names for. Oh, baby, there was that tight six-pack she'd been wondering about.

The sandwiches dropped from his fists in soggy piles near his boots. He set the pop bottles down. "It's coming down cats and dogs out there!"

Cats and dogs coming? Sunday knew for a fact that cats came hard. But that was another subject entirely. And one she would do best to put from her brain. Mustn't get her hopes up.

Okay, so her hopes were already so high they'd burst through the stratosphere. Sexy stranger stranded in her garage? The fantasy possibilities were endless. Too bad most men didn't go in for *paranormal* fantasies.

Weird was not a requirement—all Sunday needed was flesh on flesh, hot and sweaty and furious—but often weird was inevitable.

Still cussing about the rain, the man shook himself off. Methodically. Working from head down to hips he shimmied efficiently and expertly. Sunday had never seen a *person* shed rain in such a manner.

He glanced at her, and his eyes caught the overhead lights and reflected—

"Oh, hell, no."

It wasn't something she would have picked up about the man on sight. But she'd seen the shake, the mirrored eyes and now noticed that his five-o'clock shadow had actually grown to become stubble.

Sunday marched across the cement floor and lashed out. A threatening hiss accompanied her defense—claws across his square jaw.

TWO

The man growled like a dog and snapped his jaws as Sunday swung through the move. Blood pooled in three thin lines.

"What the—?" He touched his bleeding jaw.

Then his eyes changed. The gold orbs grew darker and the pupils widened. An animal snarl preceded his lunge for Sunday.

Pushing her against the wall and pinning her wrists by her head, he then shoved his entire body against the length of hers to contain her struggles.

She hissed again, not caring that it sounded animalistic. Instincts reacted before common sense, always. "You're a damn werewolf!"

"Ah." He tilted his head and those dimples deepened. "How'd you guess that one?"

"Normal men don't shake themselves off like that. Your eyes are wild. And your beard's growing faster than mold on cheese. Let me go!"

"Oh, no." He pressed closer. She felt his erection against her mons. *Mercy.* "You always greet your customers with a kitty-cat scratch like that? Oh, wait one moonlight minute. You know about me because—"

He eyed her curiously, sniffing at the air before her. Sunday watched the claw marks on his jaw heal over until they were but crusted blood.

"You're a familiar?" He released her and jerked away as if she were made of silver. Brushing both palms over his scalp, he splayed his hands in frustration. "So I had the cat thing right?"

Wishing she had a piece of silver to crush against the creep's forehead, Sunday rubbed her wrists. She bruised easily. Sweet, though, that she'd drawn blood. That'd show him she wasn't afraid of much. A werewolf? Not exactly on the top of her list, but she wouldn't flee with her tail low—not this cat.

It couldn't get any weirder than this.

Stalking before him, flexing her fingers into fists, she lowered her head and looked up through her lashes. "I think you need to leave."

"You fix my truck?"

Stating the obvious wasn't going to help his case. It was the throttle cable, and she didn't have a replacement. The man had no means to leave.

"I called in to town for parts. A shipment arrives tomorrow morning."

"Then it sounds like I'm staying the night, whether I like it or not. Don't worry." He shot her a wink and a cocky smile. "I can play nice with kitty cats."

"Call me that one more time and I'll scratch the other cheek. It's a pretty face. I'd hate to leave you all scarred and mangy."

"Ooh, you like it rough? So do I. We can talk scratches if that's what gets you off."

She huffed. Getting her off would leave him with a hell of a lot more than mere scratches.

"Come on, Sunday, you can't stop checking me out. You want to spend a rainy evening getting it on?" He gestured toward the tremendous downpour twenty feet away. "Not like we have anything better to do."

Now he was just making her…hot. What she wouldn't like to

do with those rock-hard abs and that long erection that she could still feel pressed against her.

But she didn't do dogs. They were off her radar. Not that cats and dogs couldn't have sex, they just never mixed well. A wise cat walked a wide path around a canine.

"I think it's best you lope off to town, wolf. There's a motel at the edge of the freeway. They let all sorts in."

"Name's Dean. And I'd love to wolf out and scamper off to town, but the wolf hates rain."

Sunday rolled her eyes.

"Roll 'em all you like, kitty cat. You're stuck with me. And if you know what's good for you, you'll put aside your prejudices and start being a little nicer to the guest."

"I'm not prejudiced. I just don't do dogs. Especially not dogs who think they can seduce a woman by shoving her around."

He held her by the shoulders in less than a blink. Despite what she'd just said, it did send a titillating shiver through her every time he touched her, rough or otherwise.

"I'm not a dog," he said on a tight growl that pulsed the tense muscle in his jaw. "Got it?"

She nodded. He didn't release her, and for a moment the twosome remained fixed in a challenging stare-down.

She could give him a ride to town, but they'd run out of gas halfway. That would still leave them stranded, and one of them walking with a gas can in the downpour. Why didn't he like rain?

The only other option was to let the randy wolf stay.

She'd wanted him before she'd known what he was. And, Lord, but she still did.

You think you're dangerous having sex? Probably having sex with a werewolf trumps the few mishaps you've had, Sunday.

Rational thinking was never rewarding.

"All I can offer is the extra room up the stairs. It's got a cot. You can spend the night. Then, when the part arrives in the morning, I'll send you on your way."

"You going to hunker down beside me?"

"In your dreams, wolf boy. I've a cozy bed up at the house. And if you're as freaked by the rain as you claim, I guess I'll be safe from the big bad wolf sniffing for a treat."

"Can't do the overnight thing without you, Sunday."

"Is that a fact? Anyone ever tell you your seduction skills lack finesse?"

"Yeah? Well, try this."

He tugged her around and pulled her over to the office window where the calendar hung. Stabbing today's date with his finger, he pointed out the small white moon shape at the bottom of the entry.

Sunday didn't need a lecture to know this night was going to be a trip. "Oh, crap."

THREE

Sunday paced to the edge of the garage. Sheets of silvered rain poured down from the south. The garage door faced north, so she didn't get wet. She didn't mind the weather, and could make a dash to the house whenever she wished. But if the wolf didn't do rain, that meant Dean was literally stranded inside the Quonset.

The *were*wolf.

Man, she had to fine-tune her instincts. Should have known he wasn't right when she picked him up. She had felt that twinge of him being different. Yet it hadn't been an *emergency, stop and flee* sort of feeling.

Most paranormal sorts could tell their own species—vampires had the shimmer, witches had a knowing, weres and familiars could tell by scent—but determining someone not your species was next to impossible unless they bit you or tried to take your head off.

Or you recognized a feral shake and mirrored eyes.

But he was here now, looking like her dirtiest and hottest fantasy, and Sunday had to deal with the fact that when the full moon was high in the sky, Dean Maverick was going to wolf out.

And if she knew one thing it was that wolves did not like cats. She'd be supper for sure.

Unless the werewolf was kept at bay. Which went a long way in explaining his randiness.

Werewolves—in their human, or as they called it, *were*-form—could tame the beast by having sex the night of the full moon. And while she'd been fooling herself earlier about taking the man home and having her way with him, now reality pulled the needle sharply across the vinyl.

There were reasons she hadn't had sex for close to a year. Scary reasons. Even scarier than a raging werewolf.

A touch to her elbow made her jump. "Watch the sneak, wolf!"

"Sorry. Didn't mean to scare you. We need to talk about this."

"There's nothing to say." She strode to his truck and yanked down the hood, slamming it loudly. "I can't help you. Not with your truck. Not with your..." Her eyes wandered to his crotch. "Oh, mercy."

Snapping her gaze away from the awe-inspiring sight, she wondered now if she might have the engine part buried in one of the junk piles out back. It would be worth the headache of digging if she could get this guy out of here before midnight.

"You can't help—or you're just not interested?"

She smirked, but didn't turn to face him. Because that would require more fortitude than her sex-starved skin could manage right now. "Can't."

"So that means you *are* interested? I can work with that."

"Yeah? Well, you do your thing. I'm going to take a look around, see if I can snake out the part from the junk I've got sitting around here."

She wasn't giving him the official "no." *Can't* didn't necessarily negate *interest.* Dean swiped a hand over his jaw. Another few hours and he'd have a full beard.

He didn't mind wolfing out, but not around strangers. And only when at home, where he was familiar with the terrain, and knew where he could wander without fear of encountering humans. The werewolf didn't mangle or kill humans—it stuck to small animals. But it was never wise to let the mortals know that a creature they believed imaginary was real.

And if he were at home, he'd be in bed having sex right now. He had a female posse he relied upon to appease the werewolf. Call them girlfriends; call them a means to an end.

Yeah, he was getting tired of the booty call. But rarely did a male wolf find the atypical female wolf to take as a mate these days. And mortal girlfriends were out. They couldn't handle the freak factor.

Made for a lonely life. But he wasn't complaining. Much.

The dangerous thing about this situation was that if he didn't have sex—and soon—the werewolf would emerge, take one look at Sunday and know what she really was. A shape-shifting familiar who, when not in human form, was a cat.

The wolf put cats on the same level as rabbits and squirrels—sustenance. Realizing his entire musculature had tensed, Dean shook out his shoulders and arms. A tilt and snap of his head served a wolflike means of putting it all off. He had to stay alert, but not strung so tight something minor would set him off. He muttered a prayer for the rain to stop. He didn't pray often, but it was always worth a shot.

A radio in the office blasted a Nickelback song that he liked. The pounding rhythm competed with the rain clattering on the corrugated steel roof. Toward the back of the garage, Sunday dug through a wooden pallet crate, tossing clanking metal parts aside.

Beyond the grease and oil and gasoline a very distinct scent tendriled into Dean's nose. It had toyed with him while he was sitting in the tow truck, and he'd been unable to pinpoint it in the house. He closed his eyes, wishing it away, but knew the more he tried not to think about it, the more it would fix deep into his pores.

Gingerbread?

"No luck."

Sunday perched on the edge of the wood crate, fitting the toes of her Doc Martens down the slats. Dean paced before the garage door, a beast caged. The sky was dark, and she couldn't see the moon from this side of the garage. The clouds and rain would likely keep it out of sight all night.

But out of sight did not imply safety.

If the rain would let up, he could dash off to town and settle in a motel. Which, she decided, could be dangerous to the townspeople. What kind of havoc would a lone werewolf cause in the tiny town?

She didn't want to consider the options. Nor did she owe it to anyone in town to keep them safe from a crazed wolf on the hunt.

Sighing, she shrugged her fingers through her hair. It intrigued her to watch him. He paced such a focused path that she could almost see the animal loping back and forth, frantic for escape.

"You bake cookies today?" he called across the garage.

"You saw my kitchen. Sandwiches are as creative as I get. Don't tell me a cookie will tame you."

"No, I smell gingerbread on you. Makes my mouth water."

Huh. Must be the spicy shower gel she'd used this morning.

He paused and looked up, his broad shoulders blocking out the distant yard light. "I have a craving for gingerbread."

"You always get what you want, wolf boy?"

"Usually."

Dimple alert. He was so confident and brimming with easy charm that Sunday smiled. It was hard not to like a man who reminded her a lot of herself. Stubborn, insistent and not about to let anyone tell him what to do—all served up with a *kitten in cream* smile. Or in his case, *the dog with the mountain of chew toys* smile.

"Maybe you need a lesson in denial." She jumped from her perch. "Sucks to be you, eh?"

"It's going to suck even more for you. And I'm not trying to be a jerk, I'm just stating the facts."

"I repeat, seduction skills—zero. Hand me one of those root beers."

She twisted off the bottle top and tilted it back.

"At least I give seduction a go. You catch a lot of men with your charm?" He nursed his own bottle.

"What makes you think I need to catch them?"

"So they fall all over you? I can see that. Can't understand why a sexy looker like you is stuck in this dirty old garage in the middle of nowhere."

"What, you think I should be wearing a little black cocktail dress and flirting over an appletini?"

"Works for me."

Sunday rolled her eyes. "If that's your taste—"

"My taste is for gingerbread, kitty cat." He winked and took her empty bottle from her.

"Because you've no other options. Tell me you'd even be interested if you weren't in such a dire situation."

"I would." He stepped close, and the heat of him radiated to permeate her thin shirt and tease her insides. Gold eyes took in her features, slow and sure. "Not too many women can pull off the greasy mechanic look as well as you. And I gotta guess this is like a dream of yours. You really love your cars, and this is what makes you happy, and screw anyone who scoffs."

She lifted a brow.

"I like a woman who knows exactly what she does and doesn't want. You don't want me? I can dig it."

"I didn't say I didn't want *you.*" It wasn't even the werewolf that disturbed her. It was the familiar.

"Yeah," he said, leaning in closer. "I kind of thought you liked me."

He brushed his cheek against hers. The soft stubble sent a tickle tracing from Sunday's face down to her breasts. Goose bumps prickled her skin in the wake. Her fingers curled but she resisted reaching up to pull him closer.

"Damn, you smell good. Sure you won't let me have a taste?"

Oh, hell, yeah. But tastes always led to sips and suckles and then to something akin to devouring. Which sounded *so* not bad that Sunday blurted out, "I've never kissed a wolf."

"I've never kissed a familiar." Ambient light glinted in his eyes. Too warm and inviting for a man who was still a stranger. "Is it true what they say about familiars?"

"What is it you've heard?"

"About the sex thing and…you know, the demons."

Relieved she didn't have to introduce that six-hundred-pound gorilla, Sunday nodded.

"We are a bridge for demons to this mortal realm, yes. But familiars can control that entry, and usually need a conduit to bring the demon through, like a witch to conjure a summoning or speak a spell."

"That's what I've heard. So you, er…do that a lot?"

"Does it creep you out?"

"No more than a werewolf clawing at your back door would creep you out."

Which put things in perspective.

Sunday tugged the pop bottles from his grip, and spun to go toss them in the recycle bin at the back of the garage.

FOUR

Dean paced before the truck. Every bone in his body wanted to run away, to lope across the fields and put himself as far as possible from the sexy woman behind the office window.

But an even bigger part wanted to remain with his boots planted on the garage floor.

When he'd stood close to Sunday, rubbed his cheek against hers, he'd tasted her sweetness with every pore. Her gingerbread and calendar-girl, come-give-me-a-try essence had moved slowly through his veins, thickening his desire. She wasn't one of those fragile tea sippers who worried about lipstick or runs in their nylons. Cell-phone texting and cocktail hours were way off her radar. Her naturally red lips and sensual energy put all the women he'd had previously to shame.

And that excited him.

If he closed his eyes he could already imagine running his hands over her supple body. Sloping them down her neck and taking a dive from her shoulder, he'd trace the smooth insides of her elbows down to her wrists. With his tongue, he'd stake claim to her nipples, stroking the rigid peaks and feeding upon her excited moans. He'd ease his hardness inside her, pulling her roughly to his hips so he was fully hilted.

Such thoughts only made him harder, if that was possible.

A sharp crack and a spray of sparks jolted him out of his reverie. Swinging around, he scanned outside. A burning odor invaded the curtain of rain. A snapped power line snaked upon the ground. The lights in the garage blinked to darkness.

Sunday's vision adjusted to the dark. She found a flashlight in the top desk drawer and walked out to hand it to Dean. His mirrored eyes flashed as the light swept his face; she knew hers flashed, as well. "So you don't trip and fall."

He pulled her toward him and whirled her to land against his chest, the flashlight pressed along her spine. "Bet I can find you faster in the dark than daylight, kitty cat."

She turned to face him, and placed her hands on his muscular upper arms. Her fingers curled and she vacillated, digging her nails in, but the hard pecs beneath her palms invited interest instead of retreat. Flesh like suede warmed under an oppressive sun, pearled with dew. One lick would never quench her thirst.

"Cat got your tongue?" he asked.

"I *am* the cat," she whispered. "And don't you forget I snarl and scratch when I'm put in a position I don't like."

"You seem pretty comfortable right now."

His hand glided up her back. At the illicit touch, her spine curved, arching her torso and pressing her breasts against the fire-honed sculpture of his chest. The thought niggled that she still hadn't gotten that kiss.

Dean murmured on a husky growl, "Your hard tits feel good against me. And I can smell your want."

Sunday didn't move from his embrace. "What does *want* smell like?"

"Gingerbread, motor oil and sex. God, Sunday, if you're not interested then you should stay back. Go on up to the house. I can't touch you and then stop. You don't understand what's going on inside me. When the werewolf is so close, it ratchets everything up a notch. Every touch is felt tenfold, and, hell, my cock just can't stand the pressure."

She nodded over her shoulder. "You need to go take care of business in the office?"

A growl preceded the hard kiss. It was a blissful attack of want, desire and raw need. Such demand at his mouth. Did he seek to control her?

Sunday answered with equal determination. She would not be owned.

The hand at her back skimmed lower, cupping her ass. Dean lifted and set her on the wood pallet without breaking the kiss. Root beer tainted his breath and the surprising sweetness spurred her to take as greedily as he did.

He bruised her defenses. Softened her will. He wanted to possess, to get inside and stake a claim.

Sunday wrapped her legs about his hips. He growled and shoved his hard-on against her pelvis, grinding, making her know he was in this for the payoff.

But she couldn't deliver.

"No." Sunday pushed away and leaned back. There was nothing but a stack of car parts behind her.

Dean caught her before she fell. "Yes, say yes, please."

Her legs still clasped his hips. His hardness pulsed against her groin, insistent and needy. Sunday wanted to unzip him and put her hands all over the rigid prize. But if she couldn't deliver then she had no intention of teasing.

"I can't." She extricated herself and jumped down, fleeing to the edge of the garage, where one dash into the downpour would keep her safe from the lusty wolf.

Outside, the live wire lay coiled on the ground, snapped from the overhead lines. Would it spark all night, even in the rain? It was how she felt. Sparking and coiling inside, one ember away from igniting a fire.

Dean remained bent over the pallet crate, head bowed, hand

easing down the front of his jeans. She'd already stirred him into some kind of frenzy. She took no satisfaction in being a tease.

Stepping out into the pummeling rain, Sunday shouted out her frustrations.

Strong arms grabbed her in from the rain. "Are you crazy? There's a live wire out there!"

Hugging her, Dean possessed the shivering woman, wrapping his arms across her back. He pressed his nose into her hair, closing his eyes. She'd been so close to getting electrocuted. Damn, he hardly knew Sunday, but his heart pounded as if he could have lost a mate. A real mate. Someone he could grow old with.

Was that some kind of crazy thinking? The last person he should take as a lover—let alone a mate—was a familiar.

"I wasn't thinking," she said. "Let me go."

If only she'd let *him* go. Because he was bound here by something beyond the rain and a malfunctioning truck. The beating of his heart measured the minutes he wished to remain.

One, two, three…endlessly.

Was it lust? He should have taken off walking in the rain. He might be far from any humans by now; the werewolf would just have to deal with the storm.

The two squared off at the edge of his flimsy prison. Soaked, water streaming down her face, Sunday didn't make a run. Her shirt, completely drenched, caressed the pebbled texture of her nipples.

Dean sucked in a breath and stopped his twitching fingers from reaching for her—and then he said a mental *screw it* and did reach.

His thumb rolled over her hard nipple. Her startled gasp ended in an abrupt cry as he clasped her hip, claiming her, keeping her close. He was ready to discover what it was that wouldn't release him from her ineffable draw.

"What are you struggling with, Sunday?" He leaned in and nipped her hard bud. "Talk to me. You know my deal. No sex? The werewolf comes out. What's yours?"

She squirmed as he slid a hand under her wet shirt and rolled it up to expose her bare breasts. "God, they're perfect."

Her fingers snaked across his scalp and pulled his head in as he licked her. The move said, *don't stop.* And yet she wasn't making this very easy.

"I..." The scrape of her nails through his hair sent shivers down his neck. *Do it some more* shivers. "That's so good. I need this."

"Then let's do it. No more fooling around." He pulled her shirt over her head and tossed it out into the rain. His shirt followed.

Sunday lunged to press her hands to his pecs. The touch snapped through him as if the live wire outside had tapped flesh. He wondered if he wouldn't give off his own sparks from the electric connection.

"Tell me you want this," he begged. She grazed his nipple with her teeth. Dean sucked in his upper lip. Mercy, what a wicked feline. "I'm going to take no answer as a yes," he warned.

She shot away from him. The shadows held color. Even in darkness, his acute vision found her. Her breasts were high and rosy, and long white hair spilled wetly over the gorgeous globes.

Shoulders back and a wistful look casting her eyes to the side, she said, "It's not right. I can't do this. I'm so sorry."

She turned to walk away, but Dean raced after her. Passing her by, he pressed his back to the hood of the truck as she charged into him. "Look at me, Sunday."

Her blue eyes fixed defiantly on his. She sighed and hooked her thumbs in her belt loops.

"You're so gorgeous," he breathed. Half bared and proud of it, she defied his need for command, for mastery over others. A fine match to his aggressive nature. Most others usually took what he gave, and didn't ask for more. Yet her reluctance fed his eagerness. "It's because this feels wrong to you, right? Like you're just servicing a need I have?"

"No, I have that same need."

"Then let me take care of it." He dropped to his knees, licking down from her belly button as he did. Her shivering skin softly abraded his cheek. The softness of her seemed surreal as he knelt here in the shop perfumed by motor oil. Pressing his stubbled jaw to her zipper, he raked his fingers around and across her ass. "Kitty cat sounds real good to me right now."

"Yeah, well, demons don't." She lifted a boot and kicked his shoulder, landing him against the wheel of the truck.

"I can't do this," she said, turning to put her bare back to him. "Because I can't control it. If I have sex, a demon will bridge to this realm. And there's no telling if it'll be good, bad or homicidal."

FIVE

Sunday stared at the power line coiled on the ground before the garage. Sparks had ceased, but she was all too aware it could prove deadly. The world stood in darkness, save the pale flashlight beam that glanced across the floor from under the truck where it had rolled.

She contemplated fishing for her shirt with a long stick, but it was muddy. She wasn't cold, and the fine mist that hissed out from the rain curtain felt like faery kisses against her breasts.

It would feel much better to have Dean's mouth at them again. His strong arms embracing her, moving her to positions that pleased him. Drawing from her kisses the energy he gave back to her threefold.

A wild animal proved mysterious, graceful, bewitching to behold. Dean was electric, spellbinding. Feral. She'd never imagined what it might be like to make out with a wolf. In her lifetime she'd had one demon lover; the rest had been mortals. Scared witless mortals after the climax part.

She didn't think a demon would scare Dean. But dealing with the brimstone bastards after they'd bridged here was no day at the park. And when she did climax, she then usually shifted to feline shape—without volition.

This was why she didn't do boyfriends.

Yet why should she be cursed to not enjoy sex?

"Gotta get that bridging thing under control," she muttered.

In familiar years, she was yet young, at an actual mortal twenty-five years. Most familiars didn't master bridging until their second lifetime—yes, they had nine.

It wasn't as if she had opportunity to practice. Surely if she and a partner took things slow, allowing her to focus and get a handle on the ineffable force that opened her to demons, she might achieve control.

"I'm destined to die a lonely old kitty cat. At least in this lifetime."

Sighing, she perked her ears to listen. Back by the truck, Dean paced again. She could feel his urgency, the agonizing restraint of his desire, float through the air on a tangible wave of sensual musk.

Closing her eyes, she willed the rain to stop, to release him from the anxiety, and her from the awful dilemma she didn't want to face.

Was she scared of ending up with a fully shifted werewolf? Yes. A lot. She didn't want to get tossed around like a stuffed animal and likely mauled. Scribble that one under least preferable ways to die.

"I could give it a try." The voice sounded softly at her side.

Dean stood just behind her. The heat of his presence tickled down Sunday's spine, leaving an indelible tattoo in its wake. *Yes, mark me. Make me yours as no other has.*

"I could make a run for town. It's the wolf that doesn't do rain. But in this were-form, I can."

Were was the man. Wolf meant the animal that walked on four legs. And werewolf? Man and wolf combined.

"And what would you do in town? Molest some innocent woman?"

"I don't harm humans, Sunday."

"I didn't mean to imply you would. Sorry." But hearing him say it eased a wonder she hadn't known she had. "I just, well, I suppose it's better that you stay here, blue balls or not, than risk the werewolf stalking Steele."

"That had occurred to me. I won't kill 'em, but I will freak them all out. And it's getting so close to midnight, I'd never have time to romance a woman into my arms."

"Romance? Is that what you're trying with me?"

"Hey, give a guy a little credit, the booty call is out of this area code tonight."

"Booty—so that's all I am to you?"

"I shouldn't have put it that way. Hell, Sunday, I don't claim to be a smooth operator. And I don't have roses or chocolates—"

"I don't need material things to be romanced. Just honesty. You've been very honest with me. I appreciate that."

"You have, too. Probably haven't been too many times you've wanted to reveal your *condition* to a potential lover. So…you can't control it?"

She nodded and rubbed her arms. "It's not a condition. It's simply who I am."

"I'm not afraid of demons."

Sunday smirked and cast him a look over her shoulder. "That desperate for sex, eh?"

He lifted his shoulders and sighed.

"So what's it like for you with other guys? I mean, seems like your dating life—"

"Sucks the big one. Trust me, men don't come looking for another date after they've seen me climax."

"Maybe it's not mortals you should be dating in the first place." He touched her back, but didn't do any more than that. Bless him. She was strung high enough as it was. "The taste of you is in my mouth. I need more."

"I want you, too, Dean. It's just not feasible. Don't take this personally, okay?"

"I'll try not to. Why don't you step over here and let me hold you? Want me to fish out your shirt for you?"

"I'm fine. I've a spare shirt in the office."

A step put her back against his chest. The man was hard and soft at the same time. Muscles of stone yet flesh of suede. Warm arms wrapped under her breasts and held her possessively.

Could she mark him across the chest with the invisible tattoo he'd pricked down her spine? Yes, let everyone know he was hers. For now. A stranger stranded in her heart.

Sunday snuggled her cheek against his shoulder. This quiet contact felt good. And for the moment, unthreatening. "So, your truck. It's a classic. You take good care of her, I can tell."

"The outside. But I obviously don't know what the hell I'm doing when it comes to the mechanical stuff."

"You must have been racing the moon to get home, eh?"

"You know it. The werewolf is best only released on its own territory."

"You speak of that part of yourself as if it's another entity."

"I don't remember what's gone on after I've been the werewolf. Makes it difficult to feel as if it's a part of me. Do you feel like the cat is you?"

"Always. Unlike you, I do remember while in cat shape. I don't shift often though. I enjoy this human flesh too much."

"It is some fine flesh. Soft and smelling like gingerbread."

"Too bad wolves don't get along with felines."

"Yeah." He rested his chin on her shoulder. "Or so they say."

"You with a pack?"

"Nope. There's only one left in Minnesota, and Severo—an old werewolf with control issues—keeps a tight rein on that pack. I prefer freedom and quiet, and don't get into pack politics."

"Must be lonely though. I spend a lot of time by myself, and…sometimes I just want to belong, you know?"

"Understand completely. It's not easy being what we are in this world of humans. Rarely do we find someone who can relate to the utter separation from the majority. I know what it's like to be different."

Sunday canted her head back across his broad shoulder. "Yeah, different."

She'd always been the different one. The one humans stepped a wide path around, even not knowing what she was, but somehow sensing it. She didn't mind being a familiar—she'd known nothing else—but sometimes she wanted to be accepted for what she was, and not have to hide.

Dean's hands moved to caress her breasts, and she allowed the easy, lingering strokes. It felt terrific to be touched by a man—one who was not afraid of her danger.

A man who presented his own, equal danger.

Maybe the risk would be worth it for the earth-shattering sex she knew they could have. Even now, as he massaged her nipples, her sex grew hot and moist. She squeezed her thighs together, sending a shimmer of sensation through her system.

Dean's hot tongue traced the side of her neck, gliding along the jugular. Now, vampires she did not tolerate, and she would quickly stake a sexy night brooder, with little regret.

"You thinking about vampires?" he asked, his mouth still at her neck.

She chuckled. "Hate 'em."

"Me, too. Glad to know we share the same priorities." He nipped at her vein. Hugging her, he lifted her feet from the ground briefly. "Damn, I can't *not* touch you."

She turned and pressed her breasts just under his stone-hard pectorals. The sound of his sucked-in breath bolstered her confidence. They could do this. She wasn't about to let the opportunity slip through her fingers. "Maybe foreplay would be enough?"

"I don't think so."

"Then what if I get you off? That would work."

"And deny your own climax? Uh-uh, no way. This man doesn't work that way. I want you shuddering and moaning, Sunday, nothing less."

"But it's the only way."

"Actually..." He stepped back, releasing her hand and the dimples at the same time. "I have an idea."

Sunday flinched at the sound of the shotgun chambering a bullet into the barrel. Dean stood proudly, holding the sawed-off he'd retrieved from the cab of his truck.

"You really do suck in the romance department. Is that supposed to be sexy?" she wondered aloud.

"Hell, no. It's for killing demons."

"A rifle will only piss most demons off."

"Yeah, but it'll blow off body parts long enough for you to get your act together and reverse the bridging. Yes?"

He was on the right path. She needed time in order to focus and reverse the bridging—and a witch to control the demon. She'd never tried it on her own. But maybe it would work. Anything was possible.

The man certainly did want sex. And so did she.

She crooked a finger at him, and he followed her silent command to approach. Dean's mouth fit over her breast and he lifted her with one hand. Wrapping her legs around his back, she let loose a shivery murmur as he carried her to sit on the truck's hood.

The shotgun barrel banged her elbow. Sunday grabbed the gun and set it aside on the hood. "Guns and sex don't mix for me, big boy. Keep it close, but don't think it's some kind of toy that'll get me off."

"Wouldn't dream of it." He kissed her hard along her neck.

No soft, tickling kisses from this man. The intensity of his quest captured her in the rush, the excitement, the need to move forward faster. Everything was high-octane and furious. Exactly how she liked her cars.

"You said there was a bed up the stairs?"

"A wobbly cot. But there's a wool blanket we could toss in the back of the truck bed."

"I like the way you think. Don't move. I'll be right back."

SIX

Rain still mercilessly clattered the steel roof. Navigating the garage in the darkness was instinctive. Dean found the extra room. A sharp pine odor erased Sunday's sexy-sweet scent from his sinuses. A tree-shaped air freshener hung from the pull chain below the bare lightbulb. An army-issue folding cot supported by six narrow wooden legs stood in the corner. A shove made it wobble.

"This thing is only good for careful sex." He grabbed the blanket. "I like my sex a bit more dangerous."

And the woman waiting downstairs was about as dangerous as they came.

He jumped over the top-floor banister to the garage floor, landing with a deft squat.

"Show-off," Sunday said. He tossed her the blanket. "Let me put this down."

She'd let down the truck gate and leaned over to spread the blanket across the steel bed. Dean grasped her hips and eased his erection against her fine ass. She didn't have much of a booty, but the curvy hips were just right.

"We going to play this my way?" she asked.

He lifted her onto the truck bed. She slid up to pull him in for a deep kiss. Man, she could put him to his knees with this kiss.

There was something about a woman who did exactly as she pleased that fired all his worship reflexes.

"What way is that?"

"We satisfy you first, and worry about me later."

"I don't like that idea, because I want you to take your pleasure, too."

She slipped a finger down behind the waistband of his jeans, and skimmed his erection. Now that was a knee-worshipping-worthy move. "You won't be able to deny me pleasure, wolf boy. But I like the idea of holding back my climax as long as possible. Because once I come, then the party is so over, I promise you that."

"All right then. Deal." He grimaced.

A familiar spark snapped through his limbs. It had nothing to do with lust. Dean clutched his gut.

"Dean? What's wrong? Hell, your beard is really getting thick. What time is it?"

"Close to midnight, for sure."

"Hang on. There's a clock in the office."

She slipped from the truck bed and scampered off.

"No, Sunday!" He gripped the wool blanket and gritted his teeth.

"Idiot. The clock is electric." Sunday pounded the desktop alarm with a fist. Pulling open a drawer, she shuffled about in the darkness. "I know there's a watch in here somewhere."

She shouldn't be wasting time looking for, well, the time. It was apparent the man was going to change soon. Maybe that was why she'd fled?

"You're not afraid," she tried confidently. Her breath shivered out on a reedy whimper. Sunday clasped her hands before her chest. Her lungs seemed to clamp shut. "Maybe a little. No. Not afraid of the big bad wolf. Just..." She was unsure of what was really happening here. Because it was more than two lusting bodies furiously going at it. There was something about Dean Maverick. She really liked him. And Sunday hadn't liked a man for ages.

She was startled that they were so similar. They listened to the same music. Appreciated classic cars. Drank root beer. Hated vampires. They were both loners who wanted to be accepted.

A familiar and a wolf? It just wasn't right,was it?

Her fingers played across a cracked plastic strip. She tugged out the watch, but even with her excellent night vision it was impossible to read the small face.

"Now," Dean's voice thundered from the doorway.

Sunday started to turn, but Dean grasped her from behind. Their collision pushed her against the desk, and she caught her palms upon the gnarled wood surface.

Dean's hot breath rasped in her ear. "Changing. Quickly." His entire body thrust against her, wanting to become one with her. "Gotta do this…" He let out a strained cry, half excitement, half frustration.

Now or never. Face the wolf or bring forth demons. Hell of a choice. But easy, because she knew she wouldn't be denied the pleasure she craved. Or the connection she wanted with this man.

"Yes." Sunday slid her hands behind and over his bare hips. He'd removed his jeans. She unzipped hers. Soft denim slid down her thighs. "I'm ready for this."

"Are you?" He bent her forward over the desk. He grunted as his body convulsed against hers, obviously reacting to some inner torment. "Ready? To take me?"

Her heart raced. Her body hummed. Fear had decided to strike. But it was still small. Moreover, she was hot for this half-crazed man who simply had to have her—or he'd become a beast.

"I—" he growled "—can lock myself upstairs. Maybe… Sunday, please!"

He was still trying to protect her, even as his body fought against the moon's insistent command.

She bumped her butt against his cock. And then she ground hard against his straining thighs and abs, inviting, promising she was in for the wild ride.

Dean groaned and slapped a hand on the desk near her arm. Claws jutted out from the fingers. Knuckles bulged and flesh stretched. The entire hand began to lengthen. Fingers curled, breaking wood and tearing easily through the desktop.

Another hand—paw—slapped across her stomach in a tight clutch.

"I love you for this," he growled.

Her feet left the ground briefly as he impaled her. He entered her hot core with a forceful glide. His thickness abraded her insides in the best way. Sunday gasped at the delicious fullness.

His intensity filled her, coursed through her being—the connection, the slap of flesh upon flesh, desire conquering need.

Pinpricks pierced her stomach. Claws lengthened. He was still changing.

"Faster," she cried. "We can do this."

He took directions well. Dean pounded into her, his harsh gasps and moans increasing, along with his speed. Wolf or *were*, she couldn't even know. No matter which he was, he was still Dean. A man she had come to know a little about and to crave more than the dry earth had needed the rain.

But this wasn't about her, it was all for him. And she loved sacrificing to tame the wolf. If it would work. It *had* to work. If it didn't, she might die, blissful and never regretting her decision to pick up this desperate stranger.

Dean pinnacled the edge, that moment when his body tensed and every fiber of him prepared, anticipating, opening and succumbing. The hand on her stomach relaxed and slipped away. Her lover climaxed with a shudder. The growl near her ear was a man's voice, not an animal's.

The claws digging into the wood retracted. The wolf had been put to heel. That didn't stop Dean from howling a triumphant cry into the stormy night.

Dropping her arms across the desk and collapsing forward,

Sunday smiled with relief and because she'd just had some awesome sex. With a werewolf.

"God, you're so tight. Made for me." He wrapped an arm across her shoulders and brought her up to cleave against his panting body. "That was amazing. The werewolf was so close."

"It'll stay away for the night?"

"Not sure." He huffed. A teasing bite tweaked her shoulder. He followed with a kiss that sucked in her flesh and would surely leave a love mark. Another shudder pulsed his muscles against her sweaty flesh. Dean gasped. "Might have to go a few more rounds to be safe."

"I'm up for that."

She turned in his embrace and kissed his perspiring throat where the Adam's apple throbbed. The dark beard had receded to stubble. They'd been so close. *He* had been beyond close, half changed, those claws tearing through the desk as if it were mere tinder.

But they'd made it. "Together," she whispered, breathless.

He pressed his forehead to hers. "We rock." He touched her stomach. "Oh, hell, what's this?"

"Just a scratch. You barely grazed the skin."

"Sunday, I don't want to— I'd never intentionally hurt you."

"I know that. I trust you, Dean."

"You should never trust me as the wolf. Know that. Promise me, if it gets close like that again, you'll hop in your truck and head for the hills."

She nodded, but the idea of running from this man—even as a werewolf—did not appeal to her. He'd entered her, become a part of her. "Sure. So, it looks like you're ready to go for round two."

His erection bobbed when she glided her palm over the bulging head. Suddenly airborne, Sunday landed over Dean's shoulder.

He turned and headed toward the truck bed. "Time to make the kitty cat purr."

* * *

"You are some kind of incredible woman." Dean laid Sunday on the blanket in the back of the truck and crouched over her. Tendrils of long hair spilled over her breast, and he dragged them away with a lash of his tongue, making sure to glide roughly across her nipple. "To risk the werewolf?"

"Maybe I'm as desperate for sex as you are."

A good excuse, but he figured differently. Sunday was strong, capable and wasn't the sort of woman to suffer a werewolf just for sex.

He respected her for that.

"If that's your story, we can stick to it," he said, and moved up to kiss her. Her mouth was hungry for his, and he danced his tongue with hers.

"Love being inside you." He teased his tongue along the underside of her upper lip. "Never felt so good as this."

"Never?" she whispered. She grasped his length firmly.

Dean moaned into her mouth. "Never. Mmm, you've got a good grip."

"Comes from torquing lug nuts for a living."

"Well, don't torque too hard." She moved his bulging head to her moist heat. "You're going to tame me again?"

"But you like it." She sucked in his lower lip and bit not too softly.

Dean's arms shook as he strained not to rest completely upon her body. Flesh to flesh, the rasp of her nipples grazing his skin alternated with the giddy hug of her around his erection.

"I like anything you have to offer," he groaned out. He wanted to push himself completely inside, but her fingers manipulated and stroked his length, keeping him from fully entering. The sensation made him dizzy, threatened to push him beyond rational.

"You make me feel less alone, Dean."

"Woman like you should never be alone. You deserve to be loved and sexed every day."

"Sexed?"

"Not a word? I'm making it one. Let's get you sexed, kitty cat."

He'd intended to make her purr. Wasn't fair to deny the woman. But he couldn't fight the rush that coursed through his system.

Her touches reduced his words to gasps and grunts. Sunday bit his jaw, nibbling down under his chin to lick his throat. He clutched her breast, loving the soft handful and knowing the minute sting as he squeezed the nipple sent her into some crazy kind of squirming delight.

The tilt of her torso pushed out his cock. He gripped himself and rubbed the head over the sensitive spot that made the cat retract her claws and expose her belly.

Head diving backward, Sunday splayed out her arms and gripped the blanket. A cry of mounting pleasure segued to gasping, shuddering purrs.

"That's what I wanted to hear."

But before he could bring her to climax, she gripped the hand he had about his cock. Her legs clutched his hips and forced him down and inside her, where the world was warm and right and all rational thought fled.

Dean came instantly. Again, she'd brought him to heel.

Was it too much to ask to abandon anxiety while a gorgeous hunk of man made love to her?

Sunday stroked her fingers over Dean's tense shoulders as he climaxed above her. His skin was hot and dewed with sweat. Gasps and nonsyllables sang like mating calls she answered readily. She had been close to orgasm—and then panic had chased away the prize.

There was a fifty percent chance when she did bridge a demon that it would be benevolent, probably a bit disoriented as to how it had suddenly arrived in the mortal realm and more than willing to return to its own realm.

But the other fifty percent were nasty and so ready to wreak havoc. And much as she wished she could just let them dash off on their own, Sunday did feel responsible for any bit of nasty she brought into this world.

Because if she thought loneliness was tough, the witch hunt that would gather should the world learn the truth about her and other paranormals would make being alone seem like a surreal dream.

Dean rolled off her and onto his back beside her. The metal grooves in the truck bed did not make for a comfortable surface, but the blanket was thick and warm.

"Still raining," he said on a sigh.

"I love the rain."

"It's growing on me," he offered.

"Why doesn't the werewolf like rain?"

"I was trapped in a rain sewer years back. Chained, actually, during the full moon."

"Chained?"

"It's a long story. I pissed off a witch. Learned my lesson, though. Enough about my anxieties. Why'd you do that? Let me come again?"

"You're questioning my ability to bring you to heel, wolf?"

"Hey, don't get me wrong. I can go another ten rounds if that's your game." He rolled to his side and stroked her breast with soft fingers. "But I think you're trying to stop the inevitable."

"We stopped the werewolf. That was inevitable."

"True. Sunday."

Her name, whispered in his deep, raspy voice, worked like a touch to her sex.

"I won't be put back," he whispered in her ear. His fingers skated purposefully down her stomach. "I'm not afraid of a demon. And I sure as hell won't let a girl show me up. You can stand fearless before a werewolf? Let's bring on the demon."

So now it had become an issue of male pride. She'd let him have that. But it seemed an awful way to end a perfect evening. Great sex with an extraordinary lover, cut to a bloody halt by a nasty demon.

His fingers glided over the landing strip that led to her aching core. "Say yes, Sunday." Gently, teasingly, he traced her upper thigh. The strokes hummed inside, outside, up and down her soul. "Tell me you'll sacrifice for me."

"Oh, Dean." She rocked her hips, hoping to redirect his tracing journey, but he avoided her heat, instead teasing his finger pads low on her stomach. "Is it possible to form such an intense bond with a stranger?"

"It is."

"What about us? Cats and dogs."

"I'm not a dog, but a wolf."

"Dogs drool," she said lightly, "wolves rule."

He laughed and kissed her shoulder. "You're avoiding the subject." He skimmed over her aching bud. "Purr for me, Sunday. Surrender to the wolf."

"Yes," she said, and it wasn't a thought, but more a visceral response to his touch. "Sex me."

Most men never really learned the ways to satisfy a woman in a lifetime. Dean was attuned to Sunday's every flinch, her every murmur and moan. He used his tongue as a spear, a gentle feather, a quick paintbrush laying strokes across her skin. He expertly mastered her body and knew when to alter his touch from light to hard, or from slow to fast.

She lifted her hips, grinding her wetness against his fingers. Kisses covered her breasts. The hard column of his erection fit into her groping fingers. She began to stroke him, but the world slipped away as orgasm overwhelmed her.

It attacked so fiercely, Sunday cried out. It was too good to contain. Too remarkable not to surrender to. As her body hummed with joyful success, the dark tickle of warning went unnoticed.

It was too late. An ashy cloud gushed forth from Sunday's pores. And above her and her lover, the demon formed.

SEVEN

Dean took one look at the looming black cloud that shaped overhead and spread his body across Sunday's to protect her.

As the demon coalesced, thick black horns curled about the sides of its distorted head. It landed on the floor of the garage with hooves that crushed the cement to dust. Red eyes glowered. Brimstone sickened the air.

"I'm guessing you're not one of those friendly sorts we were hoping for," Dean called to the menacing shape. "Sunday, sweetie, hand me the shotgun."

She squirmed beneath him, and he adjusted his crab-style stance to allow her to shuffle to the back of the truck bed. He was completely exposed and didn't like it. But he wasn't about to let the thing near Sunday.

"It's not here," she said. "You left it on the hood!"

"Shit."

The demon stomped the floor and roared. It slashed a taloned appendage, cutting the air like a scythe, and catching Dean across the shoulder. Flesh split open and hot blood spilled down his chest.

Rage raced to the surface, aggravating the werewolf.

"You asked for it," Dean muttered. "Have at me!"

His rib bones popped. Flesh stretched. Toenails grew and curved. Fury numbed the pain of shifting.

Dean lunged and fit his hands onto the demon's horns. Growling, he let out a howl. The thing swung him around and rammed him—half wolfed out—against the wall.

Sunday screamed.

"Stay right there!" Dean's last words were barked out.

The werewolf slapped the demon's fist as it pummeled in for a murderous punch. And then it followed through with a full-body assault.

Crouched at the edge of the truck bed, Sunday peered over the side to the floor, where the shotgun had fallen. Unless it was filled with salt, a bullet would do little to put back the demon.

And she risked shooting the werewolf. It was the size of the demon. Thick brown-and-black hair rippled across its broad back and shoulders as it swung deadly claws and tore through the demon's black, leathery flesh. Powerful thighs and paws took to the floor. Half man, half wolf, it stalked a prey that could never have anticipated the vicious welcoming party.

The battling figures moved as shadows before the open garage door. Dean had lured the demon as far from the truck as possible. Far from her, she realized. The feeling of being protected swelled warmly in her veins.

And then anxiety defeated the brief sense of comfort. Normally, after she bridged a demon, Sunday automatically shifted to cat form. It was how familiars restored their vitality. But now the intense nervous energy moving through her veins kept her in human shape.

If the werewolf saw her now, would it recognize that she was a familiar and want to do to her what it was currently doing to the demon?

"No, only when I'm a cat," she muttered. "I hope."

Not that it mattered; she wasn't in the werewolf's sight right now.

A roar preceded the werewolf, hurtling through the air. The wolf's back hit the garage wall, cracking audibly. It landed, unmoving, splayed at the edge of the garage.

Sunday cringed.

The demon marched toward its fallen prey.

Should she risk attempting to shoot the thing? Dean didn't move. A leap would place her next to the gun. No time—

The demon lunged.

One grand slash of paw sliced the air. Razor-sharp claws decapitated the demon. Brimstone hissed out in yellow clouds. The headless body convulsed and went to the ground in a brilliant explosion of embers and sulfur.

The werewolf, huffing and heaving, jumped upright and stood over its kill. It howled, stretching its head up and back and displaying a remarkable form against the blurry glow of the full moon high in the sky.

It stomped and paced, rushing to the edge of the garage, but stopped before colliding into sheets of rain. More pacing. Low, whimpering moans echoed in the darkness.

"It can't leave."

At the sound of her voice, the werewolf swung to face the truck. Sunday ducked around and put her back against the pickup's cab. She clutched the blanket to her chest. Her scent of fear overwhelmed the musky odor of the fight.

Another long howl echoed into the night. She didn't hear it approach. Was she supposed to?

A strange yip cut off the end of the lingering howl. Claws clattered over the cement, moving quickly toward her. Didn't sound like the big, clawed paws of the werewolf.

A low growl alerted her that it was to the side and coming up around the back of the truck. Why had she thought to remain in human form?

The wolf leaped, and landed on the lowered gate. Sunday's jaw dropped. It was a real wolf, not the shifted, man-beast werewolf.

That didn't mean she was out of harm's way.

Ears back and teeth bared, the imposing animal fixed its golden gaze on her—and squinted. Suspicious.

She'd never seen a wolf in the wild—*were* or otherwise—and it was twice as large as the German shepherd that roamed the Steele grocery store. That one always growled at her when she passed.

Good thing she was too tense to shift shapes. At least in this form she had a chance of fighting off the threat. *Should have retrieved the shotgun.*

No. He was her lover. And she had to believe he would recognize her.

Heartbeat racing, Sunday slowly stretched out her arm, offering her open palm. "It's me," she whispered.

The wolf licked its maw, snapped its jaw and jerked its head as if it had heard something near the door. Had the demon risen? No, the werewolf had beheaded it, reduced it to sulfur. Bowing its head, the wolf went down on its forelegs.

Daring to lean forward, Sunday moved her hand closer. The wolf sniffed. She didn't budge to touch it. Best to allow it—*her lover*—to make that first move.

"You protected me," she said. "Thank you."

The wolf crawled forward a few inches. It nudged its nose under her hand. Its muzzle was warm and soft with dark fur. Then it lashed out its pink tongue.

"Are you tasting me?" Sunday's apprehension simmered. "You've already had the cherry on top, Dean. Let's call this one a night, hmm?"

The wolf crawled alongside her leg, onto the blanket, and lay down. She dared to stroke the fur along its leg, then to gently clasp her fingers about the thick ear. She bit back the urge to say, *Nice, wolf,* but the thought of it made her smile.

The wolf twisted its body to show its furred belly to her.

Acceptance.

Sunday shuffled her fingers across its soft fur. "This is going to sound crazy, but I love you, Dean."

And with the release of her apprehensions, the shift reduced Sunday's human form to that of a blue-eyed white feline.

The wolf startled at the sudden appearance of the feline. It yipped, and snapped at the beast.

The cat didn't flinch. It slashed out a paw and struck the wolf across the nose with a claw.

Whimpering as it retreated, the wolf tucked its nose into a curled paw and eyed the small creature. It wasn't about to nip at it again.

Seeming pleased with the big dog's submission, the cat turned around once, then settled into a coiled rest against the soft belly of the wolf.

They slept that way until the rain stopped.

Sunday woke with a smile on her face. And a serious ache in her hip. Pickup trucks were not made for comfortable sex.

The warm body next to her stirred. Her forehead rested against tight abs. He smelled great, like root beer and sex and motor oil. Weird cologne, for sure, but it did something for her.

"Sunday?"

"I'm desperate for a real bed," she said and sat up. Dean quickly pulled her down to spoon against him. "This is not comfortable in the least," she said.

"Screw comfort. You're in one piece. That's all that matters. The werewolf didn't attack."

"It annihilated the demon and saved my ass."

"And a nice ass it is." He nudged his groin against her bottom and, wonder upon wonders, he was already hard. "Didn't mean to wolf out in front of you. That's something I never wanted anyone to see."

"I can handle it. You're a very handsome beast, actually."

"You think?"

"I like the smaller wolf much better, though. One smack across the nose was all it took to tame him."

"So that's why my nose hurts. Naughty, kitty cat." He performed a deft move and slid his erection inside her with a pleasurable moan. "Mmm, like it here."

"Even when the big bads come after you? You didn't run screaming, Dean. That's a first for me."

"I don't do the scream. And I'm developing a theory about you and your demons. Maybe you need practice, time to learn to control the bridging. You probably never had a chance to get down and dirty with a man who would allow you to focus on the problem, am I right?"

"Very right. You offering your services? Thought you were on your way home."

"I am, but there's no rush now that we've beat the moon. I want to stick around awhile, if you'll have me. Rather, if you can put up with the werewolf."

"Company sounds good for a change."

"Yeah, it does. I'm glad about the rain. It forced me to look at something I'd probably never noticed before. A familiar. A gorgeous, sexy woman. Mmm, you've gotten inside me, Sunday. Don't want to get you out, either."

"I believe it's you inside me. And you can stay there as long as you like. Look at us. One needs sex to keep the beast back, the other brings up all sorts of nasties with sex. This so shouldn't work."

"Yeah, but it feels right." He pumped slowly, savoring each glide. The friction felt exquisite. "I could love a woman like you, Sunday. You'd certainly keep me on my toes."

"Sounds good in theory, but I'm very happy here in the middle of nowhere."

"Now you're lying, lonely girl. You've been hiding. Just like me."

"I have. We do. The lonely thing, that is." She sighed and drew his hand up to claim her breast. "I suppose I could do with company. But I don't do the domestic thing. And I don't do dishes."

"Do you do werewolves?"

"Oh, yeah."

* * * * *

MATE OF THE WOLF

Karen Whiddon

To all the devoted Pack fans who keep buying
the books and asking for more.

KAREN WHIDDON

started weaving fanciful tales for her younger brothers at the age of eleven. Karen now lives in North Texas, where she shares her life with her very own hero of a husband and three doting dogs. You can e-mail Karen at KWhiddon1@aol.com or write to her at P.O. Box 820807, Fort Worth, Texas 76182. Fans of her writing can also check out her Web site, www.KarenWhiddon.com.

Dear Reader,

Writing this short Pack story was such a treat—fun, fun, fun! I loved introducing the vampire element into my Pack world, and the first interspecies romance was hot! I hope you enjoy it as much as I enjoyed writing it!

Karen Whiddon

ONE

"Oh, my dog, I think I see him." Allison Berg gripped her cell phone and tried not to stare. She rose onto her tiptoes in the doorway of Shorelines bar and craned her neck to get a better look.

"Is he hot?" Her human friend Emily sounded amused. Why shouldn't she? After all, this was the fifth blind date Allie had gone on this month. Em claimed that Allie's dating stories were the only thing that got her through the chemo.

"If that's him, yes. I'll tell you about it later. Gotta go." Allie closed her phone and took a deep breath, trying to maintain her composure. She headed across the room, trying to appear nonchalant, but still feminine.

He wasn't Pack—she'd noticed the singular lack of an aura. That was odd. Jen knew she didn't want to date non-Pack men. Still, he was the best-looking man she'd ever seen, just as Jen had promised. Maybe her rule about not dating humans was way outdated.

As a matter of fact, something new might be exactly what she needed.

She stopped at the bar and ordered a glass of white wine. For courage.

"Another date?" The bartender, another Pack member, took

in Allie's trendy yellow minidress and strappy mango heels and grinned. "Who's the lucky guy this time?"

"Jen set me up on a blind date."

Chance's brows rose as he handed her the wine. "And you let her? Look what happened last time."

"I know, I know." She lifted her chin, checking out the small stage where the band was setting up. "That's why I only agreed to meet for a drink. I had dinner at home."

"Speed dating." He smiled. "Only you." His expression changed, becoming serious. "How's Emily doing?"

The entire town knew Chance had a thing for Allie's best friend. Emily had even dated him once or twice. Chance believed she was his mate, even though she was human. Allie didn't think so, especially since Emily had confessed she just wasn't that into him.

But Chance refused to give up. He'd pursued Em relentlessly. Then she was diagnosed with stage IV breast cancer. She'd undergone a complete mastectomy and started an intensive radiation and chemotherapy treatment. Sick, Emily refused to even answer his phone calls.

Allie knew how badly this hurt Chance.

"She's doing as well as she can. She has one more round of chemo before she's done. Then it's wait and see." Allie swallowed, blinking back sudden tears. Emily had told her the cancer had invaded her lymph nodes. Despite all the treatments, she was dying. Her doctors predicted she wouldn't see thirty. Emily had made Allie promise not to tell anyone. She claimed she wanted to die with dignity.

"Tell her we're praying for her, will you?" Chance touched the back of Allie's hand, bringing her back to her surroundings. "And ask her to call me."

Allie nodded. Chance asked the same thing every time he saw her. Allie always dutifully passed the message along to her friend. And Emily always nodded, then proceeded to ignore the request.

"I'd better get on with it, hadn't I?" Lifting her hand in a quick wave, Allie took a sip of her wine and moved away from the bar. Tonight she'd actually considered standing up her date. Not just because she'd had second thoughts. Quite simply, she was tired. Tired of bad dates, tired of knowing within the first ten minutes that this guy would make a great friend, but nothing more, tired of fending off men with too many arms, roaming hands, beer breath and bad come-on lines.

For the first time in her twenty-seven years, she was tired of trying to find Mr. Right.

Emily teased her, alluding to her well-known set of rules. Em was the only one who knew all of them—and she was the only human who knew that Allie was Pack. Rule number one: date only Pack members. Two: if the chemistry isn't there by the second date, don't go on a third. And three: let them down gently, avoiding confrontation at all costs.

What could she say? She didn't believe in wasting time. If nothing was going to happen, she'd acknowledge that and move on.

Still, all of her Pack friends continued to set her up on dates. Sometimes she thought they had a competition going to see whose pick would last the longest.

Jen had insisted this guy would be the one. Allie had tried to refuse her but finally let herself be convinced to give it one more try.

Except Friday had turned into the day from hell at work, as she'd handled one irate customer after another, and now all she wanted to do was sit on the dock outside the marina, dangle her feet in the water and fish. Trooping around a crowded bar in heels and a dress to the sound of a band she'd heard a thousand times seemed as appealing as scrubbing toilets.

Until she'd seen him.

"Hellhounds, let that be my date," she muttered under her breath, moving across the room toward his table. The man was tall and broad shouldered, with long auburn hair and a chiseled, compassionate face. He wore a leather biker jacket and dark sunglasses, even in the dimly lit bar.

In other words, he was drop-dead gorgeous.

"He ain't from around here, that's for sure." Carrying a tray of drinks, one of the waitresses stopped long enough to comment. "Is he yours?"

"Lord, I hope so." Allie continued moving in the stranger's direction.

He watched her cross the room. As she approached his table, he removed the sunglasses.

Allie froze. Eyes like that—the color of sun-warmed amber, framed by long, dark lashes—should be illegal on a man.

Forcing herself to move forward, she was conscious of several other men staring. She had a reputation here in town—one of her dates had told her she was known as Queen Tease. The other things they called her were not so nice. Inflexible, frigid and set in her ways. Just because she had a set of rules.

Almost to his table—oh, please let him be her blind date—and intent on her thoughts—but who else could he be?—she didn't see the beer bottle someone had dropped on the floor until her heel caught it.

One leg went left, the other went right, and she heard the sound of tearing cloth as she fell. Her elbow caught a passing waitress's tray, upending a pitcher of beer all over herself. Soaked to the skin, Allie made an inelegant pirouette, trying to regain her balance, and fell against the table, knocking it into the man she'd been trying to impress. Her wine shot out of the glass she'd somehow managed to hang on to, splashing all over him.

Her last thought before she slammed her head into the table and crumpled to the ground was that this was one hell of a way to start a blind date.

TWO

The woman in the bed blinked sleepily, staring at him from her gorgeous blue eyes. Her tousled, jet-black hair and slightly flushed complexion made Kane Webster think of other things one did in beds. Things he hadn't wanted to do in a long, long time. Decades.

"I'm so sorry," she gasped. "Are you all right?"

Leaning back in his chair, he nodded. "Better than you, apparently."

Her eyes widened upon hearing his voice. Most likely she was shocked at his clipped British accent. Since he'd been in this country, he'd noticed women either loved the accent or hated it. No middle ground.

"So, I guess you're him?" she asked.

"Who?"

"My blind date." Swallowing, she blinked again. "I'm Allison Berg."

Kane had never been anyone's blind date in his entire life—all four hundred years of it. Suddenly, for this woman, he wanted to be. "Yes," he answered, enjoying the rush of pink that deepened her cheeks.

Her heartbeat accelerated, beating a butterfly flutter in the delectable hollow at the base of her throat. He wanted to taste her there, in the age-old courtship ritual of his kind. The fact that her kind was practically forbidden to him did nothing to stifle his desire.

He had a serious case of the hots for a shape-shifter. That could be a problem. Vampires and shape-shifters generally tolerated each other, nothing more. Despite the uneasy truce between their two races, a lot of animosity remained. If the Vampire Council found out, the repercussions could be serious.

She made a sound, drawing his attention. Focusing on her exquisite face once more, Kane realized he didn't care what she was. He hadn't wanted a woman like this for centuries. Though she didn't know it yet, she would be his. That was all that mattered.

"You hit your head," he told her, a bit unnecessarily since she'd raised her hand to feel the white, turbanlike bandage. "The fall knocked you out and you have a nasty cut, but they don't think your low-grade concussion is serious. They put in some stitches and said you ought to be fine. The nurse is looking for a doctor so you can be released to go home."

"Why are you here?" she asked. "I mean, I'm a bit surprised to wake up and find you sitting by the side of my bed." Again, rose suffused her cheeks. "You don't even know me."

"I felt somewhat responsible."

"Responsible?" Her self-conscious laugh sounded a bit forced. She appeared nervous—of him? "You're not responsible. That's ridiculous. I'm very sorry I knocked the table into you and spilled my wine all over you." She sighed. "I guess I can add 'clumsy' to my online profile."

"Online profile?" He raised a brow. "MySpace?"

If anything, his question made her blush deepen.

"Matchmaker.com. It's an online dating service."

Staring, Kane shook his head. "Why would someone who looks like you have to use an online dating service?" He felt a stab of jealously at the idea. He didn't want other men looking at her online and thinking they could possess her.

"I work for a family-owned insurance agency and this is a

small town. Since I'm not likely to meet anyone at work, and I know most of the guys around here—" she made a face "—Matchmaker.com seemed like a good idea."

Leaning forward, he watched her nostrils flare as she tried to catch his scent. Since he was undead, he had no bodily aromas and, unless he doused himself in men's cologne, gave off no odor of any kind. From the narrowing of her long-lashed eyes, he could see that puzzled her.

"You're different," she stated flatly. "I'm not sure I—"

Deliberately letting his gaze roam over her, he gave her a slow smile, careful to keep his fangs retracted. "You're not sure you…what?"

After a moment's hesitation, she smiled back. If he'd had a still-beating heart, Kane thought it would be pounding in his chest. This woman had no idea how she affected him. Worse, despite his lack of scent, she apparently believed him to be human. She exhibited none of the animosity her kind normally displayed toward the undead.

"Never mind." Shaking her head, her expression bemused, she swung her long legs over the side of the bed. "Would you help me stand up? I feel a little dizzy."

He knew an instant of sharp, bitter longing. If only this gorgeous, sexy shape-shifter woman could have been of his own kind. Eternally beautiful, a vampire like her he would never forget. No man with a sharp set of fangs ever would.

"Of course." He held out his arm, sighing when she placed her small hand on his skin.

"Have we met?" she asked suddenly, wrinkling her nose and frowning. Even that he found endearing.

"No."

"I didn't think so. But you look familiar for some reason. I thought maybe I'd seen you on TV or something. Are you an actor?"

"An actor?" He chuckled, resisting the urge to lean in and press a kiss on her full lips. "No. I'm in the music business. Recording industry. That's why I was in that bar earlier. I came to check out the band."

"The Digests? They're a local band, pretty good." She blinked, frowning again. "Then you aren't my blind date, are you?"

For a moment, he couldn't answer. Everything about this woman, from the arch of her neck to the way she tossed her hair, aroused him. Creamy skin, hair the color of night, graceful, athletic build. Her eyes were the most unusual color, like sapphires with a coating of gold flakes. He felt the pull of her beauty and hoped—no, believed, from her heightened color and rapid heart rate—that she felt it, too.

Astounding. He hadn't been this stirred up in the past two hundred and fifty years, if ever.

Collecting his thoughts, he smiled again, still careful to hide his fangs. He used his other hand to gently help her stand. She wobbled a little, and he used that as an excuse to hold her close. He knew shape-shifters had quick healing powers. No doubt she would be fully healed before another hour had passed.

"No, my name is Kane Webster. I'm afraid I'm not your date. But if you're willing, I'd like to be. Starting right now, if you're up to it."

THREE

Rules were meant to be broken. Gripping Kane's arm, Allie knew if she'd ever be tempted to go outside her comfort zone, this man would be the one to seduce her into doing so.

Seduce. Just the thought made her nipples ache. She only hoped he couldn't tell how he affected her. Another shape-shifter would smell her desire. This human male would have no idea. Though she still hadn't figured out why he had no scent. All humans had scents, didn't they?

Maybe she didn't know as much about humans as she thought she did. Or maybe this guy was superclean.

"Are you all right?" Kane asked, his deep voice making her yearn to touch him.

"Yes." Though still wrapped in the ridiculous bandage, her head didn't even hurt—it was already healing. Being a full-blooded shape-shifter came with advantages, fast healing being one of them.

"Then go out with me. Please."

Should she? She got the feeling he didn't often say please. Glancing at her watch, she debated. Barely ten o'clock on a Friday night. Sad that she would even contemplate going home to spend the rest of the evening alone watching television when she had the most amazing man she'd ever met flirting with her.

"Let me buy you a drink?" he asked.

That wonderful British accent was also driving her crazy. "Maybe one," she conceded.

He gave that sexy, slow smile again and she melted inside. You know, perhaps it *was* time for a fling. Especially if she really planned to quit dating for a while. She might as well have one uninhibited wild fling. Even if he was human.

Hellhounds, especially if he was human. If she was going to act completely out of character, with who better than this drop-dead gorgeous stranger passing through town?

None of her friends would have to know. Except Emily. Allie told her everything. She couldn't wait to tell her about Kane Webster.

Moving silently in white sneakers, the nurse finally brought the papers. Allie signed, grateful to see that the woman's aura showed she was Pack. She didn't bother giving any health-related suggestions, aware Allie would be fine before she made it home. Before leaving, she helped Allie take the bandage off her head.

"Ready to go?" Kane gazed down at her, his eyes full of promises.

For the first time in…well, a long time, a thrill went through her, a sharp stir of anticipation. Hounds, oh, hounds, this was going to be fantastic.

"I am," she replied. Since Kane had no idea about her healing powers, she took advantage, leaning into him on the way to his car, relishing the feel of his muscular arms around her, noting how elegant his large hands were, with his long fingers and well-groomed nails.

Instead of taking her back to Shorelines, he took her to a smaller pub, one without live music and thus less crowded. He snagged a table on the open balcony, under the moonlight, overlooking the lake. Once she was settled, he went to get them drinks.

The second he went inside, Allie called Em. She knew her friend would still be up; the chemo made her restless, unable to sleep. Em would be pacing the floor, fighting the nausea—she'd welcome the distraction.

"Hello?"

Talking fast, Allie filled her in on the night's events. To her credit, Em didn't comment on Allie's clumsy mishap—knowing her so well, she knew that kind of thing happened often.

"Breaking your iron-clad rules?" Emily teased. For the past year, ever since her diagnosis, Emily had been telling Allie that her strict adherence to her dating rules was Allie's way of dealing with a situation she couldn't control—Em's cancer.

Allie suspected Em was right. Bringing order into her own life gave her a feeling of security, a haven of safety when she wanted to rage against the cruel fate intent on robbing her best friend of life.

But tonight, she'd break every one of those rules. Every single howling one.

She spotted Kane returning from the bar with her drink. She couldn't help but notice that every woman in the room watched him as he passed.

Hounds, she couldn't blame them. Just seeing the man heading toward her, his elegant stride making him seem to float, made her mouth grow dry.

"I'll tell you about it later," Allie promised. "Gotta go. He's coming back." She snapped the phone closed and slipped it into her purse just as Kane reached their table.

"Here you go." Setting her white wine in front of her, he held her gaze as he took his seat. The look in his fabulous dark eyes promised delights so sensual she nearly licked her lips in anticipation.

Hounds, how could a human man be so hot?

His drink, in a tall glass without ice, was red. A Bloody Mary, she guessed.

"Are you in town long?" she asked, trying not to appear to care overly about his answer.

"I'd planned an overnight stay." His clipped voice sounded

regretful. "But since I didn't actually hear the band, I'll be here a bit longer, perhaps another night."

Another night. Oddly enough, having a time limit in which to seduce him turned her on even more.

She'd better move fast. Already awake inside her, her wolf paced, ready for the hunt.

Her only problem was, never having actually seduced a man before, she wasn't entirely sure how to go about it.

FOUR

Watching Allison and sipping on his blood cocktail—it helped to have vampiric connections, even in a small town like this—Kane knew he'd have to move fast. Having a time limit disconcerted him—if he'd had a choice, he'd have liked a long, slow seduction, thereby building both their desires to a fever pitch, but the sun would rise in six hours or so. He'd be out of commission until the sun went down, safely tucked away in his friend Malcolm's basement coffin. Again, vampiric connections. When he'd first been turned, in the sixteen hundreds, neither communication nor travel had been so simple. He'd been on his own, roaming the streets of London at night, learning often brutal lessons the hard way. As soon as he could, he'd left the crowded streets of London for the countryside, where he'd hooked up with a band of other vampires who'd taught him most everything he'd needed to know. Some of them, like Malcolm, he remained friends with to this day.

As soon as he woke, he wanted to see her. Tomorrow night, he had to see the band, true, but he selfishly planned to spend the rest of his time in Anniversary, Texas, with Allison. Unfortunately, the longest he could extend his stay here in town would be a few days. His record label had a big meeting scheduled and Kane had to be there. At least, he did if he wanted to keep this job. And he liked this particular job more than any other he'd had over the centuries.

Which meant he had, at best, two or three nights in which to make her his. This might be more difficult than he'd first thought, especially since she still didn't seem to realize he wasn't human. He debated showing his fangs, though he didn't want to scare her off. Normally he would welcome the thrill of the hunt, but right now Kane wanted to make every second count.

Reaching across the scarred wooden table, he took her hand, caressing her index finger with his thumb.

"Tell me about yourself, Allison."

Her full lips curved. "For starters, you can call me Allie."

Bloody hell. His already engorged body hardened even more. To cover his discomfort, he took a gulp of his drink, knowing he'd need the blood to give him enough energy for what he planned to do with her.

He wanted to give her a night of lovemaking unlike anything she'd ever had. Judging from the size of his arousal, he'd have to use every bit of willpower he possessed to keep from losing his own self-control.

"I'm more interested in hearing about you," she said, then rolled her eyes and laughed. The husky sound of her laugh sent another jolt straight to his groin.

"What?" he managed to ask, puzzled.

"I can't believe I just said that." Tugging her hand from his, she lifted her glass and drank the rest of her wine down in one fluid swallow, then set the glass back on the table. "It sounded like a bad pickup line from some cheesy movie."

"Pickup line? Are you trying to pick me up?" He couldn't resist teasing her. Just talking to this woman made him feel startlingly alive. He'd actually forgotten how good such a thing could feel.

With an uncertain look on her face, she pushed to her feet.

"Please excuse me. I've got to go to the ladies' room. I guess I'm not very good at this after all."

That said, she fled.

Moving across the wooden floor as fast as her high heels would allow and ignoring her inner wolf's howl of protest, Allie rushed to the ladies' room. She wanted Kane so badly she couldn't think, yet she couldn't bring herself to blatantly say what was on her mind.

Fear of rejection? Or was it the fact that she didn't want him to think she was…fast?

"Allie, wait." His voice, directly behind her.

One hand on the restroom door, about to push it open, she hesitated.

He touched her shoulder, a light touch, but it still made her shudder.

She turned to face him, then lost all rational thought when she found him much closer than she'd expected.

Belly-rubbing close. Her heart rate shot into overtime.

"Allie," he groaned, and then his lips covered hers.

His kiss struck a match inside her. Hot. So hot.

When he pulled her close, almost roughly, and she felt the force of his arousal, she burned inside.

Everywhere her body touched his, she tingled.

Locked together in the most sensual kiss she'd ever experienced, they stumbled backward into the single-stall ladies' room. Somehow she saw he had the presence of mind to kick the door closed and push in the lock.

He slid his hand from her neck and shoulder down the curve of her hip to her belly. His touch felt electric, making her body ache for him to continue his downward path.

"I want you," he growled, pushing against her.

"I want you, too," she managed to gasp, already wet, craving the feel of his fingers *there,* as a prelude to what his hugely aroused body promised.

"Excuse me?" A series of swift knocks against the bathroom door made them freeze. "Are you going to be much longer?"

"A little bit," Allie managed to croak. "A few more minutes."

"I'll check back in five minutes." The woman sounded huffy.

Five minutes. Not nearly enough time.

"Allie..." Kane's mouth against her ear.

"We can't do this here," she managed to gasp, even as her body arched of its own accord, still yearning for his touch. Her wolf had gone strangely silent, as though she approved.

She felt rather than saw him nod. "You're absolutely right. This is not the right place for this. Our first time together should be in a bed, unhurried, not rushed."

If he only knew how badly she wanted to feel his body pounding inside hers... Even thinking about it made her hot all over.

"My place," she told him, stepping away and attempting to adjust her clothing. "It's not far."

"Are you certain?"

Manners were the last thing she wanted from him right then. She gritted her teeth and attempted to quiet her newly agitated inner wolf.

"Absolutely positive." Taking his hand, she led him from the room.

The woman who'd interrupted them was waiting outside. Her eyes widened and her mouth opened when the two of them emerged, but one dark look from Allie quelled anything she'd been about to say.

They rushed through the bar and outside to his car. As Allie slid inside, the cool leather like balm to her overheated skin, she thought she might be about to experience the best sex she'd ever have—sex any other encounter would always be measured by.

Oddly quiet, Kane started the car. "You'll have to direct me. I'm not familiar with your town."

At his dispassionate tone, she felt as if the air had been taken from her lungs. Had the interruption given him second thoughts? Had he changed his mind about wanting to be with her?

FIVE

As a centuries-old vampire, Kane had grown used to many things. Like never seeing the sunlight and sleeping in coffins and other odd, airless apparatuses. It had taken him decades to get over the sensation of not having a heartbeat, and the fact that a cut didn't make him bleed still sent shudders of disgust through him.

Meeting this gorgeous little shape-shifter rocked his world. Allie's effect on him surpassed anything and everything that had come before. She made him feel as if he was starving, as if he hadn't had sustenance in weeks. He wasn't quite certain he liked the way she made him feel. He didn't let anyone or anything have that much power over him.

Now, for the first time in decades, he missed his former group of vampire friends. Maybe he should talk to Malcolm about this situation with Allie. Kane didn't know what to think. He worried— him, the master of willpower—that he wouldn't be able to maintain his self-control around her. Every second with her, he felt it eroding fast. Too fast.

Allie both intrigued and frightened the hell out of him.

For one thing, he couldn't stop touching her. He felt *compelled* to touch her. Even now, driving his powerful sports car, he kept one hand on the steering wheel and the other around her slender shoulders.

Technically he'd been dead for centuries, yet when he wasn't touching her, he felt as if he couldn't breathe, as if all the air had been sucked out of the world, the way a vampire drained blood from a corpse. It was the damndest thing.

Worse, he wasn't one hundred percent certain he affected Allie the same way. That frightened him even more.

The glowing numbers on the car's dashboard clock showed 1:01 a.m. Time was slipping past far too quickly. He felt a fierce desire to stop the clock, stop the earth from turning, the sun from rising, just so he could spend more time with Allie.

And he didn't even know how she felt about vampires.

A few minutes later, following her directions, they pulled into a driveway in front of a small brick bungalow. A single spotlight illuminated the front yard.

"My house," she said, sounding unaccountably nervous. "Everything's really close on this side of town." Breathless, she wouldn't look at him.

Bloody Hades.

He didn't know how he'd feel if she announced she'd had second thoughts. Akin to burning eternally in the fires of hell, he suspected. What was with his reaction to her?

"Are you coming?" Allie asked, opening the passenger door.

Moving with vampire speed, he got out, went around the car and made it to her side in time to take her arm and close her door after her. Just those brief seconds without contact had made him feel lost, like a bat without a cave.

Terrifying. Yet exhilarating, too.

Then she reached for him and he forgot all his fears. Standing on tiptoe, she breathed a kiss onto his mouth and he was lost.

She broke away and, still clutching his arm, led him up the walkway. Side by side, shoulder to shoulder, they made it to the front door. He waited while she fumbled with the key, wondering how to let her know he couldn't enter unless she invited him in.

Door unlocked, she went inside. Feeling like an untried youth, tongue-tied and anxious, Kane hovered on the doorstep, hoping against hope he wouldn't have to tell her the truth right this instant.

"Are you coming?" she asked. When he didn't answer, she gave him a puzzled frown. "Come on in, Kane."

That was all the invitation he needed. Inside in a flash, he kicked the door closed and kissed her again. Bodies bumping, lips locked together, they fell onto the couch, shedding their clothing as best they could.

Sensations flooded him—*sensations!* Sensations were, to a vampire, akin to strolling in the sunlight unburned and unharmed. He hadn't felt sensations since he'd been human, before he'd been turned, so many centuries ago.

He wanted to stay locked in her arms forever, to let these sensations—velvet and cream and musk and heat—overwhelm him. He wanted to drown in feeling, bury himself in it, until he felt like a quivering mass of raw nerve endings.

Instead of rushing straight to intercourse, he wanted to prolong the foreplay, savor the appetizers, so to speak. Minutes stretched into an hour, then another, yet time seemed to fly past. They touched, they kissed, they tasted, they sampled, skin and tongue and teeth. He brought her to climax with his fingers and then with his mouth, refusing to allow her to touch him more than briefly.

Each time her hand closed over his rigid arousal, he groaned out loud, savoring her touch, before he found another way to distract her. He knew if he let her continue to stroke him, he'd lose the last of his control and bury himself deep within her.

"This is the best foreplay I've ever had in my life," she murmured, going limp against him after climaxing yet another time. Yet a few more kisses, a caress of her breast and a stroke of her inner thigh, and she was ready and eager for more.

Meanwhile, managing to keep himself from exploding, from

yanking her moist, hot and ready body up to straddle him, knowing he could impale her on his arousal, was akin to the worst torture he'd ever endured.

Yet worth it, for her. Only for her. Again he felt a prickle of alarm at his thoughts—what was so special about this particular woman?

Occasionally, he eyed the clock, knowing he'd have to time things carefully. He wanted to make love to her with enough time remaining before the sun rose. After that, instead of allowing himself to go to sleep in her arms as he longed to do, he had to drive over to Malcolm's on the other side of the lake and descend into the basement while darkness still colored the sky the shade of jet.

Finally, when the clock on her mantel chimed three, he knew the time had come to let himself go.

Then her cell phone rang. Or rather, sang. Allie froze in his arms.

"That's Em's ring tone," she said, almost to herself. "Emily wouldn't call now unless something was wrong."

Pushing him away, Allie scrambled up from the couch, snatching the phone from her purse. "I'm sorry, I have to take this." She flipped open the cell phone, said hello and listened.

The rosy flush drained from her face, leaving her as pale as one of his own kind. She swayed on her feet, then took a deep breath. Closing her phone, she turned to him, her sapphire gaze dazed and afraid.

"That was my best friend, Emily. She's at the hospital and they're going to admit her. She needs me right now. I'm sorry, but I've got to go."

SIX

Disbelieving, Kane watched as Allie glanced about wildly and began scooping up her clothes and pulling them on. Once she was dressed, she picked up her purse and got out her car keys. A look of utter dismay came over her expressive face.

"Um, could you drive me back to Shorelines so I can get my car?"

Body still throbbing and fully aroused, he had to hold back a laugh. Fate, always fond of finding some backhanded way of getting him when he least expected it, was probably laughing her black-hearted ass off. "Of course." He sounded as though he'd swallowed a mouthful of rusty nails. "Give me a minute to get dressed."

As he started to dress, her cell rang again, the same musical tone. She answered, said hello and then not another word. After she'd finished listening, she snapped the phone closed.

Chest heaving, she faced him, her huge blue eyes full of tears. "That was Emily's mother. Em's gone into shock."

Clearly on the verge of going into shock herself, Allie began shaking. "They think this might be the end. I've got to get to the hospital right now if I want to see her before she dies."

He felt a fierce urge to hold her, to offer comfort. Yet somehow he knew she wouldn't want that, not now. He would help her the only way she'd allow.

"Let me drive you," he said, using vampiric speed to get into the rest of his clothes, guessing Allie was so distraught that she wouldn't notice how fast he moved.

As they headed for the door, the clock on the mantel chimed three-thirty. The sun would be rising in a few hours. If Allie had been anyone else, he'd have dropped her off at the hospital and continued directly to Malcolm's.

But he couldn't leave this woman while her best friend lay dying. No way, no how. No matter how much risk staying with her might put him in, he'd wait until the last possible moment before leaving her side.

What in the name of Hades was going on with him?

Though she barely knew him, Allie was glad that Kane hadn't bailed on her. Emily's mother, Cora Ralston, had revealed that the Ralstons were completely out of funds. They'd taken a second mortgage on their house, and now they were tapped dry. Since Em didn't have health insurance, they were paying for everything themselves. Mrs. Ralston had sobbed when she'd told Allie they were going to lose their daughter because they couldn't pay for more treatment.

As Kane drove to the hospital, Allie put her head on his shoulder and worked on not weeping. With her local office job, she herself was far from rich. She'd already organized several fund-raisers to help her friend. The treatments had sucked up that money like water.

Still, she couldn't cry. Em wouldn't want her to cry—Em would be positively *appalled* to see tears. For Em, Allie would have to be strong.

They parked near the hospital's emergency entrance. With the lateness of the hour, there were plenty of spots. Kane put his arm around her shoulders as they headed inside, and she let him, glad to have his strength to draw from.

That was odd. Supposedly only a mate—as in, another shape-shifter meant to be her one and only man—would be able to share his strength with her this way. She must be imagining things.

Inside the E.R. waiting room, which was more crowded than she'd expected, Allie asked about her friend. The nurse directed her to a chair, instructing her to be patient. Emily's mother was with Emily now and they couldn't allow anyone else back just yet. All Allie could do was wait. They'd let her know if anything changed.

They took two chairs in an alcove near a thin woman holding ice to her sallow face. Kane continued to massage Allie's shoulder, and she was glad. Through her fear, she felt such a rush of *rightness* that she almost turned to ask if he felt it, too. But Allie had never been a fool, or rash, so she said nothing, leaning into his touch instead and waiting for news of her friend.

She must have fallen asleep because the next thing she knew, Kane was gently shaking her. Groggy, she opened her eyes to find Mrs. Ralston standing over her and holding out her arms. Since Emily and Allie had become best friends back in elementary school, when Allie's parents had gotten divorced and her mother had moved away, Mrs. Ralston had joyfully become Allie's surrogate mother. Being without her own mother had been extremely painful, and her mother's excuse—that she'd spent years with the wrong person and needed to find her true mate—didn't help ease the pain. Mrs. Ralston did.

Allie flew into the older woman's arms. They hugged tightly before Mrs. Ralston stepped back and wiped at her eyes. "They're going to keep her overnight, but they think she's going to make it. She had some kind of allergic reaction to this last round of chemo. You can see her, but she's sleeping."

Allie smiled, brushing away any lingering tears. "I'll just look in on her for a moment."

She turned to Kane, surprising herself by leaning in and giving him a firm kiss on his lips. "I shouldn't be long. Do you mind waiting for me?"

As she'd suspected he would, he told her, "Of course not." But she couldn't help but notice the way he glanced at the wall clock after he answered, as though he were on a timetable. It bothered her more than it should have. After all, though they clicked so well that being with him felt perfect, they barely knew each other.

Shrugging off that thought, Allie followed Mrs. Ralston back to the ICU. Since only one visitor was allowed at a time, Allie entered her friend's room alone.

Surprisingly, Em was awake. She patted the chair next to her bed and demanded Allie tell her all the details of her date, leaving nothing out.

Stunned, Allie realized she really didn't want to. The rapidly developing thing with Kane was one of a kind, special. She wanted to hold it to her heart, take it out only when she was alone, and not examine it too closely. Things this wonderful and beautiful were often fragile, and she was afraid it might break.

"I don't think there's time," Allie stammered, aware of the ICU nurse standing guard at the nurses' station across the hall.

"Of course there is. I almost died," Em said. "If anyone can make demands, I can. Now spill. Don't leave anything out."

"He's waiting for me out there. We—"

"Surely he won't mind waiting a little bit longer." Em smiled expectantly.

Feeling strangely reluctant, Allie sat down and began talking.

SEVEN

Watching the hands on the wall clock inch toward four o'clock, then four-thirty, Kane began to pace. Soon he'd have no choice but to leave Allie here, though he hated to do so without at least telling her the truth. He'd finally realized he had to; his rapidly developing feelings for this woman were so strong, he knew she needed to know before they made love.

But did he have time? Again, he glanced at the clock.

Already he seriously doubted he could make it to Malcolm's before the sun rose. If he waited too much longer, he might as well go stand in the parking lot and wait to be turned into a smoldering pile of ash.

Four thirty-five, four-forty. At four forty-five, heart heavy, he gave up and turned to go.

"Kane!" Allie's voice sent a stab of pure joy through him. He spun around, waiting as she rushed across the waiting room and flew into his arms.

Like a damn sentimental greeting-card commercial, he caught her, glad and relieved and amazingly comforted the instant he touched her. This further cemented his growing wonder at the possibility of what he'd found. She was special, so of course she could make everything all right.

But could she stop the sun from rising?

"What time does the sun come up here?" he asked, trying to keep the urgency from his voice and failing.

"In June? I don't know. Five-thirty, six? I'm not sure." She gave him a puzzled look. "Why?"

"I'm allergic."

"What?" Her well-shaped brows rose.

He took a deep breath. Though he hated to, maybe it was time to tell her the truth. He'd hoped she'd get the hint and finally figure things out, but people only saw what they wanted to see. She wanted to believe he was human, so she did. The possibility of him being vampire had probably never occurred to her. After all, he'd been in this town two days and had yet to meet a vampire other than Malcolm. Even if Anniversary had been teeming with the undead, most shifters avoided them like the plague. Vampires were probably completely outside her experience, which would explain why she hadn't realized he was one. He wondered if Allie had ever even *seen* a vampire before.

Oddly, in his crazed state of mind, he would actually be pleased to be her first.

He hated her to find out so abruptly. If he had a choice, he'd break the news to her carefully, when she was less emotional. But it was nearly 5:00 a.m. The urgency of his situation left him no choice. He'd spent last night at Malcolm's. No way he could make it there before sunrise. He had to tell her now. And quickly.

"Do you mind if we go back to your place?" He'd tell her there. When her eyes widened, he gave her his most reassuring smile. "No, not to resume where we left off. I'm really tired. I find myself in urgent need of rest."

Maybe it was his proper manner of speaking, or the clipped tone to his voice, but she relaxed and nodded. "Of course. I could use a nap myself."

Once the sun came up, he'd be dead to the world. He wouldn't exactly call that a nap. But beggars couldn't be choosers, so he smiled and nodded.

"Let's go." Gallantly, he held out his arm. At least he'd be with her when he woke. How she'd feel about him then might be another story.

On the short drive back, she told him all about Emily's illness and financial troubles. Emily was her best friend, and Allie had dedicated herself to helping her beat her cancer.

He found he admired her even more. Lust and admiration was a dangerous combination. Throw in the fact that he also thoroughly *liked* her, and he knew he was in trouble indeed. As a matter of fact, though the possibility was so remote he should be staked for even thinking it, he had begun to suspect she might be the one he'd been searching for all these centuries. Vampires had a word for that, but he didn't want to jinx it by even thinking the word.

Once they were back at her house, under pretense of wanting a tour of the place, he scoped out nooks and crannies. Her bedroom had floor-to-ceiling windows on either side of the bed, so that was out. Even with the heavy thermal drapes closed, he couldn't take the chance that she might open them once she woke. The slightest bit of sunlight on his skin and he would be toast.

Her large, walk-in closet would be his best bet. The windowless room was large enough for him to stretch out on the floor, even with the five shoe racks that lined the walls. He didn't bother to speculate why she had so many—one thing he'd managed to learn over the centuries was that one must never come between a woman and her shoes.

She saw him looking at her footwear collection and laughed.

Now. He had to tell her now. Already he could feel the pull of slumber tugging at him. Though he wasn't sure of the exact time, he had to say the words quickly. Once the sun started on its journey up the horizon, he'd be dead to the world.

She turned to leave the bedroom, making some comment

about getting them both a glass of iced tea. He opened his mouth to tell her to wait, but a wave of dizziness hit him hard.

Crumpling to his knees in the closet, he held out his hand, trying to croak out a few words, anything, enough to let her know the truth before he passed out.

As she vanished around the corner, still chattering, black spots danced in his vision. He struggled to stay conscious, managing to call her name, praying she would hear.

Allie chattered the entire way to her kitchen, loving the comforting sense of domesticity she felt. Even now, after the stress of Em's close call, just being around Kane sent yet another buzz of desire humming in her blood. She'd begun to realize he was different, and the very real possibility of what they could be to each other had her dizzy, so dizzy she couldn't think straight. But she'd have to tell him she was a shape-shifter, and ideally she should do it before they made love. If he wanted her, he'd have to know the truth about what she was and what she could become. If he wanted her, he'd have to see her change.

Inside, her wolf wanted to change *now.* Since changing was often sexual with her kind, Allie couldn't help but wonder how their lovemaking would affect her need to change. Once she and Kane did the deed, she felt certain she'd be sated, exhausted, in a good way. So she needed to change first, to show him her wolf. She could only hope it wouldn't scare him away, because she so badly wanted to make love with him.

Which they would, sooner or later. For now, they'd climb into her big bed together, slide beneath the cool, cotton sheets and spoon. Maybe they'd even drift off and doze a while, but sooner or later one of them—probably her—would wake, stretch languidly and begin touching the other.

She could picture herself, half-awake, more than half-aroused, with the prime male specimen of Kane stretched out beside her. Just thinking about what she'd do to him made her insides heat.

Realizing she was now fully aroused, she wondered exactly *how* exhausted Kane actually was. If she judged from her past experience with men, he wouldn't be too tired for what she had in mind as a prelude to sleep. Of course, she'd never been with a human before, and they might be different, but somehow she doubted that.

Speaking of humans, she had to figure out why Kane had no scent. Something she'd heard, or read, nagged at her, but she couldn't remember what. It lurked in the back of her mind as she poured them each a glass of iced tea.

Concentrating on trying to remember, she bumped the second glass with her elbow. It crashed to the ceramic tile floor, shattering. Without thinking, she bent down and reached for it, slicing open her palm. Instantly, blood welled.

"Kane, would you get me a—" Turning, she saw that she was alone. Odd. She could have sworn he'd been right behind her. "Kane?"

"Allie." His voice, sounding faint.

Cut forgotten, she dripped blood as she rushed back to her bedroom. She hurried over to her closet and saw him crumpled in a heap on her floor. "What's wrong? Are you all right?"

When he looked up at her, fear warring with disorientation in his beautiful eyes, she felt a stab of terror. "Kane?"

But he was staring at her hand. Slowly she lifted it, noticing how his gaze tracked the movement.

"Are those *fangs?*" Backing slowly away, she stared at his mouth with both apprehension and fascination. "Are you a—?"

Self-preservation instinct took over, and she dropped to the carpet, bloody hand forgotten. The change began instantly, tearing her clothes as it rippled through her. Her bones lengthened, her skin grew fur, and as her eyes changed and her snout lengthened, she peered at him through the sparkling swirls of color that heralded the change.

Wolf now, her small wound instantly healed, she eyed him, uncomfortably aware that now neither of them had any secrets left.

"I'm sorry," he spoke fast, stumbling over the words in his mumbling haste. "Waited too long. Sun's rising. No choice but to sleep. Allie, I knew you were a shifter. I should have told you sooner. I'm a vampire."

Then, as she stared at him from her lupine perspective, trying to digest his words, he fell backward, completely gone.

Gone. As in *dead to the world.* Literally.

Shocked, Allie changed back to human and hurried over to him. Naked, she dropped to the ground beside him, cradling his head in her hands. Even now, she couldn't keep from touching him. Smoothing the hair from his brow, she arranged him so he could lie more comfortably.

Oh. My. Dog. Kane Webster, the man she'd thought all along might be The One, wasn't a human. He was a vampire.

Of course. That completely explained his lack of scent. Du-uh.

Backing carefully from the closet, she tried to form a rational thought. What was she going to do now? Vampire and Pack unions, while not strictly forbidden, were frowned upon.

How her friends would laugh if they knew. After years of bitterly complaining about settling for the wrong person, only her mother might understand. Allison Berg, despite all her careful plans and romantic dreams, had fallen for a blood-sucking, eternally living member of the undead. A vampire.

Fallen for, past tense. Because in the instant he'd gone unconscious, she realized what she hadn't wanted to admit to herself all along.

She loved him. Kane Webster was her mate.

EIGHT

Kane came instantly awake, wondering if he'd find Allie nearby, clutching a cross. Or worse, a stake. Although the vampire–shape-shifter truce still held, there were those who found getting past the old prejudices difficult. He knew quite a few himself, centuries-old bloodsuckers who viewed the Pack as nothing more than a council of crazy, half-wild dogs. That might have been the case centuries ago, when they'd roamed the wild forests of Europe as werewolves, but personally he thought that these days the Pack had become more organized than the Vampire Council. Of course, he'd stopped dealing with them back in the mid–eighteen hundreds. Too much bickering for him.

Yet his little Allie had thought he meant to hurt her. She'd become wolf in self-defense, believing he meant to attack her. How could she think such a thing? As if he could hurt the one who was becoming more important to him than— He cut off the thought, aware of a sharp pain in his chest, in the area where his heart used to be. He had to find Allie, find her and explain.

They could work this out. They *had* to.

He sat up, worried when he saw no sign of her anywhere. Rising, he padded from the closet. Her unmade bed looked untouched, unslept in.

A quick tour of her house proved she had gone. Where?

On his way through the living room, he noticed her answering machine light flashing. The digital readout showed one message, but when he pressed Play, the machine played two more.

All of them were from women who were apparently Allie's friends. Every single one of them had called to excitedly tell Allie about a strange man in town, a bounty hunter named Terry Holt who was offering fifty thousand dollars for a man named Kane Webster. Unfortunately, Terry was someone Kane knew all too well, though the last time he'd seen the man, Kane had gone by a different name and lived in Europe.

Terry wasn't a bounty hunter. He was a vampire hunter—one of the most successful, if one judged success by the number of kills. He'd been after Kane for a long, long time by human years. Worse, his father had been after Kane, and his father's father before him. Terry Holt came from a long, long line of vampire hunters dedicated to eradicating vampires from the face of the earth

Terry was determined to succeed where his forefathers had failed. And apparently, despite Kane's best attempts to stay below the radar, Terry had finally learned about Kane's move to America and his name change.

Terry wanted Kane dead. And he'd stop at nothing to achieve that goal.

Despite her shock at learning Kane's true nature, Allie had managed to get about five hours of sleep before the calls started coming in. Though she hadn't answered the phone, she'd woken up enough to hear the messages.

First Michelle, then Nikki, then Jen called to tell Allie the gossip around town. Every one of them knew about Em's desperate need for money. And because everyone knew everything in a small town like Anniversary, every one of them had heard about Allie meeting up with a stranger the previous night. Because of Jen, they also were aware that she'd stood up her blind date. All of her friends wanted to know if the man she'd hooked up with was the one this bounty hunter sought.

They seemed to have wholeheartedly bought this Terry Holt's story. But Allie, though not well rested, had slept enough to have her wits about her. Knowing what she now knew, she understood the truth. Terry Holt was not a bounty hunter, oh, no. He was a vampire hunter.

And he wanted to kill Kane.

What she didn't understand was why he'd tracked Kane here, to her little town in the middle of nowhere. If Kane truly was in the recording industry, as he claimed, his name would be fairly well-known. So why hadn't the bounty hunter gone to L.A. rather than Anniversary, Texas?

Intrigued and with nothing better to do until Kane woke, she went to hear Terry Holt talk. From Jen's message she'd learned that he had a town hall meeting scheduled for that afternoon at one. What she'd heard had shocked her—the man actually offered to pay fifty thousand dollars to anyone who could give him Kane Webster's location. Then he'd passed out flyers showing an enlarged photograph of Kane with the caption WANTED MAN. Terry claimed Kane was wanted in his native England, where he'd operated under an entirely different name, for crimes too heinous to mention. Terry had been looking for this criminal for a long, long time. He'd finally tracked him to America, and this time would pay well to ensure Kane didn't slip through his fingers.

Allie knew better. The Pack was hunted, too. She'd been around the man—excuse her, *vampire*—enough to sense that whatever else he might be, Kane wasn't a criminal. But the sum of money Terry offered as a reward definitely gave her pause. Fifty thousand dollars would go a long way toward helping Em pay her medical bills.

Allie considered Emily her sister. In the horrible years following her parents' divorce, when her father had turned to alcohol and her mother had abandoned her, Emily's family had become Allie's, saving her sanity and her spirit. She loved them more than her own mother, who salvaged her conscience with monthly phone calls.

In Allie's mind, there was no question of what she had to do.

NINE

Though Kane's first instinct was to flee—to climb into his souped-up sports car and drive fast and furious across the country—he wasn't willing to leave Allie. At least not without an explanation. And if he were completely honest with himself, he didn't know if he *could* leave her. Just thinking about doing that made his chest hurt even more.

A quick look around revealed she'd taken his car, so he couldn't leave even if he had wanted to.

Of course, now that she knew his true nature, she might order him to leave, not wanting a vampire cluttering up her world. If she did, Kane suspected it would break what little was left of his heart.

What an oxymoron. Everyone knew vampires didn't have hearts. True…at least until they found their Svetla.

Finally, he allowed himself to think the word, even whispering it out loud. *Svetla* meant gift—a gift from the Fates. A Svetla was the one person a vampire could happily remain with throughout eternity, and legend held that finding a Svetla was the closest a vampire came to having their former humanity restored. While nothing could make the shriveled-up muscle resume beating in a vampire's chest, finding his one true mate brought a small spark of life there, forever burning. Now he understood why his chest ached so badly.

Flipping open his cell phone, he called Malcolm. An ancient, curmudgeonly vampire eternally housed in a handsome thirty-year-old's body, Malcolm was older than Kane, probably by several hundred years. And he lived right here in Anniversary, Texas. Very few knew of his existence, and he could kill a vampire hunter easily. If Malcolm had been nearby when Terry had been chasing Kane in England, Kane never would have left the country.

Malcolm found the news of Terry Holt's arrival amusing.

"I'll take care of him immediately," Malcolm promised. "This Terry Holt won't bother you any longer."

Terry Holt, Vampire Hunter, was as good as gone. Kane hung up the phone with a feeling of satisfaction. At least one thing had gone well tonight.

A moment later, he heard the distinctive rumble of his car as it pulled into the driveway. Steeling himself, Kane went to stand near the front door, leaving the lights out. He knew a shape-shifter could see much better in the dark than a mere human.

She opened the door slowly, then quickly stepped inside and closed and locked it.

He stood stock-still while her eyes adjusted.

When she finally saw him, she tilted her head. "Why didn't you tell me sooner?"

The spot where his heart used to beat ached. Keeping his hands clenched at his sides so he wouldn't touch her, he answered as best he could. "I was afraid." Admitting fear cost him much—he who'd become so powerful over the years that other vampires feared him. "When I saw you, I went a bit insane. I didn't want to admit who you were, what you were." He swallowed, unable to say the word just yet. "Things moved fast after that, Allie. I'm sorry."

Arms crossed, she continued to stare at him, her face expressionless. "You do realize this causes all sort of problems, don't you?"

"Of course." He wanted to ask her if problems really mattered when they had finally found each other, but the words stuck in his throat.

"Of course, problems are meant to be solved," she said, making him feel as though she'd read his mind. She sounded bemused. Then, to his disbelief, she crossed the room to stand in front of him and cupped his face in her hands.

"You're so beautiful," she said. "Vampire or no. And you know what I am."

He still couldn't speak, so instead he nodded.

"For years, I've dreamed of meeting you. Gone on date after date after date, trying to find The One. I never gave up, never quit looking…" Her voice broke.

Unable to help himself, he kissed her. This was a different kind of kiss than the hot, deep ones they'd shared before. He meant the soft touch of his lips to be gentle, to reassure her. But the instant their mouths connected, fire flared between them.

"Oh, my," she gasped. "Do you have any idea what you do to me?"

"I do." Pulling her close, he held her, and kissed the top of her head. "Because you do the same to me."

She took a deep breath, pulling back a little to look up at him. "Kane, you've got to get out of here. There's a vampire hunter in town. He's tracked you here and he's offering a fifty-thousand-dollar reward."

Joy bloomed in him. Joy and hope and love. Definitely, overwhelmingly love. "You don't want the money?" He had billions, of course, and would pay whatever it took to help her friend. But he didn't say so. Not yet.

Staring at him, shock and outrage and anger flitted across her expressive face. "Of course I want the money," she said, sarcasm and reproof in her voice. "But I would never betray you, Kane. Not for anything."

He had to be sure. "Not even for Emily?"

A shadow crossed her eyes. "Not even for her. She wouldn't want to live at your expense."

Her last words were swallowed up in his kiss. He kissed her long, he kissed her hard, he kissed her deep, showing her with his tongue how he wanted to make love to her.

When they finally came up for air, she could barely stand. Kane had to support her.

"Hellhounds," she said in bemusement. Then, appearing to collect herself, she shook her head. "Seriously, Kane, you've got to go. I don't want to take a chance of that vampire hunter finding you."

Grinning, he told her about Malcolm. "Believe me, Terry Holt will never know what hit him."

"I'm so glad." She touched her nose to his, wolf-style. "We need to talk."

Since her serious tone was full of love, he nodded. Though they needed to discuss their racial differences, he really wanted to find out if she realized the truth now, as he did—the truth of what they were meant to be to each other.

He was her mate, and Allie was his Svetla, his own personal gift from the Fates. Among their own kind, such a thing was so rare, so life-changing, that vampires honored it above all else. Despite centuries of his own searching, Malcolm himself had never succeeding in finding his Svetla.

Kane didn't waste time wondering how such a thing was possible. Allie was his, and he was hers. Even if they were of different races. Even if this gift, this mate, was supposed to be another vampire, not a shape-shifter. Truth be told, Kane didn't much care. If she was willing, he'd turn her so they could be together for eternity. They'd deal with the consequences later.

"You first," he told her, unable to keep grinning. This time, he let her see his fangs. He wanted to kiss her again, but thought he'd wait to hear what she had to say.

As she opened her mouth to speak, her cell phone went off.

"Not again," she groaned, then went rigid as she recognized the number. "It's Emily's mom."

Answering, she listened, then closed the phone. Tears filled her eyes, spilling down her cheeks. "Emily's had a relapse. Her body's shutting down. This time, they don't think she's going to make it."

Suddenly, Kane realized he could give her a gift—but only if she and her friend were willing. "I may be able to help," he said slowly. "Emily doesn't have to die."

TEN

Despite the liberating joy of realizing no matter what his nature, Kane meant the world to her, once she was at the hospital again, Allie had to struggle to stop crying. From what Mrs. Ralston had said, Emily had gone into a coma and hadn't regained consciousness. The family had begun to gather, alternating between standing vigil and praying. Chance came, too, his determined expression warring with the grief and pain in his eyes. He'd come to say goodbye to the woman he loved.

Emily was truly dying. Unless…

Did she really want to let Kane turn her best friend into a vampire?

Did she have a choice? It was dead or undead, when all the rationale had been cut away. Not much of a choice after all. The way she saw things, being a vampire was infinitely preferable to being dead for eternity. Emily had accepted Allie's shape-shifter nature without reservations. Though they'd never discussed vampirism, Allie suspected that Em would embrace her new life wholeheartedly. After all, Em had never liked the sun. It always burned her pale skin.

If Kane was an example, vampires weren't bad at all. In fact, she'd venture to say that they were just like everyone else, human and shifters.

Once more she glanced at the man—er, vampire—she loved. Kane would be Em's teacher. Who better?

Going to Mrs. Ralston, Allie begged to be the next one allowed in Em's room. Grief-stricken, the older woman agreed, not even noticing when Kane went with her. Chance saw and opened his mouth to question, but a sharp look from Allie deterred him.

Except for the machines and their beeping, Em looked as if she were sleeping peacefully.

"Are you ready?" Clear and full of love, Kane's dark gaze contained a question. Allie knew that once he started, he wouldn't be able to stop. Emily would die and then, upon feeding from Kane, be reborn as a vampire.

Allie nodded. "Hurry. Before someone else comes in."

He reached out and punched a button on one of the machines. "To stop the alarms from going off when she dies."

With one last loving gaze at Allie, he bent over and fastened his mouth on Emily's pale and slender throat. As he drank from her, her blood would circulate through his body, enabling him to feed her back. When his fangs punctured her skin, her body jerked. As he continued feeding, she jerked once, twice, and then a third time, smiling as the last of her lifeblood drained from her body.

Then with a quick gesture Kane used his fangs to slash at his wrist, holding it to Emily's mouth. As the first drop of blood touched her tongue, she came alive, fastening her lips to him and sucking greedily, the way a newborn baby takes milk from its mother.

"Let me help you," a deep, masculine voice said from the doorway.

Allie spun. "How did you get in here?" she gasped. "Who are you? What do you want?"

"Allie, it's all right," Kane said, gently removing Emily's mouth from his wrist. "This is Malcolm. He can move in shadows, so no humans see him. He'll give Emily great strength if she feeds from him. To be allowed to drink the blood of one so ancient is a great honor."

Malcolm barely looked at them. All his attention was focused on the newly made vampire in the hospital bed. He moved toward her as if in a daze, then cut his own wrist and held it to her mouth. As she resumed drinking, he turned to look at Kane, his expression humble and full of awe.

"You have found my Svetla, my friend. For this I am eternally in your debt."

"Svetla?" Allie didn't understand.

"Among our kind, that means *gift.* Gift from the Fates. She is his mate, as you are mine," he said.

Stunned, Allie looked at her friend, who was now awake and staring up at the dark-haired man with obvious adoration.

Chance stepped surreptitiously into the room, likely having evaded the nurses to be there. He glared at Malcolm. "Mates? That's not possible. She's—"

"Mine," Malcolm told him, his tone full of certainty. "For eternity."

"Eternity?" A quick look at Allie and Kane, and the realization of what they'd done hit him. "You made her a—?"

"We saved her life." Kane took the shifter's arm. "And look at her, man."

Em's face was full of love as she gazed at Malcolm. She didn't even spare Chance a glance.

"That's because he made her." Furious, Chance rounded on them. "That's the only reason."

"He didn't make her. I did." Again, Kane tried to steer him toward the door. Again, Chance resisted.

"That doesn't make sense. Unless they're...what is the term?"

"Svetlas. They belong to each other."

Taking her eyes from Malcolm, Em gave Chance a gentle smile. "I'm sorry, Chance. I never felt this way about you."

Bowing his head, Chance accepted her words. Then, back straight and face averted, he left the room.

Staring again at Malcolm, Em didn't even watch Chance go. Malcolm leaned in and kissed her. She kissed him back.

"I feel like an intruder," Allie told Kane. "Maybe we should...?"

Before she could finish the words or the thought, Kane took her arm firmly, steering her toward the door. "Now someone has to tell her mother," he said. "I think that should be you."

"The truth?"

He shrugged. "That's up to you. But you'll need a cover story to give her family. Miraculous recovery, and all that. Also, a decent reason why she can't go out in the sunlight, and why she sleeps during the day."

As soon as they exited the room, Allie crossed to Mrs. Ralston. She told her only that Emily appeared to have recovered, knowing Emily would want to tell her mother the truth in her own way and time.

That done, Allie returned to where Kane waited, taking his hand and leading him down the hall.

"Did you mean what you said back there, about me being your gift?"

A look of such passion, such hunger, crossed his handsome face that it stole her breath away. "What do you think?" he growled. "Can you live with a vampire as a mate?"

"You know you'll outlive me," she said. "Turning shifters into vampires is expressly forbidden."

He swooped down to kiss her, letting her feel a tiny bit of his sharp fang. "When have you or I ever cared about the rules?"

A thrill went through her at the thought, as did a rush of desire so strong she wanted to jump his bones right there in the hallway.

A door to the right caught her eye. An empty room? Marching over to it, she peered inside, a surge of joy going through her to find it unoccupied, the bed made up as if just for them.

"Come here, mate," she ordered, pulling him inside, closing

the door, and locking them in total darkness. Shedding their clothing took only an instant. He was hard and ready and she, soft and welcoming.

"It's about time." His throaty growl ended on a groan, as she pushed him onto the bed and straddled him the way she'd wanted to back on her couch. She clenched her body around his, thrilling to the possession of him.

"Let me show you what it really means to be a wolf's mate," she said.

And, to both their pleasure, she did.

* * * * *

CAPTURED

Lori Devoti

Dedicated to everyone who wanted to know more.

LORI DEVOTI

grew up in southern Missouri and attended college at the University of Missouri–Columbia, where she earned a bachelor of journalism. Now she's proud to declare herself a writer for Silhouette Nocturne. Lori lives in Wisconsin with her family. To learn more about what Lori is working on now, visit her Web site at www.loridevoti.com.

Dear Reader,

For those of you who have read the books in my UNBOUND series, I really hope you enjoy this look at a slightly different side of the UNBOUND world. "Captured" actually shows a part of this world very few realize exists—an unsavory side. "Captured" also features a character you have heard of before but who has never been named—Leve. She was once owned by Lusse from *Unbound*, and is in fact Venge from *Wild Hunt*'s mother.

For those of you new to my books, this story stands completely on its own. But I do hope it intrigues you enough to want to learn more about hellhounds and the worlds they inhabit. Either way, welcome to the nine worlds. To learn more about them and hellhounds, visit my Web site, www.loridevoti.com.

Lori Devoti

ONE

Gray Barsk spread his fingers over the dry, caked dirt beneath him. His head was pounding. Still, his mind darted from one event to another, over what had happened this evening, what he'd done wrong, how he had landed in this cell…

He was a hellhound, one of the legendary forandre, shapeshifters, meant to run the wild hunt. Only gods and other forandre were a match for his kind—not Svartalfars, dark elves. Still, the mercenaries of the nine worlds were known for their cunning, a characteristic that had obviously been at play here.

The dark elf had caught him off guard. Poison or magic must have graced the tip of his blade. Gray wouldn't have fallen so quickly otherwise. But the poison wasn't all of it. His instincts had been dulled, too.

Even drunk, he should have been able to defeat one little flea of a dark elf. And he wasn't drunk. He'd had one mug of beer; that was all.

No, the bar was a setup, a trap. Gray realized that now. What he didn't know yet was if it was designed with only him in mind, or if he was just another hapless victim.

Hapless. Not how Gray was used to thinking of himself. It incited his anger all the more.

Footsteps shuffled nearby. The cell where Gray had been tossed was dark—too dark even for his hellhound vision to penetrate, or perhaps that was a side effect of the dark elf's poison, too. Realizing his vision wouldn't help him, he closed his eyes, concentrated on his other senses instead.

The place smelled of the dry earth he felt under his palms, compacted, smooth like concrete, but... He scratched the ground with one thumbnail. The feel of dirt clumping under his nail confirmed the place was dug into the earth, not poured in place. He started to straighten his arms, to shove himself up, but a new scent, female and laden with wary expectation, stopped him.

Tensing his muscles, he stopped moving. Hoped he hadn't already given away that he was awake and aware that somewhere in the darkness a female crouched waiting, watching.

For what?

Not again. Leve wouldn't go through this again.

She sniffed the air. Blood, sweat, the smell of male. She'd seen the flash of light as the top of the chute was opened, heard the hellhound's body being rolled down the metal ramp, felt the impact as he collided with the ground.

He was unconscious. He hadn't moved since his elegant arrival.

She crept closer, moving on the balls of her feet, using her hands to keep her balance. It was poor form to kill a hellhound while he was blacked out, against the rules of the "kamp," but she wasn't in the Kamp Arena right now. She wasn't scheduled to return until after she'd been impregnated by this male, or whoever followed, until after she'd borne a son or daughter who would grow up to fight as she did now—every day for the enjoyment of the underground followers of the Kamp—or be sold to someone else looking to start their own pack. She almost spat at the thought.

She wouldn't lose a child again. She wouldn't.

Within arm's reach of the fallen hellhound, she slowly pushed herself to a stand. First she'd make sure he was unconscious and would stay that way, then she'd figure out the quickest way to end his life. With him gone, the immediate threat would be eliminated. Then she'd wait for her captors and plot a way to explode past them when they opened the damned chute. And as she waited, she'd savor thoughts of ripping them into little bits, feeding them to the hellhounds they kept stored in these cells beneath the Kamp Arena. Perhaps she'd even let one or two live, at least long enough to be thrown in the arena, used to bait some of the most crazed hellhounds.

How would the crowd enjoy that?

A few feet from Gray's head, there was a *whoosh* of air. He rolled, grabbed the foot that was being propelled toward him and jerked. The foot's owner fell, hard, onto the dirt beside him. He wrapped one hand around a boot and grabbed a denim-clad leg with the other—a firm, but most definitely feminine, denim-clad leg.

He paused for a second—a second too long. The female let out a grunt, pulled back her free leg and jammed it into the side of his face. He spat out blood and jerked again, this time pulling her body beneath his.

She continued to fight. With a snap her head collided with his. He bit back a curse, tried to ignore the blood now pouring from his nose.

He didn't know who this female was or why she had attacked him, but one thing was perfectly clear—she was fighting in earnest and with every intention of beating him, killing him.

He growled, let the fires inside him spill into his eyes, let her see that female or not, he had no intention of rolling over, letting her win.

She growled back, let her own eyes glow. Her teeth snapped near his ear and he jerked back.

"Not again. I won't go through it again. *Jeg vil leve,*" she murmured.

I will live, he translated. The words were low, meant for her ears alone, he sensed, more a statement of conviction than threat or promise. Still, he couldn't stop his own response.

"Only if you back off," he warned, his ire growing, the bloodlust inside him igniting as the scents of anger and sweat swelled around them.

She laughed then, a cold noise, close to his ear. "But you don't want to kill me, do you? I've been here before. Survived this before. But this time, it won't happen. I won't let it happen."

How long had she been down here trapped in darkness? How far gone was her mind? He shook his head, tried to force her babbling from his thoughts. It didn't matter. Crazy or not. Tortured or not. She meant to kill him, and he had no intention of dying. His canine mind wouldn't worry about why she acted as she did, would only fight to win, no matter the cost. His canine form would end this battle quickly, perhaps saving them both.

With a roar, he let the bloodlust win out, let the magic sweep over him, let his body shift from human to hound. If only one of them could survive, he'd make sure it was him.

The wave of magic hit Leve unawares. Silly, so caught up in reliving her own nightmare, she'd slipped, let the immediate danger pale beside the memories that lingered in her mind. But now as the cell pulsed with magic, as the male's roar split the silence, she came back to herself—her present—came back to her current goal, surviving tonight, not that night so long in her past.

She bared her teeth, took a step back, then released the hold on her hellhound half, let her body and mind shift from human to canine. She let the battle shift, too. Leaving human emotions behind, she concentrated on the fight, the need to win, to survive.

Her senses immediately expanded—every smell and texture multiplying. A dozen other hellhounds had occupied this cell in the past, hundreds of battles had been waged here and remnants of each still hung in the air or lay settled on the hard dirt floor.

But she had no time to analyze the past. Just as she couldn't live in her own, she had to be in this moment, fight this battle.

The male, she could see him now, his shape, anyway, and his movements. The color of his hair was still a mystery, not that such details mattered. Her intent was to kill him before he killed her or, worse, performed the service he'd been tossed in here to complete—rape her, impregnate her.

She growled and circled to the side. Her head and tail low, she made sure he knew she wasn't playing, was more than willing to lose this fight as long as he lost his life along with hers.

Aggression rolled off the female. She'd changed to her canine form within a heartbeat of his doing so. Gray had thought to surprise her, but she hadn't hesitated even a second and seemed as eager for this fight as any *male* hellhound Gray had ever encountered.

He had never killed a female. But then, a female had never attacked him with such clear intention to destroy glowing in her eyes. He took two steps back, then lunged.

The female feinted to the left, then shimmered. Gray froze, his ears twitching, his mind alert. As quickly as she had disappeared, she rematerialized somewhere behind him. He spun, expecting her to be right beside him, or the opposite, cowering in the corner, but instead, she was hurtling toward him, using the few feet of space the cell had to propel her, to give her smaller body the advantage.

She soared toward him. He braced his feet, let her think she had him, that she would have the advantage of the surprise attack. Then while her body was still moving through the air, he shimmered, too, but only a tail's length away. She hit the hard ground with a thump and a growl and immediately began scrambling to pull her legs back beneath her body, but he didn't give her the chance. He jumped on her as she had planned to jump on him, pinned her neck to the ground with his jaws.

"Where am I?" he projected into her head.

She jerked, twisting her body so her hind feet could push into his stomach, so she could try to shove him away. He growled and tightened his grip, bit down until he tasted blood. Her movements increased, became almost frenzied. Anger and anxiety rolled off her. The scent of her emotion combined with the musk of her sex. The feel of her struggling beneath him would have sent another hellhound over the edge—completely released the beast in him. But Gray had spent the past hundred years working to conquer the bloodlust, learned to see it as the weakness it was, not the strength most hellhounds believed.

He reached inside himself, murmured a meditative chant in his head, let her hear it, too. Slowly her struggles ceased and she stared up at him, her eyes no longer glowing red.

"I won't let you win," she said telepathically.

He inhaled, realized her anger had been replaced by determination. Her heartbeat had slowed, too. The steady thump of it seemed to pound into him, each beat emphasizing the resolve that coursed through her.

Resolve for what? She was focused on something—doing or stopping something. But what?

His mouth still around her neck, his body hovering over hers, he replied, "I didn't ask for this."

"None of us did." This time her thought was tinged with sadness, a sorrow that made Gray start to pull back, to loosen his hold. But as soon as his jaws edged just a little open, she twisted again. He lost his grip. She started to jump free and he snapped down again, this time latching on to her shoulder, instead of her neck, and this time biting deeper than he had intended.

A quiver ran through her, but she didn't cry out. Instead, she seemed to pull away, pull down a shield that cut off whatever moment of communication they had shared.

Again he loosened his hold, but this time carefully, just enough to let her know he meant her no harm, but far from enough to allow her to escape. As his teeth pulled from her flesh, a new realization struck him. The flesh of her shoulder didn't give as it should have, wasn't really flesh at all anymore, but one solid mass of scar.

"What happened to you?" he asked, the thoughts more for himself than her, although he allowed them to flow into her mind, too.

She didn't answer, but he could feel her reaction—surprise, confusion—but before he could ask again, this time more directly, a metal door clanged somewhere overhead. They both froze. Gray's eyes darted toward the noise, his mind registering that he'd heard the noise before—when he first arrived here. Instinct brought his hackles to a stand and caused his muscles to tighten, but before he could react further, assess the threat, steam rolled down the metal ramp and settled all around them.

He blinked; the heavy, moist air clouded his vision and clogged his lungs. A cough built in his chest, and unable to stop the reflex, he opened his mouth, releasing a hacking bark and the female. To his surprise she didn't attack, didn't take advantage of his moment of weakness. Instead, she rolled to her feet, then shimmered, solidifying under the ramp, only her tail visible.

He staggered forward, a part of him screaming that he had to be prepared for her next attack, but another part grappling to simply focus. With each breath his thoughts grew more confused, his fight to keep control of his hellhound half harder. The steam continued to thicken. Random thoughts shot through his head—fight, kill, claim. His head swayed back and forth, his eyes searching through the fog for the female he knew waited only a few feet away.

His eyes began to glow again. He needed to do something, to fight something, to… He sniffed. The fog had subsided, no longer caught in his throat, making it difficult to breathe.

Female. She was here, and he wanted her. He could smell her, her anger, her fear and her desire. The cell was so saturated with each of the emotions he could barely stand under the onslaught.

But there was no reason to. She was here, and her emotions called out to him. He should find her, answer her unspoken request—and put an end to the lust that knifed through him.

He stalked toward the ramp, his feet plopping on the dirt, his shoulder shifting back and forth with each step. His hip swayed too far to the left, slammed into the metal chute. The female turned, bared her teeth.

"Keep away," she warned.

He frowned. Why did she say one thing when her emotions screamed something else? He took another step. She shimmered to the other side of the cell, turned and faced him, her eyes glowing, her hair standing on end. She raised her lip, revealing the full length of her canines.

"I won't be forced. Not ever again."

He blinked, pulled in another breath. The air was clearer here, not as perfumed with the enticing scent of emotion. He took another step, inhaled again. Across the room the female growled, her body tensed, ready to fight.

Gray turned his head, studied her. Something was wrong. He took another breath, pulled the air in slowly this time, analyzed it. His eyes darted to the female, then to the ramp.

The steam hadn't been steam at all, but pheromones, synthetically created emotions converted to scent. Caught up in the battle with the female, his guard down, he had sucked them in, been taken in, let them, despite his training, manipulate his actions.

He cursed in his head, let the female hear it, too.

He backed up until he could feel the wall against his haunches. The steam hadn't reached here, not as much as in the center of the cell where he had stood. Had the female realized that? Was that why she had run when the steam first covered them?

He glanced at her. She still stood in the corner, but her body language was changing. Her hair had settled back flat against her skin, and her stance was less aggressive, more submissive. The steam was reaching her, affecting her, too.

With another curse, Gray changed from hellhound to human. The pheromones would still have pull on him, but it would be less, and with the amount clogging the room, he needed every advantage he could call on.

Naked but human, he let his head hang for a second, drew on his training. When he was steadier, he lifted his gaze, checked on the female. She was still in the corner, standing and alert—watching him.

He leaned back on his heels and began murmuring the chant he'd learned to help tamp down his canine nature. Normally he would close his eyes, shut himself away from all distractions, but here he couldn't, not with the female so close. She'd attacked him before the steam had filled the cell. Now under its influence, what would she do?

Still murmuring, he stood and took a tiny step forward. His hand held out in front of him, palm up, he slowly moved behind the ramp and across the dirt floor, in a direct line to where the female lay watching.

TWO

Leve pulled her feet more fully beneath her, watched the male as he approached. He'd changed back to human. Why?

Desire trailed through her, made her want to roll over, expose her belly, let him know she wouldn't fight him. But she didn't. She wasn't quite far enough under the pheromones' control to give in. As soon as the ramp door had clanged open and she'd heard the steam, she'd known she needed to get away. From what Halla, one of the other females locked away here, had told her, the pheromones contained in the mist pumped up male hell-hounds, urged them to mate or kill, but the same chemicals subdued females, took away every urge they had except to submit. The steam stole their very will.

Leve had raced behind the ramp, hoping the air would be less tainted there, and it had been. She'd been herself for a while, but once the male invaded the space, she'd had to move again. Couldn't risk being that close to him, not after he'd taken a full dose of the emotion-laden mist into his lungs.

She'd shimmered here, hoped for some miracle to save her from the male's attack, inevitable now that he was hyped-up from the mist. She was a fighter, but she was also a realist. Her only hope for defeating a male who outweighed her by sixty pounds had been to kill him before he got a dose of the pheromones. Now with him pumped up to mate or kill and with her subdued, nothing but a miracle could stop the rape her captors had planned.

Still, she gritted her teeth, tried to focus on keeping her own mind, not letting the chemicals win. As the naked male approached, she managed one weak growl, before shifting back into her human form and rolling over belly up—submissive, exposed, beaten by her own nature.

With each step, Gray grew stronger, more under control. But as he approached the female, he was shocked by what he saw…what she did. Her eyes suspicious slits, she growled, then almost before the sound had reached his ears, she changed from canine to human and, naked, rolled over, her stomach bare and exposed. An easy target for whatever he had in mind.

His wary approach changed to hard strides. He grabbed her by the forearm and jerked her to a sit.

"What are you doing?" he asked, his fingers digging into her flesh with more force than he intended. He expected her to snarl, strike out, but instead, she lowered her head, refused to meet his gaze.

He stared at her blankly for a few seconds, unable to wrap his mind around the drastic change in her, then as his gaze drifted to the ramp, he pulled back, loosened his grip. The mist. It was affecting her, too, but in a totally different way than it had him.

Snapping out a curse, he scooped her into his arms and shimmered them both back beneath the ramp. While she sat there looking dazed, he grabbed their clothes and began pulling them on—hers first. She objected, batting his fingers away as he tried to shove buttons through holes, then just as quickly she captured his hand and began rubbing her face against his palm.

He pulled on his pants, then grabbed her face between his

index finger and thumb. "You're still in there somewhere, aren't you? Wanting to kill me?"

Something flickered in her eyes and her chin jerked—an attempt to pull away. Gray pinched her face harder, glad for the resistance but not satisfied with just that feeble effort. He stared into her eyes, forced her gaze to meet his. She lowered her eyelids and he jerked her face again, brought her attention back to him.

They continued the dance until finally she met his gaze and held it, then lifted her lip in a snarl.

Gray grinned. "Back to the bitch, I see."

She snapped her chin free and watched him out of the corners of eyes thinned with suspicion. "What happened?" she asked, her hands smoothing the sleeves of her shirt, patting the legs of her pants.

"Some kind of drug. They pumped it in here." Gray shoved himself to a stand and stalked to the center of the room, where he could study the ramp and keep an eye on the female.

"Not that." The female was in a crouch now, her eyes following his every move, her body coiled, ready to spring. "After."

He turned his gaze fully on her, crossed his arms over his chest. "You mean the part where you rolled over belly up and asked me to scratch you?"

She twisted her head to the side. A nerve jumped in her cheek.

Gray muttered to himself. He didn't have time for this. Whoever tossed them down here, then filled the place with the mist would be back. *But wait. The female had been here first, before him.*

"Where are we? Why were we put in here?"

Added tension in her back was the only sign she gave that she'd heard his questions. Fed up with the mysteries, he shimmered and bent down to grab her by the shoulder.

The meek female was gone. With no warning, she spun, her leg shooting out as she did. Gray jumped. Her leg slammed into the wall. She cursed and rolled backward, landing on her feet.

Her chest heaving, she held her hands out in front of her, ready to attack—again.

Gray tamped down a surge of anger and spoke in even, if stilted, words. "I'm not the enemy. Whoever put us here is. I want to escape—I plan to escape. Help me or keep out of my way." He turned his back on her, purposely letting her know he was bored with the games, done with them.

As he reached out to place a hand on each side of the ramp, she stopped him. "Don't. It's charged."

His hands were mere inches from touching the metal. He hadn't felt a shock when he'd been rolled down the chute. Was she lying? Was her bizarre behavior part of some elaborate act to get him not to try to escape?

He placed a hand on each edge of the chute. Power, blue hot, shot through him. For a second he couldn't even let go of the ramp, but just stood there, voltage blasting through him. Then it became too much; his hands blew free, his body catapulted across the room and thudded into the rock-hard dirt wall.

The air next to him turned to waves, and as he struggled to pull air into his lungs, the female appeared beside him, nudged him with her bare foot and said, "Way to take my help."

With a groan, he rolled over, pretended to curl into himself. Then as she started to stride away, he grabbed her by the leg and jerked her down onto the dirt beside him. His hands wrapped around her wrists, his body straddling hers, he replied, "Want to help? Start talking."

Leve barely kept the panic out of her eyes. She'd let the male catch her, had trusted him for a minute. *Stupid. No way to survive.* She knew better.

"Why should I?" she asked, keeping her tone cool, undisturbed, while inside her heart pounded.

The male narrowed his eyes, leaned down and stared into hers. "You need to work on masking your emotions. The amount of anxiety you're putting out would send any other hellhound into a frenzy."

"But not you." She laughed, but with no humor. There was nothing funny about where she was, what she might have to do, but she'd live. She always had before.

The thought brought her no relief, hadn't for years.

The female's chin angled up slightly as she held his gaze, but Gray wasn't fooled, no hellhound would be. She reeked of anxiety. She might play at nonchalance, but she was terrified.

He leaned down just to emphasize his point, but a flash of alarm shooting through her eyes stopped him. She was afraid—of him.

He released her hands, and rolled off her. She scrambled to sit up and shoved herself backward until her spine touched the wall.

"I'm not going to harm you," he said, still working through his surprise that he needed to say the words. She'd attacked him, almost before he'd even known she was in the cell, and now he was reassuring her?

Her eyes cold and disbelieving, she braced her hands on the floor. "It may not be up to you."

He frowned. "You mean…the mist? What do you know about it? Where are we?"

"The mist." She stared into space. "It changes all of us."

"Not me." He crouched down, crept closer so he could speak more softly, keep their words from being overheard—assuming the space wasn't bugged or some kind of magic being used to watch them.

She waved a hand. "Don't bother. They don't listen to us. Why should they? None of us has ever escaped. They have us completely under their control." She spat out the last word.

Control. Not something many hellhounds were good at, but losing control to another being? And being held in a cage?

He stood up, placed his palm against the solid wall.

That was something every hellhound, including himself, feared.

But Gray wouldn't let it happen, wouldn't give in to his fear. He curled his hand into a fist and slammed it against the wall. Letting his anger soak into his voice, he said, "So you've given up?"

She looked at him, her mouth opening, then closing into a tight line.

"You playing along with what whoever's behind that door wants? You working for them, helping them to house-train new hounds?" He crouched again, got in her space. "What exactly is your role here? Assassin or seductress? What hoop was I supposed to be jumping through by now?"

The flash was back in her eyes. "You'd have to ask someone else that question."

He looked around the empty cell. "Any suggestions?"

"Go fu—" The metal door rattled. He slapped a hand over her mouth, leaned in and whispered next to her ear, "What do they want? What do they expect us to be doing? What will get rid of them—at least long enough for us to figure a way out of here?"

Her body tense, she darted her gaze to the door, then back at him. Her indecision was almost palpable. He waited.

As the door above their heads inched open, she slapped her hands behind his neck and jerked his mouth down to hers.

THREE

The female's lips were soft, and moved with an urgency that made Gray want to jerk her form against his, feel the tension strumming through her, share it. Her body was soft, too—soft curves packed onto hard muscle. And she smelled good, pure female but bathed in anxiety, fear and determination. She was a mix of contrary emotions, a puzzle. One he would like to solve.

But, his mind warned, puzzle or not, this kiss was wrong, too out of character for what he'd seen from her so far. His mind battled with his body, telling him to kiss her. The feel of her breasts pressed against his chest, her sex cradling his, had to be part of a trick. He'd be a fool to give in, no matter how badly he wanted to.

He started to untangle her hands from around his neck, to push her away, but the door rattled louder. She pushed against him, knocked him to the ground and straddled him as he had straddled her earlier, while her lips never left his.

Then it hit him. She had answered his question. Seductress was her role and she was playing it to the hilt.

He wrapped his hands around her waist and rolled them into the center of the room, where whoever was peering at them from the top of the chute would be sure to see them.

She grunted as they rolled, an objection, but one she covered by running her fingers down his bare back, letting her nails scrape over his skin.

Despite knowing it was an act, one that would end as soon as the door slammed shut, a charge ran through him. He pulled his lips from hers, puffed out a breath and began trailing kisses down her neck, nibbling at her throat.

She reciprocated, grabbing his hair and holding his head still while she flipped them over again. Back on top, she traced the line of his throat with her tongue, blew on his damp skin.

A shiver raced over him. Triumph glowed in her eyes.

She'd upped the game. She was playing him. He couldn't let that pass.

He ran his hands up her sides, cupped breasts uncontained by any undergarment. Her nipples hardened. He could see them through the thin material of her shirt, and she could feel them—he could see it in her eyes. With a smile, he bent forward, ran his thumb over one hardened peak and caught the other with his mouth.

A gasp escaped her lips, and he smiled against her breast. Escaped. It was the right term. Her reaction to him was killing her, gnawing at her pride. He rolled his tongue over her nipple. She sat up straighter, pressing her sex harder against his, rock-hard and ready. A groan passed his lips before he could stop it, and she laughed, a low, mocking sound meant only for him.

He flipped them over again, lowered his hand to the zipper of her pants. How far would she take this?

She wrapped her leg around his thigh, pinning his body to hers, and dropped her own hand to the top of his jeans.

Above them the door clanked shut.

The sound of the door clanging shut rung in Leve's head, shook her back to reality. Somehow, and she'd have sworn to her last breath this would never happen, she'd gotten lost in the arms of a hellhound, forgotten what had been taken from her in the past and just enjoyed the game, played with him.

His hand, hovering over the zipper of her jeans, paused. She tensed, waited. Had she misstepped? Would he now try to take from her what others had taken before?

He curled his fingers into a fist, shook his head and rolled off her. Lying flat on the ground beside her, he said, "Maybe it's time we introduced ourselves."

For the first time since she had been dumped in this place, for the first time in decades, Leve relaxed, felt her lips curve into a soft smile. "Maybe we should," she replied.

He responded with a low laugh, then placed his hand on hers. She tensed, but didn't pull away. Then after a few seconds of just lying there, her fingers held lightly by his, she began to enjoy the feeling of warmth. His fingers pressed against hers and she returned the squeeze.

She was sharing a moment with someone who less than an hour earlier she'd been determined to kill. What had happened to her? What had she allowed to happen to her?

"Gray Barsk," he murmured.

"Leve."

"Leve? As in live?"

She shrugged. It was a name she'd given herself. To the dark elves who ran this place she was nothing more than a number. The witch who had owned her before had given her a name, but Leve refused to use it, to even remember it. She had never had anything that belonged to her, not her body, not her children—taken from her before they were even weaned—nothing. But she had given herself a name, a purpose. To live. To prove she could survive anything anyone dished out to her.

Bad memories poured into her, and she tried to pull her hand away. He held on, ran his thumb over the back. "It's a good name."

She nodded, stared up at the ceiling for a second. "They'll be back, checking to make sure things are going the way they want them to."

"Why?" he asked. "Why go along with them?"

She turned her head sharply to look at him. "Go along with them? I don't go along with them. I've fought them every chance I've had. I've done nothing but fight my entire life." She thumped her head back against the dirt, narrowed her gaze. She should have killed him.

He pushed himself up and glanced over his shoulder at the door. "It doesn't matter to me. All that matters is that you don't get in my way. I'm not a captive. I'm not staying here."

She widened her gaze at his arrogance. "Well, since you put it that way, let's go." She sat up, stared around her. "Oh, I'm sorry. I seem to have misplaced the door."

He growled. "I didn't say it would be easy." Arms folded over his chest, he stared at her. "What's your story? How did you get in here? What's the point of us…" He waved his hand between them.

"The free hellhound-matchmaking service?" She breathed out, dropped her gaze to the dirt. Bickering with him wasn't going to help her, and stupid though it might be, she trusted this male… Gray. He was different than the others. For one thing, he hadn't raped her.

She looked him in the eye. "You are in a mill—a breeding factory. Under the Kamp Arena, where hellhounds fight for other beings' entertainment. I don't know who owns either. I only know that dark elves seem to be the preferred hirelings."

His mouth opened, and even in the dim light she could see the shock on his face. "So, you…?"

"Get thrown in here every so often. Have a romantic interlude." She shrugged, pretended she didn't care. "You get the idea."

"And the children?"

She turned away then, pulled her knees to her chest. "Disappear. Sold, maybe."

"Sold." The word fell flat, like a bird shot from the sky. His arm wound around her shoulders, and to her surprise, she felt her body give, felt herself leaning against him. He didn't say anything, didn't touch her in any way with the exception of the band of his arm supporting her, comforting her.

Leve dropped her chin to her chest, and let one tear, then another roll down her cheeks.

Gray had never been more shocked, or impressed, in his life. How had Leve stood this? Being captive, being taken, her children stolen from her. How did she not only survive, but still have the strength of will to fight her captors and him?

He wished he knew something to say, wished they had time to let her heal, but the dark elves would be back soon—Leve had said so herself.

He waited another minute, one more than he felt comfortable with, then asked, "Have you ever tried to escape? How long will they leave us here? They'll have to move us at some point."

She took a deep breath, seemed to gather herself, then turned to face him. The arm he'd kept around her fell from her shoulders, but he didn't remove it completely. He liked the feel of her close, liked still touching her.

Her eyes told him, however, he *wasn't* going to like her answer.

"They'll come back after..." She tilted her head to the side.

He nodded; he didn't need her to spell it out.

She licked her lips. He could tell she was thinking back to the other times. He reached down and took her hand in his. Her fingers were cold. He held them tighter, willing warmth and strength into her.

"They'll bring food. The males..." She shivered.

He resisted the urge to pull her against him. She knew he was here, hopefully believed he wouldn't harm her. If...when she wanted more from him, he'd be here, but caught in the memories, any further advances needed to come from her.

"The males are ravenous after. The mist, I guess. They don't even seem to know I'm here. They just move from one base need to another." She licked her lips, but sat up straighter, seemed to grow stronger. "After they eat, they pass out. They may be—" she glanced at him "—dead." A furrow formed between her brows. "But I don't think so. It wouldn't make sense, would it? Why kill them? They could be used again, put in the Kamp—or sold."

Sold, continued captivity. Continued loss of power over your own destiny. Gray couldn't think of a worse fate, except—Leve's hand moved in his—what Leve had been through.

"Are there others?"

Her brows dropped lower, confused. "Hellhounds?"

He was thinking of females, trapped like Leve, used like Leve, but— "Yes, like you and me, held here somewhere?"

Her jaw jutted to the side; she nodded. "There are others. I've talked with them, telepathically through the walls, but I've never seen them."

"How long?" How long had she endured this hell, alone, except when thrown in with a drugged-up, lust-driven male?

"Years, fighting in the Kamp. Two pregnancies here. There was another before..." Again she faded away, her mind somewhere else.

He held his breath, forced himself to be patient.

She shook herself and came back to the moment. "They keep me in a cell like this, but smaller. There's a door. There." She pointed to the space under the ramp. "It's connected to a tunnel. There are other doors off it. One leads to my cell. When they've brought me here, they've drugged me beforehand, and after...well, I'm not myself."

The mist's sedative effect he'd witnessed earlier.

"Could we fool them? Make them think I was out and you were under?"

She caught his gaze. "We can try."

FOUR

Gray's arm had fallen to the small of Leve's back. The weight of it was reassuring, letting her know she wasn't alone, not anymore. Escape. Was it possible? She'd never allowed herself to dream of such a thing. She'd always stayed focused on just surviving. But now, after seeing how Gray had fought the mist and didn't succumb to its allure, how he'd pulled her from its grip, too, she couldn't help but feel some flicker of hope. Maybe let into her heart the idea that merely surviving wasn't enough.

She wanted to live—really and truly live.

But to do so, to fool the dark elves, she'd have to open herself to another risk.

She blew a breath through the circle of her lips. "We'll have to convince them…" Her decision made, she grabbed the hem of her shirt.

Gray pulled back, surprise in his eyes.

His silence made it easier. She closed her eyes and pretended she wasn't in the packed-earth cell, pretended she was free. And she was, in a way. This was her choice, her idea.

She placed a hand on Gray's chest. His skin was warm and smooth, but she could feel the muscle underneath.

"You don't have to do this," he said.

"That's why I can," she replied.

The metal door rattled. Leve jerked the shirt over her head. The cool air hit her breasts, making her nipples pucker, but she resisted the urge to grab her shirt and cover herself back up. Instead, she reached for Gray.

As the door clanked fully open, she pushed him to the ground and covered his mouth with hers.

His lips were soft, encouraging, not demanding. She ran her hands down his sides, prayed what they were doing looked believable. The other times, she'd been aware of so little, except that she was unaware, lost in a fog. Then later when she came out of it in her own cell, she'd remember bits and pieces, the ugly mosaic of what had happened.

From those bits, she knew what passed between her and Gray wasn't the furious, pheromone-driven mating she'd experienced before. Hopefully, the guards wouldn't question the difference, would just be satisfied that their breeding was under way.

The door stayed open longer this time. Sweat formed between Leve's breasts. She put a hand on Gray's jeans, began unzipping them.

He placed his hand on top of hers. "Slow down," he whispered. "They expect me to be the aggressor."

He was right. She had a role to play, and to do that she had to give up control. The thought caused a new twinge of panic, but she squelched it and allowed him to flip her over, to lie on top of her.

She waited, expecting him to become aggressive. To portray a bloodlust-driven hellhound he would have to, but he simply kissed her again, ran his hand up and down her side in long strokes that made her almost forget the dirt clinging to them both, the dank smell of the cell and the eyes watching from behind the open door above.

Almost.

The door creaked, not closed, but closing.

Gray murmured sounds of reassurance in her ear, reached for

the closure of his pants. The zipping noise seemed unnaturally loud, startling. She twitched beneath him. He pressed tiny kisses around her ear, down her neck, and to her surprise, her back began to arch, and something—longing—began to build inside her.

Gray had never fought a battle as difficult as this one. Holding Leve in his arms, pretending they were doing what their captors expected—mating—while hiding from Leve the emotions inside him pounding to get out.

Trapped in this dirt cell, watched like an animal, treated like an animal, he couldn't stop his body from reacting to Leve's soft curves and the strength obvious in the muscles beneath them. Just as he couldn't stop his emotions from reacting to her story and the pain he'd caught wafting off her as she recounted her tale.

He wanted this female—sexually and emotionally. And there was no way he could make love to her and not hurt her more—not now.

The door clunked shut.

He lowered his head to Leve's chest, resisted the urge to rub his forehead against her sweat-damp skin, to gorge himself on her scent. "We need to be naked when they get back, make it look like we're done." His voice was rough, the words choppy, and he couldn't stop himself from pressing a small kiss to Leve's chest, hoped she accepted it as just more of the act.

For a second Leve didn't move, and he froze, too, worried he'd gone too far, pressed too hard. But then she relaxed, put her hands on his back and began to knead his tight muscles. The movement was natural, as if she didn't realize what she was doing.

"Will that be enough?" she asked. There was a tremor in her voice, and Gray cursed whatever gods had set them up for this, put their destinies on a path to cross in this no-win situation.

"Yes," he replied. He wanted to escape, knew she did, too, but he wouldn't violate the bit of trust she'd given him by asking her to do more than what was absolutely necessary.

Quickly, silently, they removed the rest of their clothing. When they were both naked, Gray held out his hand. Her fingers slipped into his, and she stretched out on the dirt beside him. He braced himself on one elbow and waited.

When the door creaked again, he leaned over her and whispered. "If things get too close, fight me, let me know." Then he lowered his body until their skin touched, until he could feel her heart beating against his chest.

Her smell, feel and taste almost overwhelmed him. His groin still hard from before, engorged even more. He groaned with real pain and desire, rubbed his length against her mound, hoped it appeared from above that he was inside her—as he longed to be.

Leve played along with him, lifting her sex, rubbing her hands up and down his back. A moan fell from her lips.

He gritted his teeth, barely controlling the passion he yearned to set free. Leve's lips danced over his chest; her tongue flickered over his skin. He wanted to whisper that her actions weren't necessary, that the dark elves thought she was drugged, subdued, but he didn't think he could form the words. He could barely hold his thoughts together enough to keep from capturing her lips with his, from putting his knee between hers and sliding his erection between her soft folds.

The image of encasing himself inside her brought another groan. His sex pulsed anew, and he knew he couldn't stop his body from finishing what he and Leve had started.

He slipped his hands under her body, pulled her tighter and whispered hoarsely in her ear, "Now." It was all he could get out as the need to move faster overcame his resistance. He pressed down against her mound, put the lure of being inside her aside, concentrated, instead, on the feel of her mound rubbing against his length, of hearing the tiny pants of her breath, faux though he knew them to be.

She played along well, arching against him, murmuring, even nipping at his throat, and finally as his orgasm hit him, as he felt his release, she quivered in his arms, made him feel that she was there with him.

Leve clung to Gray, unable to believe she'd forgotten where they were, that they were playacting for some demented dark elf. Her body tingled with awareness, wanted more. She'd been close to losing herself, closer than she had ever been before. She had never understood the males' need to mate, what drove them, but after "pretending" with Gray, she more than understood the need; she shared it.

As the door shut again and Gray edged away from her, it took all her strength to let him, to not insist he finish what he'd begun.

"Now what?" he asked. He turned his back to her, kept his gaze on the door.

Leve winced and covered her breasts with her arms. She'd never felt uncomfortable being naked, most forandre wouldn't, but suddenly she felt cold, exposed.

As if sensing her discomfort, Gray turned back. "I'm sorry," he said. He ran a hand over his face. "Are you okay?"

She leaned forward, pressed her palms on the dirt floor. "I'm fine." Now that he was looking at her, talking to her like an equal, she felt all right. She shook off the moment of unease. "They should be back soon. We need to take our places. I'll lie here." She pointed to a place not far away.

"No." Gray shook his head. "Over here." He gestured to the other side of the space. "It's farther from the door." He glanced at where she had told him the door to the tunnels would open. "I'll make sure they have to get past me to get to you. And they won't."

FIVE

Gray watched as Leve positioned herself out of the way. Then he began roaming the cell, roaring and muttering, slamming his fist into the wall—acting like a thousand hellhounds he had seen caught in the out-of-control spiral of bloodlust.

His efforts paid off. Within minutes the door at the top of the ramp rattled open and a tray laden with meat slid down. He jumped on the food, pretended to shove it into his mouth as quickly as he could, sliding it under his shirt, which still lay on the floor, instead. As he pretended to chew, he continued to roam, stumbling past Leve, who lay curled on her side performing her own act of the drugged, submissive female. She went as far as to cringe when his foot brushed her hair, and for a second he stopped, forgot she was acting, too. But when her eyes darted to the side, he remembered himself and his role.

He let his steps drag, his body slump, until he fell to his knees, then over, face-first in the dirt right between the hidden entrance and the ramp.

They lay there, Gray breathing in the smell of dirt and desperation, Leve curled on her side, uttering a low hum that changed to a keen as the minutes ticked by. The sound pulled at Gray. The idea that she had made that sound before, when she had lost her child, stabbed at him, made it all the harder to stay in character and wait.

But he did; they both did, and after what felt like hours, after Leve's lament had softened to a whimper, the secret door behind Gray slowly edged open.

He didn't stir. A dark elf, reeking of licorice, crept into the room. He stopped by Gray. Gray could feel his gaze, smell his annoyance. Gray wasn't where he was supposed to be, was in the elf's way—just as Gray and Leve had planned it.

The elf muttered under his breath, then turned, the light patter of his footsteps telling Gray he'd returned to the doorway, probably signaling for help.

Gray counted in his head, kept his mind busy so his body didn't react too soon. The more guards who came into the room, the more opponents who'd be taken down, accounted for.

He hadn't asked Leve how many manned the mill, guessed she wouldn't know, but it stood to reason the operation wasn't watched by a single Svartalfar. There would be others. Everyone he took out here was one less to wonder about later.

Soon the dark elf returned, with company. His companions shared his scent, more Svartalfars. Was this a totally Svartalfar operation or were the dark elves just easy hires for whoever was in charge? Dark elves were known for their mercenary tendencies. If any beings' loyalty could be bought, it was theirs.

Gray stilled his mind, concentrated on the sound of the guards, their footsteps, their heartbeats. There were three of them, one older than the others, more experienced, if his slower, calmer heartbeat could be trusted.

Gray focused on him. Take him out first and the others would panic.

The original guard walked up to Gray, stopping only inches away. "Want to move him first?" he asked, his voice low, but with an edge of bravado.

"No, stick with the plan. Get the bitch locked up. She's where the value is."

"Humph."

The second guard drew closer, knocked Gray with his foot. Gray grunted and made a drunken, sleepy swipe with his hand, missing the Svartalfar by a foot.

"See? He's out. Rem said it took three slashes to get him down enough to get him here. I tripled the dose in the meat. He won't be up for days."

"Get the bitch." The older guard seemed unimpressed.

Tension rolled off the younger pair, but they stepped away, toward Leve. As Gray had suspected, the third stayed close.

Again he counted, gave them ten paces—until he estimated they were halfway between where he lay and Leve. Then he attacked.

Leve let her eyes flutter for a second, took a peek at what was happening in the cell. Three Svartalfars had entered. Two approached her; the third stayed near Gray, his gaze on the guards walking toward her.

Silent as the mist that had filled the cell earlier, Gray rose and grabbed the dark elf near him by the neck. One quick savage twist and the Svartalfar slumped in his arms—dead.

As he fell a gurgle escaped his crushed throat. The guards nearest Leve spun toward the sound, cursed.

Leve didn't wait. She leaped to her feet, threw herself on the back of the closest—the one who had tossed her in here. Without a flicker of regret, she followed Gray's lead and snapped the slim Svartalfar's neck.

That left one.

The dark elf panicked—never a good move. He started to run, then froze, unsure which direction to dart, his body twitching one way, then the other. Nowhere was safe, not for him. Just as this place had never been safe for Leve, offered no safety for any of the hellhounds brought here, not even the males.

She stepped over the dead guard she'd killed, moved to grab this one. He pulled a sword from the belt at his side and rushed at her. She widened her stance, ready to meet him head-on, almost hungry for a fight against the beings who had held her, watched her torment. But as the dark elf lunged for his first thrust, Gray roared and charged at him from behind.

Holding his weapon seemed to have calmed the guard, and he spun, graceful, smooth. Kept his sword in front of him, the tip steady and pointed at Gray's heart.

Leve could have attacked him then, from behind. But she knew better. Gray wouldn't appreciate her help, and she trusted he could take care of one mercenary guard by himself.

The guard slashed his sword to the left. Gray hopped to the side. The guard danced forward. Gray moved again. The dark elf changed his stance and seemed to settle in for a long, serious battle, but as he did, Gray shimmered, solidifying behind him. One arm around the guard's chest, the other gripping his chin, Gray jerked and the last guard crumpled to the ground.

"Sorry. No time for games today," Gray muttered to the dead Svartalfar. Then he looked up, grabbed Leve's gaze. "Let's go."

With a nod, she stepped over the dead guards and led him from the room.

They stepped into a hall. The walls were lined with some kind of metal. Gray placed a palm against the cold, smooth surface.

"To stop shimmers?" he asked.

Leve lifted one shoulder. "Or communication. The guards seemed to think I couldn't talk with anyone else. We never told them differently."

Gray's jaw hardened. He stood in the center of the hall, his eyes ticking off the doors on each side. "Twenty. Are they all full?"

"I don't—"

Gray cut her off with an upraised hand.

Farther down the hall, past a turn, came the sound of music—flutes and drums. Svartalfar.

Gray turned to face her, mouthed, "Where's the exit?"

Leve's eyes narrowed. He could leave, but she wasn't going anywhere. Not without checking behind every door and freeing every female.

She pivoted, started to step back into the cell she and Gray had just left.

He grabbed her arm, his fingers digging into her skin. She stopped, stared at his hand, gave him a second to let her go.

He didn't. Instead, he stepped closer, whispered in her ear. "You get out. I'll stay and get the others."

She pulled her arm away and continued back into the cell. At the first guard's body, she stopped and searched his pockets. Nothing. Breathing deeply through her nose, willing her mind to stay calm, she went to the next one—the one with the sword. Tucked into a slot on his scabbard was a metal card. She pulled it free and hurried back into the hall.

She tapped it against her thumbnail. "We'll need this."

Gray started to shake his head, but she held up the card. "You know what these females have been through? You think they'll trust a male hellhound?"

Anger, then resolve flitted through Gray's eyes. "Okay. I'll look for an exit and see if anyone's listening to..." He jerked his head toward the music.

Leve slid the card into the first door. As the lock popped, Leve flinched. Just like it had every time one of the guards had opened her door, never knowing if this was the time she would be taken back to the cell.

But the guards were dead—she glanced down the hall toward the music that still played—or would be soon. She didn't have to fear that sound again. It had greeted her on every arrival, every trip to a cell where she would be attacked, raped. And no other females would have to fear it either.

With the thought held in the forefront in her mind, she pushed the door open. A pregnant female, her hands wrapped around her swollen belly, lay propped against the wall. Her lip was curled into a snarl and her eyes burned red.

Emotion caught in Leve's chest. "Halla?" she whispered.

The female's eyes widened, the simmering glow dimming. Leve took another step, held out one hand. "We're leaving, escaping. You won't lose your baby, not this one."

Halla's face began to soften. She reached out, too, grabbed Leve's hand. "It's true," Leve said. "We're going to save you. Save everyone."

A tear rolled down Halla's face and she struggled to stand. Not pregnant, the female would have outweighed Leve by thirty pounds. Nine months pregnant, the difference was closer to a hundred. Still, Leve held Halla's arm, tried to leverage her own weight against the pregnant hellhound's.

It wasn't enough. Halla began to fall, taking Leve with her. Then Gray was there, helping them, giving Leve the chance to catch her balance and cradling Halla against his chest.

Leve breathed out a sigh—of relief, of joy at having someone to help her and not having to be strong all alone. But before she could take in another breath, Halla changed from stumbling to spitting and raging. She twisted in Gray's arms, went for his face, fingernails flailing and teeth flashing.

Terror shot through Leve. "Don't hurt her!" she screamed, forgetting where they were, that other guards might be near, hear them.

Gray, grappling for a hold of the other female's wrists, growled out a reply. "If you don't trust me, how will she? She can smell your panic."

Leve stepped back. He was right. Anger replaced fear—anger at her moment of weakness, for losing control. She breathed in and out, forced herself to see that Gray wasn't hurting Halla, that despite the pregnant female's attempts to harm him, he remained calm, held her as gently as he could a storming mother-to-be bent on his death.

Leve placed a hand on Halla's hair, ran her palm down its length, then down the other female's back. "He won't hurt you, Halla. He's here to help. They captured him, too, but he resisted. He didn't hurt me. He won't hurt you, either."

As Halla continued to struggle, Leve continued to stroke the pregnant hellhound and concentrate on keeping her own mind calm, projecting trust, hope, things most of the mill's inhabitants hadn't felt or smelled for years.

Slowly, Halla's muscles relaxed, her eyes calmed, and her breathing slowed.

Leve put an arm around her waist and looked at Gray. "You can let her go."

He cocked an eyebrow, but released the exhausted female. Leve staggered under her weight, but didn't fall. Together they stumbled into the hall.

"No more guards, not now, anyway." Gray pulled the metal card from Leve's fingers. "And I found the exit. You can't shimmer here. I tried. But once out of this area—to where the music is playing—you'll see another door to another hall. It leads outside. Take her."

The two stared at each other, both realizing they needed Leve to calm the women, but neither wanting to leave the other behind, perhaps to get trapped here again.

"I'll go on my own," Halla murmured, her hands clutching her stomach. "I'll be slow, anyway. You may beat me." Licking her lips, she began shuffling down the hall toward the music.

"It will take her forever," Leve murmured.

"Will she let me carry her?" Gray asked, but he didn't wait for the answer. They both knew Halla wouldn't. She might not let another male touch her ever again, and the last thing they needed was for her to panic once more and go into labor with them stuck in the mill.

So Leve turned her attention away from her friend, concentrated instead on saving others, getting as many out as quickly as they could. She and Gray worked as a team. He opened the doors and stood watch. Leve slipped inside and whispered to the females. Then pointed them down the hall toward freedom.

When the last female had been freed, Leve held her arm and walked with her to the end of the hall. Gray followed, but at the doorway, where the females quickened their pace, smelling fresh air and freedom, he stopped.

Leve stopped, too, waved the last female on ahead.

"We're there. We're free. What are you doing?"

"There's another hall. I haven't been down it, but I heard a noise. There's a hellhound held there." He took a breath. "A male."

A fist closed around Leve's heart; her shoulders pulled back. She opened her mouth to tell Gray to leave him, that the male wasn't worth saving, deserved what he got, but Gray's knowing gaze stopped her.

"He's as much a victim as any of you. He didn't choose to come here, didn't ask to by hyped-up on whatever they pump into that room."

"Are you sure? You resisted." Leve's hands opened and closed, grasping for something that wasn't there, something to squeeze, some way to let the hate that roared through her escape without screaming at Gray.

Gray turned on his heel and started down the second hall.

Leve clenched her jaw, started to turn away, to follow the last female as she shuffled out the door to freedom. She took one step and stopped. Gray was wrong. Saving the male was wrong, foolhardy. The mill was empty now, the guards who had been on duty dead, but more guards would come. Leve had been here long enough to know there was more than one shift.

When would the next group arrive? She had no way of knowing, had lost a sense of time soon after being deposited here.

If they arrived while Gray was still inside, he'd be trapped, and while they hadn't beaten him the first time, they'd figure out a way. They'd make him into one of the monsters.

She shoved her fingers into her hair and cursed.

Then she followed Gray.

Gray knew the minute Leve decided to follow him, heard her tiny intake of breath, that she didn't approve, but was with him, anyway. He should have forced her to go back, to stay with the other females. But he suspected that would be a waste of breath and time, time he didn't have.

In the guards' break room, he'd seen the schedule, and a clock. There had been an hour until the next shift took over. They'd spent at least half that freeing the females. Leaving thirty minutes to find and free the male and get out of here. And that was assuming no one was overly dedicated and came in early.

But if someone did, he'd deal with it. He wouldn't be captured, not again.

The hall veered to the right, then down. Gray had to slow his pace, point his toes and shift his weight backward to keep from tumbling over. Behind him, Leve followed suit.

Doors led off this hall, just like the females' hall, but only one cell was occupied. Gray had already pressed his ear to each door, waited to listen for a heartbeat.

If anyone was inside the other cells, they were past saving.

He stopped in front of the last door and waited for Leve. "I don't know what he'll be like," he said, giving her one last chance to leave him.

She reached in her pants pocket and pulled out the metal key card. "Guess we'll find out."

She slid the card into the lock, then stood to the side, wisely letting him face the male first.

Two hundred pounds of hellhound male charged at them. Gray stepped in the room, slamming the door closed behind him and shimmering at the same time. Unable to stop his forward motion and obviously not expecting whoever opened the door to be able to shimmer, the male rammed into the now closed door.

Gray materialized, crossed his arms over his chest and waited. The male spun, his eyes glowing.

"I'm not one of your keepers." Gray held out both hands, but the male was too far gone. He charged again.

Gray shimmered again. Under other circumstances, he would have fought back, but he was here to save the hellhound, not kill him. This time when the confined hellhound turned, a line had formed between his brows.

"Do I look like a dark elf?" Gray flexed his head to the side, let the other male see the breadth of his shoulders, the build no Svartalfar could ever develop. "Do I smell like one?"

The male paused, pressed two fingers to his temple. "Who are you?" he asked, the words coming out in a croak.

"Can't say I'm a friend, but I'm not your enemy." Gray's gaze flicked to the closed door. "I'm here to let you out."

Surprise, then suspicion, filled the male's face.

Gray held up a hand. "But first I need to know what happened here. What did you do?"

The hellhound reached for the door.

"It's locked. Talk to me, or you don't get out." Gray kept his gaze steady, sure, and prayed silently that the door had locked behind him and that Leve wouldn't open it without hearing his voice.

The male tried the door anyway. When he was sure it wouldn't open, he placed both hands on the door and rested his forehead on its smooth surface. "What did I do? Hell if I know."

"You don't remember?" Gray remembered being sliced by the dark elf's knife in a bar in the human world, then very little more until he was shoved down the ramp into the cell with Leve.

"I got in a fight." The hellhound pushed his body away from the door, turned to face Gray. His eyes were blue—no sign of the telltale red, but his posture was far from trusting. "Nothing new for our kind." He cocked his head. "You going to open the door now?"

Gray smiled, back on known turf, talking with his own kind, battling even in conversation. "What about here? What happened to you here?"

The hellhound stared at him for a second, then shrugged. "Beats me. I got rolled down some kind of slope into another room. The place reeked of emotion…" He dropped his gaze, looked at the ground. "I don't know what happened, but I doubt it was pretty."

Gray rushed forward, grabbed the male by the throat and shoved him back against a wall. "You better be telling the truth. There are twenty females out there who'd like to chomp you into kibble, and if I get a single sniff that you're lying to me, I'll truss you up like Sunday dinner."

The male blinked; confusion streamed from him, tinged with a touch of anger and resentment.

Satisfied that if the hellhound had attacked any of the females, he hadn't done so under his own mental power, Gray strode to the door and yelled to Leve.

Leve couldn't stop the growl that came to her throat as the male hellhound appeared in the doorway. Gray's hand on her shoulder kept the rumble from turning to a full-on attack.

"How do you think whichever of those females he attacked are going to react?" she muttered to him as they walked behind the male.

"What makes you think those females are anywhere near here?"

Leve twisted her mouth to the side. He was right. There was no reason the females would wait outside the mill's entrance and risk being recaptured. While she had spoken to many of them through the mill's walls, they weren't a pack and they had every reason to scatter as soon as their feet hit free ground.

The hall they were walking in turned to a round-sided tunnel, then began to pitch sharply upward. The male in front of them scrambled up and out. Leve followed, stopping at the top to let her eyes adjust to the blinding light.

She closed her eyes and pulled air into her lungs, enjoying the sharp scents of fresh dirt, pollen and every animal that had scampered by in the past months.

Gray touched her from behind, a light press of his fingers against her back, just letting her know he was beside her, sharing the moment.

She turned, happy to have him there, ready to thank him. As she moved, something fell from above, landed with a clump. An arm caught her around the waist, almost cutting off her air, and her feet shot out in front of her as Gray jerked her from behind, pulling her back into the tunnel.

With her back to Gray's front, her eyes facing the freedom she had barely tasted, she saw the hellhound they had rescued covered in a glimmering net. He rose on his knees and roared, anger and frustration pouring from him. She reached out, thinking she could somehow save him, but as she did, a dozen dark elves dropped on the ground beside them.

Behind her Gray cursed and began to shimmer—shimmer them both—but before she'd felt more than the first tingles, the space in front of them darkened and hardened, formed into a solid wall of magic.

Gray saw the door in front of them darken, felt the loss of fresh air, but he kept with the shimmer, determined to get Leve and himself out of the mill.

It didn't work.

He and Leve solidified still inside the tunnel. He gritted his teeth, his mind spinning, grasping for another plan.

Another exit, a fire exit, something. There had to be. He grabbed Leve's hand, prepared to tug her after him.

They got fifteen feet, maybe less, and ran into another dark mass of magic.

Trapped. The end of the tunnel was rigged to stop an escape; maybe all the tunnels and halls were like this, shut down right now into fifteen-foot segments.

Her feet still moving her forward, Leve knocked into him.

"We're trapped," he said.

"We can't be."

The doom Gray felt was apparent in Leve's voice. Gray and then Leve attempted everything they could think of to open the passageway—shimmering, pounding against the barrier, running the pads of their fingers and nails around the outline of what used to be the opening, searching for a crack—but nothing worked. They could find no weakness.

"Trapped." Gray turned, pulled Leve into his arms, didn't ask this time, just knew he had to. She shook against him, but not from fear. Rage.

"This can't happen," she said. He pulled her closer as if his body and calm facade could soak up her anger.

Maybe it did. Slowly she relaxed against him. She burrowed her face into his chest. "What can we do?"

He shook his head. Her hair tickled his chin. "Wait. There's not much else we can do. There seems to be air coming in. And we know they want us alive. Eventually they will open up one of those doors."

"Or pour more mist in with us."

They stood in silence for a second. Not knowing what drove him, only that he didn't want to be alone, didn't want Leve to be alone, Gray placed one finger under her chin, tipped her face up to his and captured her lips in a kiss.

Gray's was gentle, undemanding, asking only for what Leve was willing to give. She didn't hesitate to reply. She placed her hands on his shoulders and parted her lips, meeting his tongue with hers.

She was going to make love with him, and the decision was wholly her own. She was going to savor every detail, hold it in her heart. If the choice was never hers again, she'd have this.

His hands didn't move; he didn't pull her closer. So Leve took the next step, rubbed her breasts against his chest, ran her fingers through his hair. It was long, and brushed his shoulders. She wondered briefly if it was by choice, or if he'd been roaming and therefore had no time to care for such niceties.

She knew so little about him. But what she did know was important. He cared—for her and the other hellhounds. He placed their freedom before his own, and he was strong, able to resist what Leve had never heard of any hellhound resisting before. But maybe most important, he'd given her back a piece of herself, something she'd thought was long gone—the ability to trust.

How could she not love him, not want to be with him?

Her fingers wandered down his chest, pausing to trace each bulge of muscle and line of definition. She was glad he'd left his shirt back in the cell, didn't want to waste time removing clothes or doing anything except being with this male while she was still free, at least in her own mind.

He inhaled, and she could feel him holding back, waiting, letting her take the lead. She smiled against his lips, then captured his again, took her time, moved her mouth over his, slipped her tongue past his teeth.

The kiss was slow and seductive, and Leve had never felt more powerful. She lowered her hand, felt Gray's erection lengthen beneath his pants. She rubbed her palm over the denim, felt him harden further.

He groaned into her mouth, but didn't move to touch her. She grabbed his waistband in both hands and jerked the buttons open. His erection sprang free, slipped up under her shirt. She grabbed him by the sides and pulled his body to hers, deepened their kiss, put every ounce of passion she felt into the act.

He kissed her back, his arms tense at his sides, his body ready for action.

She slipped his pants down his hips and curved her fingers around the hard bulge of his buttocks and squeezed.

"Touch me," she whispered, barely pulling her lips away from his.

As if he'd been awaiting her words, he grabbed her by the waist, pulled her against him, his hands sliding up her sides as he did. His thumbs brushed the underside of her breasts, then the tips of her nipples. She pulled in a breath, licked her lips, then his.

Her shirt disappeared, flung to the floor with such speed she wasn't sure if he or she had removed it. Her pants followed, then his. Naked, they explored each other's bodies, their hands and lips roaming, tasting.

Leve ran her tongue down the center of Gray's chest, then over his abs. Right below his belly button she stopped, pressed a kiss to the smooth plane of muscle.

Gray kneeled, pulled her into a kiss, then coaxed her onto the ground. With her laid out beside him, he leaned over her and traced a path around one nipple with his tongue.

The air was cool against Leve's skin. Her nipples puckered, and as he continued outlining first one tip and then the other, her core contracted. She ran her fingernails down his back, along the side of his hip, reached for his sex, but he pulled to the side, and stared down at her.

She lay there, her body screaming for his touch, her heart pounding in her chest. Her breath came in little puffs.

He ran the pads of his fingers lightly over her breasts, stomach, to her thighs, then slowly slipped one finger past the hair that covered her sex.

Leve's scent surrounded Gray. His erection pulsed with the need to be inside her, but he wanted this to last, for this experience to block out every bad memory or belief she had about sex.

Her eyes rounded as he found her center. As he circled the nub, her body arched, her hands clawed at the ground beneath her, and her eyelids closed.

He ran his other hand over her breasts, pulled one nipple into his mouth, swirled his tongue around it while he continued to circle her nub, then slipped a finger inside her. Her muscles clenched around him and he groaned, bent lower, replaced his hand with his mouth.

Taste and smell, his senses were overwhelmed with Leve. She was strong, stronger than she knew. He wanted her to accept that and to know she wasn't alone. As long as he was alive, she'd never be alone again. He wouldn't leave her, couldn't. He'd die before letting the dark elves take her again, throw her into a cell to be used and forgotten.

She was his equal—equal to any of them, but she was also his…his alone.

His hands caressing her breasts, he swirled his tongue around the nub hidden between her folds. Her body tensed beneath his hands, her lower back leaving the ground, and her fingers wound into his hair.

A groan left her lips, then a whisper. "Now. I need…"

He swept his body up hers and found her mouth. Her leg wrapped around his, leaving her open to him. Unable to hold back any longer, he drove his erection into her.

An "ahh" of breath left her lips. He caught her exhale with his mouth.

Her tongue met his, and as their bodies merged, as he pulled his length in and out, as pressure and anticipation built, she clung to him, and he held her, never intending to let her go.

The air around them warmed, the scent of their lovemaking increasing their desire. Leve's skin was damp. Gray longed to lick the salt from her body, but couldn't bear to pull his lips from her mouth, couldn't bear to change anything about the perfect position of their bodies melded together, moving together as their pace increased, as they drew closer and closer to finding release.

The tension continued to build; Gray's entire body screamed for release. He moved faster, Leve moving with him.

Then, when he thought he might explode, his body began to tense and release, Leve's body tensing and releasing around him.

She pulled her mouth free of his, panted out breath, hot against his skin. He leaned back, stared into her eyes, and as the last moment of their orgasm swept over them, he rolled, let Leve straddle him, let Leve control the moment.

Her hands on his chest, she stared down at him and smiled—a smile that reached her eyes, warmed him as much as their love-making had.

He ran his hand up her neck and pulled her back down for a kiss.

Leve lay in Gray's arms, knowing she needed to get dressed, that their interlude had been foolish to start with, but unwilling to let it go and consider where they were and what they would soon have to face.

"What are the chances the male escaped?" she asked.

Gray tilted his neck, pressed his temple against the top of her head. "Not impossible, but…"

The possibility hung between them. They both knew the odds were slim that the male hellhound, even if he did defeat the dark elves and secure his own freedom, would stay and work to release them from the mill.

"Even if he or the females try, there's no way to know they can," she murmured.

Gray's arm tightened around her shoulders, but he didn't reply. There wasn't anything to say.

Gray didn't bother pulling on his clothes, and neither did Leve. He assumed she, like him, wanted to savor the moments they had—skin to skin.

And if they never escaped, this was how he wanted to go… with Leve pressed against him, her heart beating softly against his side, her breath blowing across his chest.

She'd dozed off, sleep he suspected she needed, when the wall of magic thinned and cool night air crept into their hole.

He squeezed her and she was awake instantly. Silently they both moved to a crouch.

Wide shoulders appeared, blocking what little light was left of the day. A light shone into the tunnel, blinding them both.

Gray grabbed Leve's hand and started to shimmer them past the doorway.

"Well, at least you kept yourselves busy." The hellhound they'd freed dropped the spotlight and stepped out of their way, motioning them out into the night.

Leve held Gray's hand as she walked out into the cool air, not even pausing to pick up her clothes before she did.

Outside the hellhounds waited—all of them, the male and the females. Hanging from a tree was the net that she and Gray had last seen dropped over the male hellhound now in the tunnel retrieving their clothes. Inside the net were five dark elves, dead or knocked out—Leve didn't know and honestly didn't care.

The hellhound who'd opened the tunnel handed her and Gray their clothes, then nodded to the net. "Mercenaries don't put up much of a fight. Not once they see they're facing some real hurt." He glanced at the females, his gaze cautious, but respectful.

Leve pulled on her clothes. Beside her, Gray did the same. "What are you going to do with them?" she asked.

The hellhound shrugged. "Up to you two. I don't mind killing them, but I thought you might have other plans."

"Like finding whoever hired them?" Gray glanced at Leve.

The net stirred—one of the guards coming to consciousness. She concentrated on watching him, not looking at Gray. He'd saved her and they'd had their moment in the tunnel. She couldn't expect him to think about her now, to want to stay with her longer.

"Might be a good idea." Gray eyed the swinging net, then placed a hand on Leve's back. His touch was light and unsure, but Leve's heart raced. "What do you think? Want to hang around? Hunt down whoever's done this?" he asked.

Leve smiled, glanced at the females, then back at Gray. She stepped closer, until the warmth of his body mingled with hers. "Yeah, I think I do."

His arms opened and she stepped into them, let him press her against his body.

She wasn't alone. Never would be again.

* * * * *

DREAMCATCHER

Anna Leonard

ANNA LEONARD

is the nom de paranormal for fantasy/horror writer Laura Anne Gilman, who grew up wondering why none of the characters in her favorite gothic novels ever seemed to know a damn thing about ghosts, vampires or how to run in high heels. Anna can be reached via www.sff.net/people/lauraanne.gilman or www.cosanostradamus.blogspot.com.

Dear Reader,

I always start with a voice in my head, a character asking to be written into life. But for "Dreamcatcher," that voice was different. It was the combined voices of real women, women who have shown me the true meaning of courage. Not physical courage, although there's that, but *internal* courage.

J. and S. and K. are women who battle, daily, with the fact that their bodies aren't capable of things we take for granted. They have fibromyalgia, chronic fatigue syndrome, severe Lyme disease—conditions that make daily life a daily challenge, 24/7. Yet they take weakness, and find inside it an amazing strength.

Emma was born of women who have not just courage but lion(ess)heartedness. The kind of courage that allows you to look at and not flinch away from the truth, no matter how ugly or unpleasant or difficult it might be to accept. The kind that gives you the strength to do what must be done.

For them, for all of you who battle a demon of your own body…this story is for you.

Best,

Laura Anne

Emma remembered that she wasn't always like this. Once upon a time she would jump out of bed in the morning and hit the ground running. And then she...didn't anymore. Her muscles ached, her energy was low, and there was a constant hum in her ears, like a deep voice whispering to her while she slept, constantly whispering, never leaving her alone.

You're mine. All mine. I will consume you, piece by piece, and I will never be done...

Her body convulsed around a pain centered low in her gut, like something was hollowing her out, bite by bite. "No. Please, no..."

Yes. Oh, yes...

Emma's body was so heavy, lead-heavy, limbs heavier than the floor, even her skin aching and delicate with exhaustion. Something had happened? She had been so tired all week, all month, but this was...this was worse. It was like being pushed toward a cliff and then finally going over kind of worse.

A laugh sounded in her ear, low and satisfied, and she felt a shiver run across her skin. Was that her boss's voice? She didn't like that laugh. It wasn't a nice laugh, and it was in her head, and she didn't like that, either. It made her tired just to listen to it.

"Where are the damn paramedics?" Her boss wasn't laughing. In fact, he sounded panicked. Their construction manager never panicked, not even when all hell was breaking loose…

"They're on their way," a woman's voice assured him. "Emma." A hand lifted hers, smooth cool skin touching hers. "Emma, can you hear me? Twitch if you can hear me."

Emma wanted to twitch her hand, but it was too much effort. A sigh escaped her lips, and someone squeezed her hand. "Good girl. You just stay down, and the cute doctors will come and take care of you, okay?"

Stay down. Yes. She could manage that. Emma stopped listening to the voices over her, and in her head, and stayed down in the dark, cool place where she didn't hear anything at all.

The hospital bed was too hard in the wrong places, too soft in the wrong places and too narrow everywhere. Emma was exhausted, but the bed wasn't letting her sleep. Even after they took the machines away and stopped prodding her and making her look into lights and even after they drained half a gallon of blood for endless tests, she ached too much to sleep. Arms, legs, ribs, even her scalp, ached like someone had taken double handfuls of her hair and pulled for a day and a half.

The paramedics told her that she'd passed out in the office. The last thing she remembered was reaching down for an allocation request form, then being hit by a wave of exhaustion and hearing that voice—the same one that always seemed to be whispering in the back of her mind these days.

What had it said? She couldn't remember.

Dr. Gan came in, carrying his PDA and looking professionally jovial. "And how are you feeling?"

"I want to go home."

The doctor didn't pretend not to hear her softly voiced request, the way the nurses did. "I know. But we still don't know why you collapsed, and—"

"And I have insurance, so you want to milk me for whatever you can get."

The doctor, who was fiftysomething, bald and not as jovial as his expression would suggest, closed his PDA with an exasperated snap. "Actually, I want to figure out what is making you so tired, so you can be not quite so tired, and not collapse again, and not end up in my E.R. again, so we can keep the bed for someone who's actually in need of it."

They glared at each other, and Emma dropped her gaze first. It was too much effort to argue. Her feet itched, and she rubbed the sole of one against the mattress. Alissa had brought her pajamas when they admitted her from the E.R., and the cotton fabric, usually soothing, felt scratchy under the too-thin blanket. Suddenly all the noises and smells were too much, too overwhelming. A headache formed in her left temple, a by-now familiar and unwelcome counterpart to her aching scalp.

"I'm sorry," she said quietly, trying to will the headache away.

The doctor sighed. "I know you want to go home, Ms. Roberts. Very few people appreciate our accommodations. But I can't in good conscience release you when we don't even know why you ended up here."

They had run their tests and ruled out Lyme disease, fibromyalgia, myasthenia gravis, pregnancy, thyroid disease, heart disease and an old-fashioned lack of potassium, among possible causes. The overwhelming and increasing fatigue that caused her to collapse seemed determined to keep its origins secret. Emma had done her reading of the pamphlets they gave her: chronic fatigue syndrome, the catchall for anything that didn't match up elsewhere, was probably the inevitable diagnosis. But Dr. Gan didn't seem ready to dump her into that basket just yet.

At this point, Emma would have taken a diagnosis of shingles, if it meant they'd let her go. She wasn't used to being helpless, and certainly not to being *treated* like she was helpless. It was unnerving, and made her exhaustion and headaches even worse.

There was a knock at her door, and a round, wizened face peered into the room. "You ready to give us a little more blood?"

Emma almost smiled. "Would you stop if I said no?"

"Vampires aren't known for their restraint, but for you I'll make an exception. Hopefully, you'll let me do my job, and I'll give you a lolly." Sean, the phlebotomist, ignored Dr. Gan as he came into the room, a small cart loaded with white-towel-covered instruments, tubes, sterile boxes and deflated bags. His hands were brisk and gentle, and Emma barely even noticed as he took another vial of blood from her arm, adding to the black and green bruises on her skin. As promised, he presented her with a lollypop when he was done. She smiled and let the candy rest on the bed next to her.

"Please let me go home," she said, looking up at the doctor, who sighed again, this time in resignation. He didn't have any reason to keep her there, not really, and they both knew it.

"If you promise to take at least a week off from work, to recover. No work, no running around, straight bed rest and call if you start to develop any new symptoms, and I mean *any.* Do you have someone who can take care of you for at least a few days?"

Emma looked him right in the eyes and lied. "Of course."

"Dad, please."

Her father stood at the window, looking out at the postage stamp–size yard. Her bungalow was classic Craftsman style, built in the 1920s. Emma had bought it years ago, seeing potential in the run-down building. Her job at Blackbrun Construction had gotten her the contacts—and the discounts—to restore the clean, simple lines to near-perfection.

Just thinking about how hard she had worked, sanding and painting and landscaping, made her want to weep, now.

"The doctors said nothing was wrong with you."

How would he know, he hadn't even come to the hospital... She cut that thought off immediately. He had called, twice. And sent flowers.

"They think it's chronic fatigue syndrome."

Her father wasn't impressed by the diagnosis. She hadn't expected him to be. The rule growing up in the Roberts family was "suck it up and shake it off." If there wasn't blood or bone showing or something on fire, it wasn't that serious. Being tired all the time? Not sleeping well? Suck it up and shake it off, girl!

"Dad, I..."

She couldn't stay here alone. Much as it burned her to admit that fact, it had taken all of twenty-four hours before the truth became glaringly obvious. Dr. Gan had been right. She had barely been able to get out of the cab and into the house before she needed to take a nap. The thought of being alone if she passed out again the way she had in the office...

"If you were really ill, they should have kept you in the hospital."

"I didn't want to stay there. Hospitals are horrible."

Her father cracked a smile at that. "True. Emma, baby, your mother and I are supposed to leave for Virginia tomorrow. We've been planning this trip for months. And your brothers can't be expected to drop their lives to come and babysit you. They have lives and jobs of their own."

"I know."

She hadn't expected anything else. Surprising, how much it hurt anyway.

Her coworkers were no different. They were sorry she wasn't feeling well, her passing out had scared the hell out of them but already her boss had left a message on her answering machine, saying that he knew she was only just home but would she be able to swing by the office later this week?

What was that old saying? Don't be irreplaceable; if you can't be replaced you can't be promoted—and you can't be out sick, either.

None of them matter now. You're mine. All mine.

The hint of laughter came back to her, and Emma winced. It

was just the exhaustion, the doctor said, causing her aural hallucinations. That was all. She wasn't going crazy.

"Your mother suggested that we hire someone to take care of you, while you're taking leave. I've engaged the services of a caretaker, starting tomorrow. The agency says that they'll do light housekeeping, make sure you are getting enough to eat, and don't fall down the stairs." He turned to look at her, a long, assessing stare. "Please don't fall down any more stairs. It would upset your mother."

Emma looked at her father, his well-cut suit and ruthlessly trimmed hair almost perfectly matching gray. Her mother's hair was silver—they both refused to dye their hair, wearing their decades proudly. Emma's own brunette had started to show a few strands of white a year ago, around her thirtieth birthday. She had dyed it immediately, and hated herself for it.

"Dad, I..." She dropped her gaze, and laced her fingers together in her lap. "Thank you." He was trying to be helpful. Her parents loved her, and wanted her to be safe. They just... couldn't understand. She couldn't just "shake this off." If she could, she would have already.

"We love you, baby."

"I know, Dad." They did. They really did. But they were the way they were, and always had been. You stood on your own feet in the Roberts household. That wasn't a bad thing. It was simply...exhausting, sometimes.

Emma got up, slowly, and walked with him to the door, submitting to the engulfing hug.

"Take care of yourself. When we get back, you'll be all revved up and ready to go, the Emma we all know and love."

"Yes, Dad."

What else could she say?

Give. Give. It's what you do best. And now you're mine, all mine, and I won't share...

Emma woke up the next morning with the sheets wrapped

around her, damp with her own sweat. A nightmare, that was all, triggered by her own morose and self-pitying thoughts before falling asleep. If she could just get up and moving, everything would be all right. The by-now familiar sensation of muscle quiver, though, made her want to stay in bed and not move.

The doorbell chiming downstairs insisted otherwise. That must have been what woke her up. Despite temptation, a stronger sense of responsibility—she couldn't just leave whoever it was standing out there—made her get up, pull on clothing and go downstairs to answer the summons.

"Emma Roberts?"

Emma tugged the edge of her sweatshirt self-consciously and nodded. "Yes?"

The man on her doorstep looked at her impatiently, like she was supposed to have recognized him already and welcomed him in. She had never seen him before—she would have remembered him, no matter how tired she was. Pale, which was unusual here in Southern California, and with the darkest eyes she had ever seen, like deep, still pools of black ink. The rest of the face was standard-issue handsome—squared-off chin, nice firm jawline, good cheekbones and sandy-brown hair trimmed into near-military obedience. The face of a man who was good-looking, knew it and had other things on his mind.

"My name is Matthew. From HomeHelp?"

Emma stared, her brain not quite working as fast as it usually did. By now she should have been on her third cup of coffee, sorting and shoving the office into functionality. Instead, pulling on sweats and jeans had taxed her endurance to the point where she just wanted to sit down.

"You hired me."

Oh.

"My father did. I was…I was expecting someone…"

The man—Matthew—sighed. "Female?"

"Yeah. I suppose so."

Matthew pulled out a laminated ID and handed it to her. It told her that his name was Matthew Reiden, that he was employed by HomeHelp Nursing, Inc., and that he was certified by the California State Nursing Board as a Home Health Aid. She looked at the picture, then back at him.

"Now you know who I am. May I come in?"

"Yes, sorry, of course." She stepped back, and let him into her home.

He walked in, and took over. "The referral form we got from the hospital said that you've been diagnosed with CFS?"

"Yes." She was guarded still, waiting to see his reaction.

"And you really think that two weeks are going to be enough to let you get back to your previous levels of energy?"

His tone was flat, almost unsympathetic, and she bristled. "I'm not making it up. The doctors said—"

"I didn't suggest that you were, and I'm sure that they did," he replied, placing his black case—too large for a laptop, too small to be a suitcase—on the floor. "I'm not a doctor, I'm not here to diagnose. My job's to teach you how to take care of yourself, so that you don't just curl up and die when it gets too hard. Why don't you show me where I should put my things, and then we can talk about what your expectations are?"

Emma looked at him blankly, then realized he was talking about where he was going to sleep. She had expected—assumed—that the caretaker would be female, and for a moment thought about demanding that he go away, that the company send the older, sympathetic maternal housekeeper type she had been expecting. But it was all too much effort. He was a trained professional, and his ID said he was bonded and insured, so there was no reason to have a fluttery missy fit. Right?

It was too much effort to kick him out, and have to explain to her father, and…

"The guest room's upstairs, first door on the left." She let him take the lead on the stairs, following more slowly, her hand on the wooden banister for support. She wasn't so tired, though, that she didn't notice that he had a world-class ass. Pretty faces were a dime a dozen out here—she came from a family of handsome faces—but not even the best surgery could replicate the look of a well-formed backside.

She almost laughed. The good-looking nurse and the lecherous patient, gender-switched. Hooray for social progress.

The guest room barely deserved the name; it was large enough for a bed, a small dresser and a tall cupboard, all made out of the same red-hued wood. The bed was made up with a dark blue blanket and two white pillows. Matthew took it all in with a glance, and nodded briefly. "It will do. The bathroom is down the hall?"

"Yes." Figuring it was best to get it out of the way immediately, she added, "There's only the one on this floor. Downstairs there's a half-bath."

"I'll respect your privacy as much as I can," he said.

"Thank you." It was only two weeks, and it was better than being in the hospital.

After his gear was stored, they ended up in the kitchen, Emma sitting at the table with a cup of tea he had brewed up for her immediately, ladling two spoonfuls of honey—organic, he had noted with an approval that was missing in the rest of his survey—in the mug, while Matthew moved through the cabinets, familiarizing himself with what was there and where it all was.

"No cereal," he noted.

"I don't eat breakfast."

"You do now." He didn't miss a beat, starting a shopping list on a pad of paper he'd brought with him, then bending down to see what pots and pans she had. Emma had a lashing of embarrassment at how badly her kitchen was stocked, and then shrugged it off. She wasn't a cook. So what?

"I'm never hungry—"

"Look." He turned around then and looked at her with those dark, liquid eyes. In her cozy little white-and-yellow kitchen, he seemed like an alien intruder, except for his obvious familiarity in the domestic surroundings. "You need to keep your strength up, and that means fueling the machine. Breakfast, lunch, a snack and a real dinner, every day. Healthy food, not processed crap."

"And you're going to cook all this for me?"

"I'm going to teach you how to do for yourself, without exhausting yourself. That's a balance you're going to have to walk for the rest of your life, might as well start now." His voice was deep, velvety and totally unsympathetic. Emma wanted nothing more than to throw him and his tea and his lists out the door he'd come in through.

Instead she made a "whatever" gesture with her left hand, and let him continue taking over her kitchen.

Two weeks. She could survive two weeks.

By the end of the next day, Emma wasn't so sure of that.

"Keep moving."

"I can't."

"You can and you will. Or you're going to curl up and die."

Emma would have snarled, if she knew how to do it. "I hate you."

"Good. Hatred is powerful. Hate me enough to kick me out. But you'd better be strong enough to do it first."

They were out on the patio, Matthew standing in front of her like a carved statue of Italian marble dressed down in blue jeans and a dark red T-shirt that fit like it had been tailored to fit. His feet were bare, and Emma focused on his toes; they were almost too perfect, each nail a pearl-white curve against paler skin. Everyone in Southern California spent hours in the sun, and yet his skin was still so pale…

"Again. Keep moving."

Emma lifted the weights and shuffled around the patio. Each

weight was only three pounds, but after ten minutes it felt like a ton. They had been doing this for an hour. Her arms were sore, her heart was racing, and all she wanted to do was lie down and cry.

"You need muscle to keep your body going, Emma. Muscle and fuel, sunlight and sleep, everything in balance."

"I hate you," she said again.

I will consume you.

The voice ripped through her, even as a cloud passed over the sun. The hollow pit returned in her gut, inching upward into her heart. She dropped the weights, and sat down, hard, on the patio. The stones were warm under her butt, almost too warm, but she couldn't move.

"Emma."

"Leave me alone."

Thankfully, he did.

"God, please," she whispered. "Make it stop." The exhaustion she could deal with. The bullying caretaker she could outlast. The sleepless nights and shuddering muscles, she would work around. But that voice in her head, the cold fingers of something digging in her soul, spooning out everything inside... she couldn't stand that. She couldn't survive that.

The cloud passed, and the sun warmed her skin again. A hand touched her shoulder, gently enough that she didn't jump.

"Here. Drink this."

It was lemonade, tart and sweet and not too cold from a pitcher now sitting on the patio table. She drank the entire glass, and handed it back to him. "Can I take a nap now?"

"No. Back on your feet. Two more times around the patio."

"Why are you doing this to me?" She was whining. She hated whining.

"It's my job." His voice was flat again, all that compassion wiped clean.

"Torture?"

"If I leave today, just up and walk out—what will you do?"

Emma stopped and looked at him. It was an assessing look, but he had been given worse, and he waited her out.

"I'd go back to bed," she admitted.

"You have to be strong. You have to be strong enough to deal with this."

"Why? What does it matter? If this CFS is what I'm stuck with the rest of my life, why shouldn't I just make my bed as comfortable as possible, and deal with it from a reclining position? What do I have to be strong for?"

Matthew swallowed and looked away, trying to find a way to respond to the quiet resignation in her voice.

"This isn't you," he said finally. "I've only known you a few days, and I know that. You're not a quitter. You're not the type to give up."

"You don't know me at all," she said. But she got up and lifted the weights again. That was all that mattered.

I hate you.

Torture?

What does it matter?

Emma's words echoed in his memory the moment he woke up. It was dawn; he always woke at dawn, no matter what time he had gone to sleep. The sun was his alarm clock.

I hate you. Her expression, so open and trusting. Her body, slender, golden-skinned and too frail, but a fire burning inside her, a passion that she hid from everyone. He could sense it, though. Her fire, her strength. He hadn't lied to her; when he looked in her eyes, he didn't see a quitter. He saw a fighter. Part of him wanted to build it up—and part of him wanted to break it down.

Throwing back the coverlet, Matthew got out of bed and walked to the window.

"She's strong. Of course she is. Weak ones fall over and die at the first touch." Matthew watched the sun rise outside the small window in his small bedroom. It felt like a cage, too small for him to move around in, too small to contain his restless needs. Normally he would go for a run, burn off some energy as the sun rose overhead, but he couldn't. Not while he was on a job. Not this job. She was too delicate right now, too needy. He had to build her strength back up, keep her healthy. Keep himself from damaging her further.

For two weeks, two months. However long it took.

He had wanted to be a healer, his entire life. Irony, that. There was no forgiveness for the likes of him—and no escape, either.

Pulling on a pair of jeans, he buttoned the waistband, slipped on a T-shirt and went downstairs to start making breakfast.

A sound woke her up. Emma lay in bed, feeling every ache like she was ninety-four instead of thirty-four. The noise was coming from downstairs, in the kitchen.

Matthew was making breakfast. Despite herself, Emma's mouth began to water. A few days of his cooking, and she was starting to appreciate having more than toast and coffee for breakfast. Maybe that she would keep, when he left.

She really should get up, get dressed and get downstairs. That was the rule—she could nap all she wanted in the afternoon, after exercises, but she had to get up in the morning for breakfast.

She started to get up, and fell back on the pillow. She had slept almost eight hours, exactly how much she was supposed to be getting. She was eating well, and doing moderate exercises, and getting sunlight, and she was supposed to be getting better, not feeling worse!

The whisper curled around her brain, like sticky fingers stroking her skin. *Tasty. So tasty. In the darkness I will consume you...*

"No. Leave me alone..."

"Emma?"

The woman's voice cut into the deep whisper, causing it to retreat, although Emma could still feel it, lurking just inside her skull.

Emma pulled the covers over her head. She knew that voice. She didn't want to see anyone, not today. Not Alissa, especially. She just didn't have the energy to deal with her perpetually perky coworker today.

"Emma? Darling, you have a handsome man downstairs insisting on making you breakfast, you better be wearing something slinky and smoking a cigarette, or I'll be woefully disappointed in you."

"No can do." But the words were muffled by the coverlet.

"Emma?" The bed sagged as the woman sat down next to her. "Come on, I've seen bedhead before, you can't scare me."

Emma lowered the coverlet, and blinked up at her coworker.

"Oh, sweetie." Alissa was clearly taken aback. "You, um, you look…tired. I mean, obviously, but…have you been sleeping at *all?*"

"Yeah. I just… Let me splash some water on my face and I'll be down in a couple of minutes, okay?" She liked Alissa, but the woman was a casual friend at best, and Emma was uncomfortable having her here, upstairs, in her space. Alissa was too bright, too perky, too perfect, and Emma wasn't up to dealing with her, wasn't up to being the Emma the Efficient they all expected, demanded. The exhaustion doubled in weight, and turned her joints into lead.

"Right." Alissa stood up and backed away, clearly as uncomfortable as Emma felt. "I'll…I'll be downstairs."

Left alone, Emma slid out of bed and went into the bathroom. She had painted the walls a pale rose, to complement her skin tone, but the face that looked back at her out of the mirror needed more than paint to look good. Her hair was lank and lifeless, and there were dark hollows under her eyes, making her entire face look sunken and haggard.

There was makeup in the cabinet, powders and foundation and blush. Emma looked at them, and then shook her head. What was the point?

She went downstairs slowly and stood in the kitchen doorway.

Alissa was sitting at the kitchen table, drinking a cup of coffee. Emma craved coffee, but knew better than to even ask; coffee was on the forbidden list.

"Emma, this man is a godsend," Alissa said on seeing her there. "A few days of napping and eating this food, and you'll get this out of your system and be back in the office. And not a minute too soon, I gotta tell you. You gave us a scare, but there had to be easier ways to get a vacation. We really need you back at the office. The guys don't listen to me worth a damn about keeping the space clean, and I can't find anything in your filing system."

Emma listened, and felt every word like another brick dropping on her chest until it was difficult to breathe.

"Go. Just…go away."

Alissa stopped midspeech and stared. "What?"

The words fell out of Emma's mouth. "I'm sorry I can't be what you wanted, what you need, but you can't put this on me, not now. You have to go."

Words out, she felt herself crumple inside. Saying that had taken all the energy she had, and the only thing keeping her upright in the chair was a sense of dread, pressure building from inside until she thought she might pop, like an overfilled balloon. Dimly she heard Alissa's voice, then Matthew's, and footsteps receding. Only one set, heavier, comforting, came back into the kitchen.

"I… I just… I'll be back."

The stairs were too much to even consider. The laundry room was closer, and there were no stairs to get there. Emma closed the door behind her, sank to the floor, her back against the far wall, drew her knees up to her chest, and rested her head on her arms. The warm prickle of tears came, and she didn't fight them. Each sob tore something inside her, making her body shake until it emptied itself out.

After a while the flow started to ease, leaving her drained and yet somehow less exhausted than she had felt before. It was only then that she realized that she wasn't alone in the room.

He didn't touch her, a small blessing that made the embarrassment almost survivable.

"Did she leave?"

"Yeah. She said she'd call. Later."

"Uh-huh."

"Emma…"

"I'm okay," she said.

"No, you're not."

"No, I… It lets the stress out. Crying." She didn't know why she was explaining anything to him; explanations just left you vulnerable. But his silent presence, on his ass on the floor next to her, let it all slip out. "I hate being weak like this. Tired. I'm trying, I'm doing everything right just the way the doctors said, the way you said, and nothing I do is making any difference, and I'm useless like this."

Matthew let out a soft breath, and leaned his head back against the wall with a gentle thunking noise. "You're hanging out with the wrong sort, Em. Not everyone is like that. There are people out there who don't equate strength, or usefulness, with personal worth."

"That sounds nice. I'd like to hang out with people like that, if they exist."

"They do. Emma…" There was a long silence, and the sound of him swallowing, hard. "Will you let me help?"

"Help me? Aren't you already doing that?"

"I can do more…to help you. But you have to let me."

Emma tilted her head, looking at his hands through the curtain of her hair. They were resting on his jean-clad leg, stilled for once. His hands were pale, like the rest of his skin, but they were capable-looking, long-fingered and…solid, like an artist's. A potter, maybe. She could imagine those fingers molding clay on a wheel, forcing the clay into the desired shape, wheel and hands moving in perfect synchronicity.

She wasn't sure that she liked him, not really. But…he

listened to her. He didn't think she was faking it, or overreacting. He wasn't demanding anything of her, except that she do what the doctor ordered.

She trusted him. She wasn't sure why, but...she trusted him.

"Yes. All right."

Matthew's fingers twitched once, then stilled.

"It will sound...crazy."

Emma made a laugh deep in her throat that might have been laughter. "Trust me, crazy isn't so crazy anymore."

"Yeah. All right. Here goes.

"My people have a legend, a story every child learns, of creatures that travel in our sleep, seeking someone open to them, someone whose energy can feed them. They eat away, in small bites, making the life force, the soul, last as long as possible, feeding until there is nothing left to consume...and then moving on to another victim."

Emma watched his eyes while he talked, and the starkness in his voice matched his steady gaze; her calm, no-nonsense caretaker believed what he was saying.

"That's..."

"Crazy?"

He had warned her. She shrugged. "My parents, my coworkers, they all think that *I'm* crazy, that I'm imagining all this. Even the doctors aren't willing to give me a diagnosis, or a cure, or even a treatment other than rest up and don't stress it. But they don't know what's causing it, or how to treat it. Who am I to say crazy or not crazy? You think it's being caused by something trying to eat me? How crazier is that than 'we don't know, so sorry, try to get a lot of sleep'?"

Emma paused long enough to take a deep breath, and wait for Matthew to respond. When he remained silent, she exhaled heavily, her scalp aching again, like someone was pulling on it.

"All right, say your crazy story is right. Why me?"

Matthew opened his mouth to respond, and she waved him

off. "No, that's the kind of answer that, even when given, doesn't do any good. Better—how the hell am I supposed to fight off that thing? Somehow I don't think an extra glass of orange juice in the morning's going to do it. And what about the dreams? They didn't start until after, and when the dreams come, I feel better. When they don't...worse."

Matthew shrugged, staring away from her, out across the patio. "Maybe...it is your subconscious way of fighting it off? That somehow the dreams block its access?"

"Your people don't have a legend about how to fight it?"

Matthew looked down. "Nothing they were going to put in a story for kids," he said, and Emma almost laughed; he was blushing.

"There is one way, one legend they do tell us," he said. "A gift that was given to my people when we came here, generations on generations ago. The story says that we walked up from the fire-lands in the south to the northern plains, and were stopped by an ancient medicine man, who looked into us, and saw what we were...and welcomed us anyway. The gift was from his daughter to a son of my people, an offering of friendship, to bind them together forever."

"What happened? In the story?" Not that she believed any of it, but it was different, she would give him that.

Matthew shook his head and spread his hands as though to say "that's all I got." "According to legend, they had a dozen children, and all of them got into more trouble than their parents could keep track of."

She laughed a little, just the way he intended her to.

"It's just a story, but...the gift was supposed to protect the re-cipient, a kind of defensive magic. We're all taught how to re-create it, just in case. With your permission...?"

"Just in case you're right about the monster?"

He smiled, just a little, but his eyes stayed dark and shadowed. "Just in case."

She liked the fact that he asked permission, and nodded.

* * *

That night, Emma cooked dinner for the first time since coming home, with Matthew sitting at the table and teasing her about hidden culinary skills. Grilled mahi mahi with a commercially prepared sauce, it was something a ten-year-old could have managed, but she felt triumphant as she served it up and sat down to eat. That was about all she could handle, though. Leaving Matthew with the cleanup, she made her way upstairs, where her bed waited.

A month ago she would have gone to the sofa, watched some television, fallen asleep there and then woken up at three in the morning with a crick in her neck and an unwillingness to move. Matthew had been right. Knowing that she was perfectly justified in going to bed early, rather than trying to force herself to stay up, allowed Emma to do away with the guilt and shame that had been dogging her. No matter what was causing this exhaustion, she was still putting her money on a chemical imbalance, no matter how tempting it might be to blame it on some night-flying boogie monster.

The thought made her laugh, even as she was pulling off her jeans and dropping them to the floor. As she reached out to pull down the coverlet, a splash of color caught her eye. Up over the bed, attached to the metal headboard, someone—Matthew, it had to be—had hung what looked like several scraps of colored cloth. Closer inspection showed that the strips had been woven together, the edges dangling, but the center creating a distinct pattern, like the bottom of a basket.

"A dreamcatcher," she said, touching the center delicately, as though it might disintegrate at her touch.

Well, it made sense, in a way. If the legends said the monster entered through sleep…

She was too tired to try to figure it out now. Maybe in the morning. If she actually slept, and didn't dream…

But the dreams were helping. So would a dreamcatcher stop them, or help them?

"You start thinking like that, and you *will* be getting into the crazy. Voices and erotic dreams and ancient legends…lions and tigers and crazy, oh, my."

As she pulled the coverlet up over her, Emma's gaze fell on the window on the opposite wall. The light from the patio cast it in shadows, and in those she was able to make out a strange tracing, almost like frost…in the same weave pattern as the dreamcatcher.

Crazy, the whisper suggested. *Tear it down. Throw it away.*

She might be crazy, but she trusted Matthew more than she trusted that shadowed voice. She might, when it came down to it, trust Matthew more than she trusted herself.

With the image of the reflected dreamcatcher in her mind, she lay back, a pillow under her head and another tucked into her arms, and closed her eyes.

Emma.

The voice this time didn't cause her alarm, but comfort. The hand stroking her back knew what it was doing, using long firm strokes from her neck to ass, kneading the flesh until Emma wanted to melt facedown into the bed. The tension that seemed to have become a part of her eased, and even the exhaustion was less obvious, her nerves tingling in a much more pleasurable way. The hand lingered on her ass, massaging the soft flesh, then moved down, under her hips. Without opening her eyes she lifted her body, allowing him easier access, and was rewarded by the soft touch of lip on her shoulder, the flicker of a warm tongue on her night-cooled skin. Eventually, she thought, she would turn over, open her eyes, maybe do a little exploring of her own. But right now…right now it was nice to just let someone else do all the work…

As though reading her thoughts, the owner of that hand used his other to hold her hips still and reached the thick curls of her pubic hair, agile fingers slipping over slick, sensitive flesh until she shivered, aching for something more than that gentle touch.

As though on cue, she felt the press of a leg against her own, the definitely masculine pressure of an erection sending a shiver of anticipation up her spine.

"Hrmm. Nice." Her voice was dream-drowsy, and some rational thread suggested that none of it was real, that it was another hallucination.

No sooner had she thought that then the echo of that horrible laughter sifted into the dream, and the weight of a body covered her own, pressing her down into the mattress. Instantly, the flickers of lust were flashed over by panic, as she felt herself starting to suffocate…

Wake up. Wake up and be safe.

It was a deep voice, a man's voice, but different from the one that had been haunting her for months. Different, and yet similar… dangerous, but reassuring…

She woke up, in her own bed, the sheets tangled at her feet. Expecting to be covered in sweat and hammered by exhaustion as usual, she moved slowly, swinging her feet out of bed…and halted, unsure about the message her body was sending her.

Sweaty, yes, and an aching between her legs that tied into the bits of her dreams that she remembered—her sex drive apparently required more than exhaustion and abstinence to give up—but otherwise…

Her muscles were sore, but responsive. For the first time in months, she didn't ache, didn't feel the need to sit down the moment she stood up. She felt…good.

By the time she had gotten dressed and made it downstairs, the energy had faded, and a sense of embarrassment had taken up residence. It wasn't as though she was inexperienced, but she'd never had wet dreams before, or whatever they were called when women had them.

She glowed that morning. It was clichéd, but the only way he could describe it. Vitality shone in her skin, exuded in her movements. The fact that he knew it was temporary didn't dampen his enjoyment at all.

"More weights today?" she asked, drinking the entire glass of orange juice without complaint, although her eyes still went to the coffee machine on the counter with a look of hopeful longing. No matter how many times he told her that caffeine was counterproductive, the addiction was still there.

"Not today. I want to teach you some stretching exercises. Yes, I know you know how to stretch. These are different."

"Yoga." The disgust in her voice made him laugh. How long had it been since he laughed? How long had there been anyone to make him laugh?

"Some of it. But I promise, no silly-sounding names, or poses only a limber twelve-year-old could perform."

After breakfast, they went back out onto the patio. It was private, with the hedge rising to shoulder height and her only neighbors were young professionals who left for the office early in the morning. The sunlight fell directly onto the paving stones, making the early morning air comfortable and comforting.

She had an hour after each meal to digest and relax and talk about things that had nothing to do with anything, just casual conversation. She knew that he was an only child, raised by a single father and an extended family of aunts and uncles and cousins. He knew that she had gone to college to be a designer, and discovered that she was good enough to be second-rate, and had taken her skills and become a first-rate office manager instead.

They never talked about her illness, or medicine, or what was going to happen at the end of two weeks, when he left, and she was on her own again.

He had made an entire pitcher of that lemonade, and she was on her second glass, her legs stretched out in front of her, letting the sunlight paint her skin with warmth. She was turning a pale golden brown like she had as a child, when her summers were spent by the pool, not locked inside an office. Matthew's own skin remained pale and cool, no matter how many hours he sat in the sun with her.

"All right. You ready?" He unrolled the exercise mat he had brought with them, and adjusted it to his satisfaction, then patted it in invitation. "Come here."

He smiled inwardly as she joined him on the patio stones. She was like a skittish colt, eager to please and yet worried about what was going to happen with this new routine. The opening movements calmed her and he could almost feel the life flowing in her veins as the muscles softened and stretched as she worked. The temptation to touch her was maddening; a hand on her shoulder to encourage a deeper bend, the push in the small of her back while extolling the importance of tucking in her stomach for support, the tuck of fingers under her bare knee to help extend the leg properly, and the exhilaration when she placed her own hand on his arm, to maintain her balance…

Dangerous. So very dangerous. For him, and for her.

"Push gently, not harder. The trick isn't to stress your body but to encourage it. We want to get the blood flowing again, nourishing the rest of your body."

"Including my brain?"

"That's part of it, yeah."

"We're going to have to work harder, then." She leaned forward more, bending in half so that her nose almost touched her knees, her arms stretched toward her toes, and turned her head to the side to smile at him.

He hadn't thought he had a heart left to break.

"Pay attention," he said, trying to be stern, but the smile tugging at his own lips made the effort useless. In the sunlight, with her living form showing signs of such improvement from the frail, washed-out woman who had answered the door that first day, Matthew almost forgot himself enough to hope.

His hand brushed a strand of hair away from her cheek, and then he moved away, sitting back on his heels, putting distance between them. No matter what happened, there was no way out for him, no happy ending. All he could hope for was a happy ending for her.

Emma. Emma.

She heard the voice, and turned toward it, her arms outstretched. Unlike earlier dreams, now, there was no shame here, no hesitation. Her lover made her feel cherished, protected.

He drew her down onto the blanket, so that she lay on her side, and he was behind her. A large hand smoothed the hair away from her neck and tilted her head back, then his mouth replaced the hand, nuzzling her neck, nipping gently at the skin. His voice, midnight dark and caramel sweet, whispered something into her ear that she didn't understand...it seemed familiar, but it wasn't in English or Spanish, the two languages she knew. It sounded harsher, and yet more musical at the same time, with syllables she didn't recognize.

She tried to move him, to shift them both so that she could see his face, but his arm held her down, the threat implicit—if she persisted, he would stop. Rebuked, she subsided, and his mouth moved across the back of her neck, and down her spine. Needing to do something to reciprocate, she rubbed her cheek against the corded forearm, feeling the faint scattering of hair on his skin scrape against her face, feeling like tiny porcupine quills in her dream-state hypersensitivity. She looked up, and saw a pattern in the sky, like woven clouds and shadows, the moonlight sparkling against them. The pattern looked almost familiar, and she thought she should recognize it, then the thoughts slipped away under his erotic touch, stroking down her skin.

But the sense of familiarity nagged, even as her body melted under his gentle assault. "Where are we?"

When he didn't answer, she turned her head again and nipped him on his arm, a rebuke of her own. Her teeth sank deeper than she intended, and he winced, drawing his arm away, rolling her over onto her back and descending with a pleasing ferocity, his fingers tangling with her own, stretching her arms out against the softness of their bed. The shadows obscured his face but his mouth was warm and familiar as it touched hers, and had a tenderness to it that made her willingly open her legs when his knee nudged between them. She was not surprised—this was a dream after all—when their clothing disappeared without notice, and it was heated skin to skin, the weight of his sex pressing against her lower stomach.

This was new, this intimacy; before, the dreams had been exciting, erotic, but more teasing, not so overtly sexual. This was more, more immediate, more real.

"Let me..." he whispered, and she agreed without hesitation.

"God, yes, please."

He didn't pull away, but somehow shifted enough, his hands sliding under her ass and lifting her, so that he slid smoothly into her. Even as she was exhaling in satisfaction, a part of her was mourning that this was only a dream, that only in dreams was it this easy, this easily so good.

"Shh. Don't think. Feel," he whispered against her mouth.

She could do that. Feeling was easier. Feeling didn't require any effort, it just was. *He rocked upward, moving inside her, and she arched her body forward, straining against the gentle restraint of his hands, wanting to reach every inch of that warm, male body.*

He didn't release her, but lowered himself so that her breasts brushed against his bare chest, the contact only increasing her anticipation, deepening the need. She wrapped her legs up around his hips, drawing him in deeper, keeping their lower bodies connected so tightly she could almost imagine they were one animal, the blood pulsing between them. A few more mutual thrusts, and the question of if her muscles were tightening around him or his erection was swelling inside her became a moot point because they were both caught up in the same sensation of sweet pressure winding up inside until there was nowhere to go but explode. His breath came harder, feeding her own reactions until they were both slicked with sweat. His mouth found hers again for a bruising kiss and amazingly, she felt a tidal-wave orgasm hit at the exact same moment he moaned and shuddered into her mouth with his own release.

Emma had never managed that before; had almost believed it was a sexual myth. Now, now she felt as though every sinew in her body had been cut, leaving her limp, exhausted and exhilarated.

The next morning, Emma wasn't at all surprised that she had enough energy, not only to get out of bed and take a shower, but to make it downstairs into the kitchen before Matthew. A faint snoring noise from behind the closed door of the guest room, as she walked to the stairs, made it obvious where he was.

"Good morning," she said, when he finally shuffled downstairs, his pale skin almost translucent in the sunlight streaming in through the windows. "I thought maybe pancakes this morning. With," she added before he could scold her, "whole wheat flour, and fresh fruit, not syrup."

Matthew's smile was even brighter than the sunlight, even though he looked as tired as she normally felt. He was wearing his usual jeans, and a dark red T-shirt that made his glossy dark hair seem to shimmer with a reflected blue, like a blackbird's wing. Mixing the ingredients together, she turned to ask him to set the table, and that was when she saw it.

On his left forearm, on the side of his arm, just above the wrist.

A bite mark.

Emma turned back to the counter, her request unspoken. Her brain tried to tell her that she was crazy, that she was hallucinating, that she was making wild assumptions and impossible conclusions. Of course she was. It was wild, crazy and impossible. And yet, she was convinced that if she were to walk over there, and place her mouth over that mark—crazy, impossible—her mouth would match the mark exactly.

The place where she had bitten her dream lover.

Emma made it out to the patio and sat down. Her heart was racing so hard she wasn't sure it was going to stay in her chest. That voice she had been hearing, the laugh…the dream lover who made her feel so safe… Was it all Matthew? How? And why? Why had he come into her house… Oh, God, she had let him into her house, had *invited* him in!

That wasn't all she had invited him in for.

"Let me help you."

"Yes."

"Idiot," she said now, shredding her thumbnail with her teeth until it tore off below the quick. "You invited him in. You gave him permission. Because you haven't ever seen a damn horror movie?"

A slightly hysterical laugh bubbled up. It was impossible, crazy, totally insane. There was no such thing as…whatever she was thinking he was.

"All right, stop that." She suddenly realized that her thumb was bleeding, and sucked on it absently. "You got sick. Nobody knows why, but hey, so do a huge number of women every year in the U.S. alone, according to Dr. Gan. So you're tired, and you haven't gotten laid in—oh, man—way too long, and you're having seriously hot dreams. So far, totally normal. And hey, hot guy sleeping down the hall, making you breakfast and doing the laundry which is sex of a whole different kind."

A rock dove landed on the patio railing and cocked its head at her, and she reached into the old coffee can by the side of her chair and tossed it some birdseed to keep it from flying off. If she was talking to a bird, that was bad, but better than talking to herself.

"So. Let's think this through like the evenhanded, levelheaded office manager you are, okay? You've got CFS. You're exhausted.

Hot guy caretaker is hired, shows up in my equally hot dreams. That's all. No conflation of them at all, except in your overtired brain. Because anything else really is the crazy."

The dove cooed at her, and crapped on the railing.

"Yeah. Right. Thanks."

Emma needed to talk to someone else, someone who would have more of a sense of crazy/not crazy than a bird. But who?

"Jel?"

"*Chica!* My God, you live! I live! We both live! It's been, what, three months? Four? Your job doesn't keep you that busy! And never returning my messages. Bad form, *chica*."

"I know. I am bad, bad. But I did call!" After she had made sure that Matthew was taking his day off—his first, after six days on—she had picked up the phone and called her old college roommate, now *Dr.* Jela Lay.

"Which means you've got something to talk about. Spill it, *chica*. You've been sick, I can tell already, and you didn't come to see me?"

"You're a pediatrician."

"So? You're emotionally twelve."

"I am not!"

"Are, too."

"Not!"

There was a pause, and then the two women started to giggle.

"Oh, God, thank you. I needed that."

"So what's wrong?"

Emma shrugged, playing with the folds of the tablecloth in front of her. "Chronic fatigue syndrome."

"Oh, Em…"

"No, it's okay. I'm okay. I'm feeling better, much better now. Going to go back to work next week. Probably."

"Full-time?"

"I'm going to try anyway." She and Jela had been friends for almost a decade; she didn't have to pretend in front of her. "I'll see how it goes."

"That makes sense. But you sound…tired, but okay."

"Yeah. About that. Jel…I need to run something by you. And you have to promise not to laugh, or try to commit me, or anything."

"So help me, I promise."

And with that promise, Emma told her everything, from the first sensation of someone watching her, months ago, to the discovery of the bite mark on Matthew's arm.

"So. Am I crazy?"

"Maybe. Doesn't mean you didn't bite him."

"Great. You're a lot of help."

"Look, you're asking me if I believe that someone can—do I have this right?—somehow use your dreams to get in and suck your energy? And this guy, who can maybe get into your dreams, is also the guy your dad hired to take care of you? I guess maybe he needed to be closer, in order to finish the job?"

Emma made a distressed noise, and Jela hushed her. "I'm just running with the idea, Em. So he works in a care facility to get access? Did your dad pick these guys out of the phone book, or—"

"They were recommended by the hospital."

"Ah. Never take a hospital's recommendation. They're as prone to kickbacks as any corporation. So he shows up, and gets your permission to do whatever it is he's going to do, which, yeah, is totally vampire territory, that inviting-in thing, and your dreams get all steamy…but you said you feel better when you dream?"

"Yeah."

Jela clucked her tongue. "I'd hate to hear how you sound when you feel worse, then."

"I didn't have a dream last night," Emma admitted. "Mainly because I didn't get to sleep. It happens sometimes, I'm so wiped out, I can't sleep. I've been catching up on a lot of black-and-white movies, and old sitcoms."

"So you invited him in, and gave him permission…and when

the dreams don't come you feel worse… *Chica,* I'm not saying you're crazy because, hey, I take Communion and believe in the Resurrection, and you don't say I'm crazy, but have you thought about the fact that maybe he's not the one draining you, but maybe he's the one protecting you? That maybe this dream sex isn't any kind of violation, but medicine?"

Jela finished all in a rush, then waited for her response.

Emma laughed. "That's crazy. You know that's crazy, right?"

"Bacteria was crazy once, too. Em, just do me a favor, okay? For once, don't insist on having all the solutions. You don't—" There was a buzzing noise, and the sound of something clicking. "Oh, damn. *Chica,* I have to go, I'm on call, I'm sorry."

"It's all right. Go. I'm okay."

"You're sure? You'll think about what I said, and not insist everything be making sense? Because so much of what we deal with, the stuff that is important, it makes no sense at all, you know that, right?"

"Are you trying to tell me that all we need is faith? Because I think we had that argument freshman year, and you didn't convince me then, either."

Jela laughed. "Faith and love and a bit of modern medicine, that's how my world goes round. And, *chica,* if he does anything, and I mean anything that's weird, or scary or…not in a dream, you call me no matter what the hour, and I will come and get you and kick his ass. Got me?"

"Yes, Doc. I promise. Go make your baby patients all better."

Dinner that evening was a quiet affair; she had brought energy to the phone call so that Jela wouldn't worry, but now that she didn't have to put up a front, it was almost worse than before. Matthew picked up on it, having her sit at the table and peel vegetables while he handled the rest of the dinner prep, despite the fact that she was supposed to be preparing the meals now. Only half of her attention was on scraping the carrots and shredding lettuce; the rest was content to watch him move around the small kitchen, competent and mostly familiar now with where everything was.

Strange, how quickly it had become comfortable, having him in her space. She would miss him. The thought came as a jolt of surprise.

"Has the company given you another assignment yet?"

"No." Did his hands hesitate, even a little? "I usually take a week or so off between assignments. Anyway, you're not quite ready to be on your own just yet. Another week, you'll be—"

She didn't want to hear it, not from him. "I'm never going to be okay. That's what you told me the first day, remember? That's not how it works. CFS? It's always, once it arrives. I'm just going to have to…make do."

"Don't say that." Matthew's voice was still low and calm, but it was angry, too. Like she'd insulted him, or something. His perfect back, his perfect backside, was still, like he'd frozen in place. "The doctors don't know everything. Just…keep the dreamcatcher over your bed, all right?" He turned and looked at her, those dark eyes of his almost pure black against his pale skin. "You have to trust me."

It was the perfect opening: *Matthew, are you involved in this? Is any of this real—your story, my dreams, or have I lost my mind?*

She couldn't say it, not looking at him, the way he was looking at her, like she was the only thing in his world, something valuable, precious and rare. Like something he was going to lose.

Her throat was suddenly tight and sore, and she wanted to cry. "All right," she said.

She took a bath before she climbed into bed, a sea-salt scrub bringing a glow to her skin, and lilac-scented lotion smoothing it down again. Rather than her usual T-shirt and shorts, she pulled out a silky tank and tap pants, and slid them on, feeling foolish even as she did so, like a woman preparing for a romantic date, not a near-invalid getting ready for bed.

It wasn't until her hand was reaching for the bottle of perfume on her dresser that she realized what she was about to do. She was dressing up for a fantasy. Or, worse, an invader.

"All right, it stops here and now. Dream lover's going to have to make do with my natural sleep-sweat. See if he finds that sexy."

She slipped in between the sheets, silk against cotton. As usual, her body's exhaustion had reached the point where she almost couldn't sleep, but the relaxation techniques Matthew had taught her during the stretching sessions slowed her racing heart down to where she could relax into the mattress. Once that happened, it was only a few moments before her eyelids fluttered, the now-familiar dreamcatcher pattern hovered in her eyesight, and then there was only darkness.

"Em. Emma, wake up. Come to me, Emma." Not the shadow voice, but one more familiar. Trusted.

She reached out, and he was there.

His hands were warm, his lips smooth on her skin, and once again all her fears, her worries drowned under the purely carnal sensations her dream lover created. She felt herself relax backward, falling without any fear or uncertainty, and he was there, his arms braced on either side of her head, supporting his body over hers. It wasn't a dream. It didn't feel like a dream.

"Hi," she said, before his lips were on hers again, his tongue flicking, demanding entry and silencing her voice. His knee pushed her legs apart, and he settled comfortably between her thighs, lowering his upper body so that the heat between them had nowhere to go but back down into her skin, making Emma feel like she was melting into the mattress.

The promise was tempting; all she had to do was lie back and let him drive her into sexual satiation. And he would, too. Her lover did not tease, and he did not hold back from his own pleasure, either.

"Matthew?"

She barely breathed his name, but her lover hesitated enough for confirmation.

"What are you doing?"

"Shh. Don't think, Em. Don't talk. Don't use my name. Just let me in. Feel me. Hold me. Let me love you."

"But, Ma—"

The dream shook, like someone rattling her bed, trying to climb in.

"Em, don't think. Dream. Dream of only pleasant things. Let the dream catch you. The dream will keep you safe." His voice shook with the bed, and his touch was softer, like he was slipping away, fading.

"Tell me why!" Her cry was into empty darkness; he was gone. The dream was gone. Her skin was cold, the air too dry, and the voice was back inside her head.

Mine. Mine. He can't have. I don't share. Not ever. Not until you're all gone...

"Matthew." Was that her voice? It seemed impossible that such a faint whimper could come from her body. It was the voice of an old woman, a frail stick, not a healthy thirty-four-year-old. "Matthew?"

And he was there, kneeling at her bedside, his hands warm against her too-cold skin, his voice murmuring gentle words as he helped her sit up against the pillows. Her body shook with the aches, and her head felt too heavy for her neck.

"What did you do to me?" she asked despairingly. She was too tired, too sore to be angry. She just wanted to know why—no, not why. Why her?

"I didn't," he said.

She didn't believe him. She couldn't believe him. He had been there, in her dreams. She had invited him into her home, thinking he would help her, but it was him doing this, draining her, making her so tired she couldn't move, could barely breathe because it hurt so much…

"Why?" Tears would have helped, but she was too tired for even that. "What did I ever do to you?"

"Nothing. Nothing. Em, I am so sorry. I am. I tried to help. I wasn't supposed to and I did, I did more than I should have, but you broke the web and let him back in…"

She felt him gather her up in his arms. He felt so intensely *solid,* while she was fragile, near-translucent. "Did I do that to you? Did you get so solid off me?"

"Please, stop it." He sounded like he had a bad cold. "Don't stop believing in me. If you stop believing, if the dream dies, he wins."

"He?"

He ducked his head, unable to look at her, but the dam was broken, and the words tumbled out of him, almost incoherent, terrifyingly insane. "Him. Me. We're two sides of the same coin. That story I told you. It's true, but it wasn't all… My people were cursed. Ages ago, biblical ages ago. I don't know why or by whom, and it doesn't matter. We split, every child born, damned. One side lives only in the shadows, the dark of night, stealing strength. Incubi, your people call them. Incubi or succubi, it's all the same. There comes a time in their existence when the life force they were born with begins to fade, and they must find someone and…steal her life in order for them to survive."

It was crazy, all the crazy she had been afraid of in herself. Insane, and impossible. Jela's voice sounded, a years-old counterpoint to the whispers: "Believe, *chica.* For once, for your own sake, *believe.*"

She believed. Not because it was believable, but because it felt true. It made sense, where none of the medical double-talk had.

"And you…you aid them. You help them steal life."

"No!"

His anger made her bones hurt, and he seemed to realize it,

softening his voice and relaxing his hold on her. "No. Never. I…I try to help, to make him stronger."

"So they have more to feed on. Your shadow self."

"I'm a healer, Em. I take care of people. I want to make them better, stronger. That side…disgusts me. But I can't kill him, not without killing myself, and forgive me, I want to live, too. I want to live."

She reached out to touch him, to give comfort, then pulled her hand back, but didn't demand that he let go of her. Even now, even hearing what he was saying, knowing what he had been doing to her, his touch was a comfort. If there was crazy in any of this, it was that.

"I knew when he started to fade, my darkside self. I knew he'd have to find someone, again and again. Over the years, we've… we've worked out how to do it. It takes three months, usually. Three months for all of his victim's life force to siphon from them to him. He never tells me. They never do. If I could find out who, track his victim down and keep her healthy and well through the third month…"

"Then what?"

"Then he's fed enough to survive, still weak, but she lives. If I fail, if he's satiated…they die."

"I die."

"Yes. Sometimes I…have to let him win. But you… I couldn't stand it." He looked at her then, those dark eyes red-rimmed and wet with tears. "You were so delicate, so frail, but there was so much life in you, beaten down but still beautiful, so stubborn, and nobody else could see the beauty in you… I couldn't let him win, not even a little. I kept him out. I got between the connection, and gave you strength to fight him."

"The dreams…"

"At first, yes. It was the only way I could think of, to fight him on his own ground. And then, the dreamcatcher. It was just a legend, but I was desperate, grabbing at anything. It's supposed to be a filter. I'm mortal, so I can get through but he can't. But you didn't trust me, you doubted, and struggled, and broke the dreamcatcher, and he drank so deeply last night, he was so hungry…"

"I'm dying." It was a relief actually. Death wouldn't hurt so much, it couldn't.

"I won't let you."

"Then you'll die, won't you." She almost understood that now. They both existed, or they both died, one predator feeding on them both. Feeding on her.

Once again, people were depending on her.

Matthew moved his arms from around her as though he'd only just realized they were so intimate. "It's all right. Living this way…I hate it. And I couldn't go on, once you were gone. I'll rebuild the dreamcatcher, we'll keep him out long enough. He hasn't drunk enough and there's no time for him to find someone new, not now, and soon it will be over."

"No."

"Emma, be serious."

She was, he saw that. "You walked in here…and you saved me."

"I—"

"Everyone else dropped and ran. Everyone's always dropped and run. You need me to…to die, to live. But you protected me anyway, even at cost to yourself. Why?"

He had no answer to give her except the truth. "You… You glow. Like the sun. Everything that he feeds on…so do I. I warm myself in the sun. I felt myself warming to you. The first day you were so pale and drawn and tired, and I thought all I could do was ease your passage, make sure that you gave him enough that he would be sated for a long time, and that you didn't suffer…"

"Like a calf, fatted to feed the monster." Her voice was low and bitter, and it hurt him that the bitterness was directed, not against him, who deserved it, but herself.

"Yes. I'm not proud of it, Emma. It's how we survive, the best…the only way we can, without going crazy or…

"Some of us do go crazy. They embrace the beast, encourage it. They see the rest of humanity as fair feeding grounds, using the beast's strength to augment their own lives. They turn the curse into a justification, hunting and feeding for their own benefit." He had seen it happen; seen it, and seen one possible future for himself.

"Not you."

"No." He shook his head, feeling the loss of her warmth next to him, even though she was still there. "Not yet. But it could happen. If I lived long enough, saw enough. I'd rather die. There are things I have to do to survive. But I would never take pleasure in them. I would never intentionally benefit from them. Not like that."

Emma's hand reached out for his own, and he took it almost without conscious effort, unable to resist. She was slender to the point of frailness, but her hands felt warm and capable; the hands of a woman who could accomplish anything.

Anything except save him.

It was too much effort to move. Emma rested her head against Matthew's shoulder, and he shifted so that she fit against his side more comfortably. They didn't talk, didn't fret over what was, or what might be, but simply sat on her bed and held each other.

Matthew fell asleep first. Emma knew only because his breathing slowed ever so slightly; his fingers remained interlaced with her own, as though to let go would be to let her go. Her body ached from the stress of the day, and her mind was just as exhausted from the effort of taking in everything she had learned. The temptation to curl up and let the pain and lethargy win was strong, but now that she knew what was causing it, that there was a chance to beat it, the temptation could be beaten down.

You can't win. I have you...

"No, you don't," she whispered back. "No, you don't."

Matthew thought he had to sacrifice himself to save her. She would find another way. She *had* to find another way.

Trust me.

The voice was quiet, neutral. Not the dark whisper but something cooler, filled with equal amounts shadow and light. Something familiar, trustworthy, even though she had no idea….

Trust yourself. Trust your heart.

And like that, she understood. She was surprised that it was so easy, after all the worrying. Lie down, look up into the dreamcatcher. See it, really see the colors and the way the threads tangled with each other, crossing and catching, holding and binding…

That easy, and she was not asleep, walking in a dream landscape that wasn't comforting or threatening, neither demanding nor offering. It simply *was*. And, in it, so was she.

This is your place, that unfamiliar voice told her, vibrating through her dream body. *It is yours to control. Your destiny that you shape.*

Emma looked down, and saw the red and blue strands under her feet. The voice had come from there, from the dreamcatcher.

Hers to control.

In that realization, a landscape emerged around her. A high mountain peak, gray stone and golden sunshine slanting down and creating pools of cooler shadow. Her feet kept walking until, cartoonlike, she stepped off the stone path and onto that slant of sunlight. Her body remained upright, suspended in the air between peaks as she walked farther out into the warmth of the sun.

She knew, then, that she wasn't alone.

"Come on then." She stood in the center of the dreamcatcher, feeling the strands sway underneath, like a cable bridge high in the wind. "Come here."

The dream wind wrapped around her, trying to toss her off the strands, and it should have been terrifying. Instead, the frisson of fear was like salt in a meal, making the rest of the sensations jump into sharp relief.

Hers to control. Hers to not control, to let the wind do what wind did, and know it was her own strength that kept her upright.

Heady, that sensation. Dangerous, maybe, but heady.

"I can't." Matthew stood off to the side, his feet firmly planted on the ledge of the mountain. He was dressed in jeans, as usual, but there were hiking boots on his feet, and a heavy leather jacket over his T-shirt, against the wind. By contrast, she wore only a tank top and shorts, and her feet were bare.

"Of course you can. Just step over."

"No. The dreamcatcher's damaged, Em. It can only hold you, not both of us. I'd tear it, and then he'd be able to come in again. I won't let that happen."

"It's all right. Matt. Trust me." She held out her hand, the sunlight catching on her palm and flaring brightly like fire was held within. Despite himself, Matthew swayed forward.

"Come here."

Her confidence was startling, her determination irresistible. Their gazes locked, Matthew stepped off the cliff, and down onto the brightly colored web.

And with that, the wind intensified, sweeping down off the sheer sides of the peaks, bringing with it the bitter tang of snow and the sweet coolness of rain. The smell wasn't unpleasant; it actually made Emma lift her face up into it, appreciating the sensation on her skin even as it tried to tear the strands out from under her feet and send her plummeting down into the dark crevasse.

Matthew's image wavered, shimmering as though he were under attack, and then came back, more solid than before.

He shook his head, feeling the difference. He could feel it, that he was more solid, with depths and texture, as though the artist had added background and shadows to a previously two-dimensional portrait, not changing the image so much as intensifying it.

"No!"

He staggered under the shock, then regained his footing even as she reached out and took his hands in her own, pulling him to her. Her hands were burning hot, and he was so very, very cold….

"Emma. What have you done?"

His voice had a rasp to it, like he'd been screaming for hours, and he could hear in it a mixture of horror and anticipation, mimicking what he felt inside.

"This couldn't go on," she said, her eyes tearing. "You couldn't go on like this."

"Emma… Oh, God, no!"

He could feel the hunger inside overwhelming the horror and dismay, reaching with greedy grabby hands for the life inside his lover, wanting only to reach in and pull it out, pull it into himself and feast on it until he was sated…

And she was dead.

"No!"

He tried to pull himself out of her grasp. It should have been a simple thing; he was that much stronger than she was, and fear gave him an extra rush. But in this dream space she was the master, and he was no longer the sole resident of his body.

Let her go, he warned the intruder in his own flesh. *I will destroy us both, rather than let you have her.*

The other awareness didn't even consider his threat worth responding to, so focused was he on the prize. *Mine. Mine to consume. Mine to possess, not share. Not give up.*

"I don't *think* so," Emma said, calm as though she had been talking to the shadowed one for decades. "That's always been the problem, hasn't it? Everyone wanting a piece and taking and taking and never giving back, wearing me down. That's what you saw, isn't it? That there was a chink in me that everyone else had worn down, and that's how you slipped in, that first time."

The shadow self shook his head, tightening his grasp on her fingers. *Stop talking. Feed me.*

"You can't have me. Not all of me, not the last morsel of me. Not even the second-to-last morsel. I won't allow it."

She was so strong, so determined, but the shadow self used his body and laughed. The same laugh that had echoed in her head for months now. The laugh that mocked her attempts to break free, that ridiculed her insistence on freedom, on self-worth. The laugh that had haunted her, wearing her down, taking the marrow of her strength and leaving her with nothing…

He could see years of agreeing to others' demands, of being supportive and understanding, threatened to swamp her under a violent gust of wind, mocking laughter tangling in her air. *You can't even stand up for yourself, how do you expect to stand up to me?*

Matthew could see her starting to slip away, her skin losing the healthy tan and fading to translucence, and the sight gripped his heart and throat so he had trouble breathing. He would not lose her. He would *not* let her slip away. "Emma. No. Hold on to the dreamcatcher, Emma. I gave this to you. This is your place. He can't claim you here."

Her eyes closed, and her entire body shuddered, then those blue-shadowed lids rose and she looked at him—looked *into* him—and smiled that glorious, life-filled smile, teeth white against the pink of her lips. The grip on his heart squeezed tighter, and he barely noticed.

"No. You're right. He can't claim me. But I can claim *him.*"

The dreamcatcher's voice started to hum, rising in pitch as the vibration traveled from the soles of her feet, up her legs, and into her torso, filling her rib cage with a sensation she almost couldn't recognize, it had been so long.

Courage.

The dreamcatcher protected her; Matthew had been right about that. But he was wrong about *why.* There was nothing magical about it, no counterspell to his curse. The only magic was in the making of it; his gift…his belief in her. His willingness to betray his other half, to die, to keep her safe.

Her parents loved her. Her coworkers depended on her. But nobody had ever given up anything for her. Nobody had ever announced that she was the most important thing, worth sacrificing for.

Mine. Mine. The voice was back, and the hunger in Matthew's eyes was real—and painful to see. The dark whisper and the dreamcatcher's hum collided in her sinus cavities, like a headache that wasn't quite there yet, and she squinched her eyes shut.

"Stop it, both of you!"

Silence, shocked and still.

Opening her eyes, she looked to where her hand was still holding Matthew's, their fingers, alternating tan and pale, dappled by sunlight and shadows.

"You love me." It wasn't a question, wasn't a revelation. Just a statement. A simple awareness of an impossible fact.

Need you, the shadowed voice whispered, even as the physical lips echoed her own words. *"Love you."*

Need and love and hunger and sadness were all in that gaze, and it fed her, met her own need and hunger and sadness—and love, she realized without any surprise—and gave her the strength to do what was needed.

"To bind us together," she said softly, echoing the words of the legend. "Forever."

The dreamcatcher dropped out from under them like an elevator falling, the strands reaching up even as the center sank, tangling them in the multicolored strands so that they were pressed skin to skin, unable to move, falling down impossibly fast through the endlessly deep chasm of the dreamscape mountain crevice. Terror and excitement surged, the three of them trapped together in what seemed like an inevitable death-plunge.

Stop it!

"Emma..." Unlike the shadow voice, Matthew's words were worried, but calm. "What happens when we hit bottom?"

Emma laughed, a little shaky herself. "I don't know," she admitted. "But we're all three going to hit at the same time, so I think maybe it's up to all of us."

Will not die!

"None of us have to," Emma agreed. "Or all of us will. I'm okay with that. How about you?"

It wasn't really a question. The shadowed one didn't want to die. Matthew wanted her to live. She didn't want to live without Matthew.

The sudden hard stop at the end of the fall didn't hurt as much as she had expected.

Morning sunlight coated the bedroom window, pink-hued strands creeping across the bedspread, touching the two forms sprawled there, limbs and torsos entwined. The larger form stirred, then sat upright abruptly, waking the other.

"Emma."

"Mmm?" She rubbed her eyes with one hand, then stretched, luxuriating in the feel of her body.

"We died, Em."

"Did we?"

"Em..." Matthew's expression tried for dire, but didn't quite make it. "Em, I feel... What happened?"

"The dreamcatcher caught us." She reached up and touched his face. His skin was still pale, but there were hints of an olive tone underneath now that matched his eyes and hair. "The way it was supposed to. Caught and bound."

Matthew went very still, and she could practically feel him probing the air around them, reaching out for a once-too-familiar shadow lurking nearby.

There was nothing there now. She saw that realization dawn on his face, followed by an expression she didn't know, but could guess at; the sensation of a new weight inside, a darker presence, fitting itself into the flesh. What had been sundered now was one. One man, freed from the driving hunger—but, hopefully, not the need.

The gentle man she had fallen in love with was still there, the strength it had taken to stand against his shadow self to protect her, finally enhanced by the darkness, rather than having to constantly fight it.

"How did you know?" he asked, his voice hushed with amazement and awe. "The dreamcatcher…how did you know?"

"I didn't," she admitted, still enthralled by the changes she could see happening in him. "Not really. But what you said about the gift—a gift to bind them, you said—and why else pass down the knowledge of how to make one, if it didn't have a purpose? Your parents and grandparents and great-grandparents—all those generations telling the story for a reason. Saving me wasn't enough for them to remember it—it had to be there to save you, too. If anyone ever cared enough to use it."

"Cared together, all three of us, binding us…how?"

Emma reached up to pull her lover back down onto the mattress with her. "Love, and need, and a willingness to do whatever it takes to survive," she said softly, dropping a gentle kiss on his forehead, then the tip of his nose, then his chin, then an ear before he took her face between his hands and moved her attentions to his mouth, hushing her for a moment.

"You're free," she said to him, when he let her breathe. "Finally, you're free."

"Free, yeah. But only to be trapped again." He kissed her again, fingers twining with her own, echoing the weaving of the dreamcatcher's threads. "He and I had—have—that one thing in common. We're never letting you get away."

Emma felt life surge within her, and smiled. That, she could live with.

* * * * *

MAHINA'S STORM

Vivi Anna

To all those tough chicks out there.
You know who you are.

VIVI ANNA

likes to burn up the pages with her unique brand of fantasy fiction. Whether it's in the Amazon jungle, an apocalyptic future or the otherworld city of Necropolis, Vivi always writes fast-paced action-adventure featuring strong, independent women and dark, delicious heroes.

Dear Reader,

When asked to write a story for the Nocturne Bites program, I jumped at the opportunity. I knew exactly who I was going to write about.

The toughest chick in Necropolis—Captain Mahina Garner. I love everything about Mahina, especially her direct, no-nonsense way of dealing with things. So when I was pondering what kind of story to write for her, I knew I had to throw a wrench into her life, to shake it up. I was excited to see how she would handle it. So I tossed Ren Calder at her. And boy, do things get shaken up!

A storm is about to erupt. I hope you enjoy the ride!

Best wishes,

Vivi Anna

Catch up with Vivi and all her stories about the OCU at her Web site, www.vivianna.net.

ONE

The bust was about to go down.

Captain Mahina Garner of the Necropolis Police Department peered toward the warehouse's back door around the side of the truck she was using for cover. There was no activity that she could see. She glanced at her wristwatch. Ten more minutes until her team was ready to go in.

She hoped that her informant had given her reliable information. She'd been working on this Vampatimine drug operation for a while now. And today was the big payoff. The main operator was supposed to be inside overseeing the production of the illegal street drug.

The leader's name was Richard Terry, a young vampire of ninety-five, but still powerful enough to have control of most of the illegal vampire drug business in Necropolis. Mahina had been working this case ever since a young human woman was found murdered in one of the city's seedier hotels with Vampatimine in her system. The killer had used it to subdue her. Produced from a vampire's saliva, it was the Otherworlder community's answer to the drug RBH—the date rape drug. She'd been trying to bring the ring down ever since.

The forensics team she worked closely with, headed by Caine Valorian, a vampire, had been able to find the killer of the human girl—it had also been a vampire that cowed her and siphoned all the blood from her body. The team, or OCU, was like any big-city crime investigative unit—collecting evidence, analyzing it and tracing that evidence to the perpetrators. The only difference was that the members were made up of lycans, like her, vampires and witches. It made sense for a city made up of entirely Otherworld-like beings.

But they had yet been able to track down the manufacturer of the drug. Until now.

"Garner. We're in position." Detective Ren Calder's voice crackled through the radio clipped to her jacket collar.

Mahina pressed the respond button. "Good to go in two minutes."

"Roger that."

She was happy to have Ren on her team. He was a lycan like herself—strong, quick and agile, with great instincts. He was nice to look at, too, but that certainly wasn't why she liked working with him. He was a good cop and damn good to have in a fight. She'd worked a number of cases with him before. They'd always come out with positive results and the perpetrators in handcuffs. She hoped for the same results today.

She wanted this bust so badly she could taste it. Not big on vampires to begin with—except for maybe two or three that she worked with in law enforcement and on Caine Valorian's forensics team—she despised those who preyed on the weak. Which was unusual considering her species. But there was a big difference between chasing rabbits in a park and victimizing humans and other Otherworlder species with a genetic abnormality that could produce a lethal drug.

She glanced at her watch again. One minute to go. The storm was about to begin.

Nodding to the three officers she had with her, she tapped her watch and indicated that they had one minute left. They all nodded in return and readied themselves, checking gear and weapons.

Mahina checked the clip in her gun again. She had ten shots but hoped she wouldn't have to use any of them. She liked shooting at targets in a closed range, not at real people. She always tried to avoid lethal force. She hoped the suspects wouldn't make her use her gun.

After another quick check of the time, Mahina nodded to her team. She was ready to go in.

Gun in hand, she moved out first. Checking around the truck, she then ran to the next cover—a stack of wooden pallets used for shipping. Once she was there, she gave the signal for the rest of the officers to move forward. One by one they progressed to the warehouse door.

Mahina counted to three, kicked in the door, then rushed into the building. "NPD!"

She could hear Ren call out the same initials from the front. Everyone inside the building was sufficiently trapped with no way to escape.

It was dark in the warehouse, but that didn't affect Mahina's ability to see. All lycans had built-in night vision. There were about a dozen people scrambling in front of her, each trying to find a way to fight or flee. Bags of Vampatimine were tossed, money shoved into pockets and weapons snatched off the long metal tables.

She saw Richard Terry immediately in the chaos. Standing off to the side looking around, he projected an air of boredom, as if he were above all of this. With her hackles up, she made her way straight for him, intent on knocking the arrogant smirk off his thin face.

That was when all hell broke loose.

Gunshots rang out. Mahina didn't know who was shooting at whom. Bullets whizzed by, forcing her to the ground. She rolled on the cement floor and came up behind a line of four metal drums. Ren had also found his way there, crouching down for cover.

He nodded to her. "Great party as usual, Garner. Looks like they were expecting us."

That had crossed her mind, too. Her snitch had obviously tipped off Terry and his guys. She was going to have to have a long involved discussion with him once she got out of here. And he wasn't going to like it much, especially when she tossed him into a jail cell for a few long months.

"What's the plan?" he asked, peering through a slit between the barrels.

"Take down the bad guys and don't get shot."

"The usual, then."

She smiled at him. She'd always liked his cool and casual manner. It kept her from rushing around like a mad dog. He had a quiet way of keeping her in line. An almost impossible feat that he was able to do with a little humor and a few choice words.

Peeking around the drum, Mahina spied the vampire she was after moving toward the back door. All the officers on her team were otherwise engaged and weren't watching as their quarry stealthily approached the exit. It would be up to her to bring him down.

Which was exactly the way she liked it anyway.

Adrenaline coursed through her as she prepared to spring out from behind the barrels and make a rush for the vampire. She could sense Ren's uneasiness beside her.

"Garner?" His voice held a slight edge. He must've known what she was about to do.

"Cover me," she told him as she leaped to her feet and ran full-out toward Richard Terry.

As she sprinted across the warehouse floor, Mahina was completely and utterly focused on the vampire. She didn't see or hear anything else around her. She had to take him down. Nothing else mattered.

She could hear his heart pumping as she drew near. A mixture of excitement and fear infused his scent with an acidity that made her nostrils burn. But she liked the fact that he was afraid. That thought pushed her harder and faster, urging her on.

Someone came at her from the right—a big, burly vampire

with ham-size fists. Mahina dodged his first punch, then retaliated with her own solid blow to his temple. His knees buckled and he collapsed on the ground. She leaped over his falling body and continued to sprint toward the door, where her quarry was just about to get away.

At the last second he swung around toward her. Everything after that was a bit of a blur.

"Garner! Get down!"

Ren's frantic voice exploded in her mind. She didn't have time to react before she was gathered in someone's arms and propelled to the cement floor. The impact knocked the air from her lungs.

"Are you hit?"

Trying to catch her breath, she blinked up at Ren, confused. He surveyed her face and neck.

"What?" she asked, her voice barely a whisper.

"Are you injured? Did the bullet graze you?"

"What bullet?"

Rolling off her, Ren reached for the collar of her shirt. He yanked it up toward her face. "You're damn lucky, Garner."

She looked incredulously at the burned hole in her shirt. Quickly Mahina ran her hands over her neck and upper chest. There was no bullet hole. Not even a mark.

"Where's Terry?" She looked around frantically. Had he got away?

"Don't worry. We got him."

Two of the officers had the vampire in handcuffs. A gun lay at his feet. Another of the officers picked it up carefully and placed it in a bag for evidence.

She hadn't even seen the weapon on the vampire. When he'd turned at the door, all she'd focused on was capturing him. And he'd nearly taken her out. There was no doubt in her mind that his weapon had been loaded with silver. One shot to a vital part of her body and she wouldn't have been able to heal the wound because of the silver poisoning.

Ren stood, then pulled her to her feet. He kept her hand in his just a bit longer than was necessary. An odd heat rushed up her arm. Mahina pulled away from his touch and brushed at her pants.

"Are you all right?" he asked. She could hear the worry in his voice.

"Yeah—why wouldn't I be?"

He just looked at her, and she saw concern in his eyes. She didn't like the fact that he thought there was something wrong. It made her feel weak.

Without another look at Ren, Mahina marched through the warehouse to take over the handling of the vampire. This was her bust, and she'd be the one to take him in.

He smiled at her when she neared. She knew he was looking at the bullet hole in her shirt. "Hmm, so close."

Her resolve shattered. She punched him hard in the face, sending him to his knees. "I'd say that was just right on the money."

The other officers grabbed the vampire by his arms and hefted him to his feet. He wasn't smiling when they took him, half carrying and half dragging, out of the warehouse.

The punch did nothing to dampen the feelings racing around in her mind and body. She'd nearly died. One inch lower and she'd have been down for good. Ren had saved her life. If he'd been one second slower on the uptake, she'd be bleeding out on the cold, hard cement floor of the warehouse.

For a woman claiming to have everything under control, Mahina felt as if she was unraveling thread by thread. And it scared her to no end.

TWO

Garner! Get down!

Mahina couldn't stop the words from repeating in her head. Nor could she muffle the sound of gunshots still ringing in her ears.

She gave the hundred-pound bag swinging in front of her an uppercut-hook combo, then took a step back and spun on her heel for a roundhouse kick. Sweat dribbled down her back and her arms were starting to feel leaden from the weighted gloves she wore. But it would be some time before she gave up working the bag. It was therapeutic, and right now Mahina needed a ton of therapy.

It wasn't as if she'd never faced death before. She had on several occasions and thwarted it by quick thinking and even quicker reflexes. A woman didn't work as a police captain for the Necropolis Police Department in a city full of vampires, witches and lycans and not have the grim reaper's number on speed dial. It was just that she hadn't seen the silver bullets coming.

This time someone else had saved her life.

She punched the bag again—jab, jab, cross, hook, uppercut. A tendril of brown wavy hair escaped her high ponytail to hang in her face. She brushed at it with her gloved hand.

It wasn't that she wasn't grateful; it was just that she'd never been in such a position before—having someone else save her.

Mahina prided herself on the fact that she was a tough, independent, no-nonsense type of woman. She had worked her whole life against lycan pack politics, a domineering father, absent mother and sexism within the police department to get to where she was—a captain on the police force with a reputation for being as hard as stone. Nothing could move or affect her. Nothing could scare her.

Until now.

She delivered another flurry of punches and kicks to the bag until every muscle in her body quivered with strain. Taking a step back, she wiped the sweat from her eyes. Another hour of working out she hoped would squash the frustration that gripped her body and her mind. Something had shifted in the past twelve hours. She no longer felt in control. And the dynamic between her and Ren had changed. She didn't like that situation one bit.

As if to prove her point, the door to the gym opened and Ren walked in, gym bag slung over his broad shoulder. He crossed the room as if deep in thought, but as soon as he noticed Mahina, he stopped, his cobalt-blue eyes widening.

"Hey." He nodded to her. "I thought everyone went home for the night."

"Nah, I'm not one for sleeping at night." She gave the bag a solid jab-cross combo.

"Me either." He set his bag down, unzipped it and took out a jump rope.

She tried not to watch him as he slid his hands over the rope handles, but it was hard not to. Ren was a formidable-looking man even in an unassuming white tank top and gray shorts. Standing at six-three, he towered over her impressive five-nine. He was broad in the shoulders and had one of those V-shaped bodies that men all over the world spent thousands of dollars on supplements and gym memberships to acquire. Ren possessed it naturally. A product of his lycan genetics.

He was one of the few men who had ever made her feel small.

Her study of him must have made him uncomfortable, because he asked, "Is it okay if I work out here with you?"

"Knock yourself out," she said, trying to appear unaffected by his presence. She tore her gaze away from him and put it back onto the hundred-pound punching bag where it belonged.

Jab. Hook. Cross.

But her gaze shifted toward him again as he jumped rope. Had she never noticed before the way the muscles in his legs rippled as he moved? Or how his biceps bulged? Surely she'd noticed how incredibly strong and powerful he looked. How could a woman not see how incredibly attractive he was?

Or was it that Mahina's eyes had opened for the first time?

As he jumped, his gaze strayed to her. When she saw him looking at her, she returned her attention to the bag. Inwardly she winced. She was acting like a horny teenage lycan out for her first sexual experience. She'd had plenty of bedmates. She wasn't one of those lycans who believed in saving yourself for your soul mate; no, she firmly believed in trying anything at least once. How did a woman know if it fit, if she didn't try it on?

But lately she'd been limiting her sexual interactions with others. Somehow it didn't feel quite as right as it had ten years ago. Maybe she was getting jaded. Thirty-seven was fairly old in the lycan world to be single. By her age most lycans had found a mate and settled down. She'd been getting flak on all sides about her status. Her pack alpha was on her back about it and her father, the domineering jerk that he was, constantly sniped at her for not being married and producing a bunch of grandkids for him. She hated his monthly phone calls.

Ren had stopped jumping and was regarding her curiously as he tossed the rope to the side. "Quite the day."

She broke from her reverie and started punching the bag again. "Yeah."

"Are you okay?"

His question surprised her. He'd asked her that same question at the warehouse, after almost being shot. She stopped this time and really looked at him. "What kind of question is that? Of course I'm okay."

"Hey, I'm just asking." He grabbed his white terry-cloth towel and wiped the sweat from his face and the back of his neck. "You seem a little off. You have been since it happened."

"I'm fine." She punched the bag again, as if to prove her words.

"It doesn't hurt to talk to someone about it."

"I don't need your psychoanalysis."

He smiled. "As if I had the time for that long process."

Her next punch faltered. "What's that supposed to mean?"

"It means nothing." He shook his head, then, crouching by his bag, he took out hand wraps.

Mahina tried to ignore him as she circled the bag and performed a series of combinations, punches and kicks. But once he had his hands wrapped, he stepped into her view.

"Want to spar?"

She studied him for a moment. His gaze was guarded, but he had a small smile on his face. He was goading her into it. Daring her to spar with him.

The man knew her all too well. He knew exactly how to help her forget that she'd nearly died and he'd saved her life.

"Are you sure you want to?" She stepped away from the bag and toward the practice mat. "The last guy's still getting dental work done."

"Hey, that's what mouth guards are for." He showed her the one in his hand.

That made her laugh. "Okay, you're on."

Ten minutes later they were both gloved, both wearing mouth guards and circling each other on the thin blue mat.

She'd never sparred with Ren before, so she didn't know what to expect from him. Most of her male sparring partners learned quite quickly that she never pulled punches and that neither should they, especially if they wanted to keep their good-looking faces intact. It also helped that most of her partners had increased rejuvenation powers, so no injury lasted very long anyway.

Mahina hoped Ren was as smart as she thought him to be. She really didn't want to mess up her partnership with him by besting him too badly.

After another minute of sizing him up, Mahina feinted with her right hand and struck with a left hook. Ren was much too quick for that and he easily dodged her blow. But it backed him up a little and put a grin on his face.

He pushed the mouth guard out of his mouth and said, "Hmm, you're not as fast as I'd heard."

Mahina didn't comment. Instead she showed him how quick she could be. Within seconds she'd landed two blows, one to his side and the other to his jaw. Satisfaction filled her when Ren stumbled two steps to the right.

"I'm fast enough," she garbled around the mouth guard.

He shook it off, then came at her with his own combination. She managed to deflect one punch to the head, but wasn't fast enough to outmaneuver the glove headed for her gut.

The blow knocked the wind from her and she doubled over. Unfortunately, with Mahina being temporarily winded, there was an opportunity for Ren to take another shot at her head. She was impressed when he capitalized on the chance. She would've been disappointed if he hadn't.

The blow to her cheek rattled her head. Black spots popped in and out of her vision. Her knees gave out and she dropped to the mat.

As she gained her breath, Ren approached her. She could see the regret on his face. He held out a glove toward her, intent on helping her up. "Are you all right?"

Instead of taking his hand, she swept her right leg at his ankles and took him down to the mat. She shook her head. He should've known she'd use his moment of weakness against him.

While he was still down, Mahina struggled to her feet, but Ren had other ideas.

Wrapping his arms around her legs, he tripped her up and she landed flat on her back. Air whooshed out of her lungs. Before she could move, or even think, Ren was up on his hands and knees pinning her to the mat.

She was acutely aware of his strength as he held her down. She was also conscious of his smell wafting to her. It was heady and potent. One hundred percent rock-hard male. And it was making her blood pump hard through her veins.

Breathing deeply, she took in his scent. By the dark expression in his eyes, she could see that Ren was fully aware of her reaction to him being so close.

She suddenly felt very vulnerable.

His head was near hers. Too near. She glanced at his mouth and imagined taking it hard and fast. His gaze also dipped to her lips. Sweat dripped off his forehead and dotted her cheek. A rush of hot, hearty desire shot through her body. It was enough to drive her mad.

Mahina pushed at his body. Spitting out her mouth guard, she growled, "Get off me."

He shook his head. "No. I kind of like it here. On top for a change."

"What, your woman doesn't let you play the man?"

He grinned. It was slow and easy and made her stomach do a complicated flip-flop. "There is no woman, and you know it, Garner."

"I don't know any such thing," she protested. She was maybe just a bit too fierce in her denial, judging by the amused look on Ren's face.

"How long have we been working together?"

She shrugged. "I don't know. A few years, I guess."

"And how many times have we worked a case together in those years?"

"How should I know? It's not like I keep count." *Seven,* she said in her mind.

"Seven times," he echoed. "And every time neither one of us is in a relationship."

"So?" she said. "What does that prove? It's just a coincidence."

Mahina didn't believe in coincidences. Obviously neither did Ren.

"It means something, Mahina. Don't pretend it doesn't."

She tried shoving him away again, but to no avail. The man was strong and stubborn. She sighed. "Why are we talking about this? What does it matter anyway?"

"I want you, Mahina."

His plain but blunt statement shocked her. "What?" She pushed at his shoulders again, harder this time. She needed him to move, to get away from her. She couldn't think. It was much too hot in the gym. She found it difficult to breathe.

"I want you. And I have for some time now."

"I must've hit you too hard in the head. You're rambling like an idiot." This time she shoved him and was finally successful in moving him. She scuttled out from underneath him like a crab. She scrambled to her feet and started to strip off her gloves. "Now you've ruined a perfectly good night of sparring."

Ren stood and watched her. "Why do you think Ginny left me?"

"I don't know—because you're a jerk."

"She left because of you."

That brought her head up. "Excuse me? You're blaming me for your last failed relationship?"

"She knew how I felt about you."

Mahina pulled one glove off and tossed it to the ground. "That's stupid. You've never even indicated to *me* how you supposedly feel."

"What about that night at the Blue Moon?"

As Mahina tore at the tie on her other glove, her thoughts drifted to the one night, months ago, when she and a bunch of other officers had been drinking heavily at the Blue Moon bar near the precinct. Ren had shown up late, angry and standoffish.

They'd stayed on opposite sides of the bar, both drinking tequila. But when Mahina had ventured down the back hall toward the ladies' room, she'd run into Ren coming out of the men's room. She remembered nodding to him in greeting and his return grunt of recognition.

Then it had got all very hazy and confusing. He'd grabbed her and tossed her up against the wall. Before she could move or strike out, he'd pressed his body into hers, effectively pinning her. She'd told him to back off, but instead of retorting with his own angry growl, he'd kissed her.

His kiss was hard, fast and full of anger and frustration. Mahina remembered a heat, intense and searing, racing down her body and she hadn't protested; in fact, she had buried her hands in his silky dark hair and passionately returned his kiss.

The kiss had lasted for only a few minutes. Afterward, Ren had pulled away, and without so much as a look or word to her, he had stomped back to the bar.

Mahina had continued on toward the bathroom, but instead of going into the ladies' room, she'd kept going and gone out the back door of the bar. She'd leaned against the cool brick wall outside for a while, just listening to the music and drinking in fresh air. She'd stayed there long enough so that when she had gone back in, everyone had thought she'd gone home. Ren had been nowhere to be found.

"Please, that was one kiss." She stripped off the other glove. "And it wasn't all that good, either."

Ren laughed. "I never knew you were a coward, Garner."

She eyed him then, anger at his cavalier attitude making her hands shake. "I'm no coward."

"You're running away from me."

"No, I'm not. I'm just tired of playing with you." Mahina picked up her gloves and shoved them into her gym bag.

She was finished. The only problem was she was more on edge than she had been before she'd arrived at the gym. And it had everything to do with the man still staring at her with that dark, dangerous look in his eyes. Ignoring him, she picked up her bag, slung it over her shoulder and made for the exit.

"Just like that, you're going to leave?"

"Yup," she said, not bothering to look over her shoulder at him. She couldn't and still push open the metal door and walk out.

"You're a real piece of work, Garner. You know that?"

With a hand on the door, she did turn around this time. "Hey, I already thanked you for saving my life. What more do you want?"

"Everything."

She shook her head. "Well, you're not going to get it from me." She shoved at the door and went through, letting it softly snick shut behind her.

Once she was gone, Ren shook his head and muttered to himself. God, he was an idiot. He'd never been any good at talking to women, especially *this* woman. The one woman who'd had him emotionally tied in knots for the past two years.

Shoving one gloved hand under his arm, he yanked his hand out, then proceeded to do that with the other glove. When they were off, he shoved them into his bag, picked up his towel and wiped at the sweat on his face and the back of his neck. His jaw still throbbed from where Mahina had clocked him. She had a powerful punch, but he'd expected no less. She was a tough, powerful and stubborn-as-hell woman, and he had to admit he really liked that about her. There was never a dull moment around her. She was as unpredictable as the weather.

He had been wondering where she'd gone, and had guessed she was in the gym punching the crap out of the bag instead of going home to rest as any average person would've done. In that he did know her well. She wouldn't slow down even in the face of death.

And she had almost bitten it today.

His heart had nearly stopped when he saw the vampire, Richard Terry, swing around from the open doorway brandishing a firearm aimed directly at Mahina. And she'd been charging right for him without any indication that she was going to slow down or duck for cover.

His first and only instinct had been to dive after her and get her out of the way. Pain had ripped through him as the bullet had grazed him across the lateral muscle between his shoulder and neck, but all he'd been able to think about was keeping Mahina safe. He'd deal with the injury on his own. She didn't need to know.

Ren assumed she was having a hard enough time as it was dealing with the fact that she'd had to be saved during the bust. Adding the news that he'd been injured would not comfort her. She'd blame herself.

If she found out, he'd never get a chance to get closer to her. She would push him away harder and further than she had already. He knew that was Mahina's way. She didn't allow anyone to get close to her. During all the time he'd known her, he'd never seen her with one man for long. And she'd never admitted to ever having a boyfriend.

And he'd been an idiot to bring up their one and only kiss. Out of anger at having just been dumped by his previous girlfriend Ginny, Ren had taken it out on the one woman he'd always wanted—Mahina.

What a kiss it had been.

Fueled by anger and frustration, it hadn't been any less potent. In fact, every time he thought about it, his gut clenched and his cock twitched. Having Mahina pressed up against the wall had been a little piece of nirvana. Especially when she'd given in to him and wrapped her strong hands in his hair and matched his passion.

He could still remember the way she tasted—dark and dangerous, like a walk through a mist-filled alley on a moonlit night.

Sighing, he shoved his towel into his gym bag, zipped it up and swung it over his shoulder. He needed to have a cold shower. There was no way he was going to be able to go home and sleep soundly. Not with Mahina's scent still mingling with his own. The woman always smelled like sex, the hot, raunchy variety that he loved.

Kicking open the door to the shower room, Ren decided that he didn't want to settle for a cold shower. He wanted Mahina, and he'd be damned if he was going to let her get away. Not this time.

THREE

Once she was out in the cool night air, Mahina felt a little better. There wasn't this oppressive heat pressing down on her. She'd left the cause of it behind in the gym with his boxing gloves still on.

She couldn't believe that Ren had told her he wanted her. It was a shock. Not once in the years they'd worked together had he ever given her any indication that he looked at her in any way other than as his partner and sometimes boss. Definitely not as a woman. Or a potential lover.

Or had he? Maybe she just hadn't noticed.

Their one kiss came to her mind again. Sure, it had been electric and powerful, but it had been alcohol induced. Ren had never mentioned it to her afterward, never given any indication that he even remembered it happening.

She took in a deep breath of flower-scented air and looked up at the night sky. It was a beautiful, calm evening, perfect for running. Instead of going home, she'd drive to her favorite park, shift and go for a long, vigorous run. Maybe then she'd be tired enough to sleep and not dream. She feared that her dreams would include things she didn't want to think about—death, sex and Ren Calder.

Thankfully, the drive to the park was short. By the time Mahina was out of her car, every muscle in her body was quivering with the need to shift. She hadn't even reached the entrance to the park before she'd already stripped off her shirt and bra. When she reached the dewy grass, her pants and underwear were behind her.

Stretching with a long-drawn-out quiver from the tips of her toes to the top of her head, she crouched on the ground and began to shift. It hurt like hell, as it always did, but the result was glorious.

Mahina raised her face to the air and sniffed. A myriad of scents came to her in an instant, and she was able to identify them quickly. Damp grass and leaves, dirt, lavender and freesia, the subtle musk of rodents and other wildlife. She took it all in and sighed.

Shaking out her body from end to end, she bounded into the tall grass and headed for the copse of trees. Maybe she'd do a little hunting during her run. There was nothing like the thrill of stalking prey. It never failed to ignite the most primal part of her—the lycan side that ruled much of what she was, even in human guise.

As she sprinted through the underbrush, leaping over fallen branches and craggy bushes, her thoughts strayed back to Ren. She hated that now when she most wanted to free her mind and body of all human emotion, his image flashed behind her eyes. She hoped speed and endurance would wipe her mind clear.

She ran faster, harder, pushing her wolf body to its limits. By the time she made it through the trees to the clearing, her heart thumped so fast she was panting with the exertion.

But still his image remained.

She huffed once, then twice, and a heady scent caught her attention. She inhaled deeply. A shiver raced down the length of her body and her hackles rose. She wasn't alone. Another wolf was prowling nearby.

And by the scent of him, he was no ordinary animal.

She turned just in time to see Ren leap out of the trees and into the clearing a few yards from where she stood. He was majestic in lycan form. His fur was a deep rich sable color and his body was long and lean, but she knew underneath all that lustrous fur would be ropey, powerful muscles. He was as striking a wolf as he was a man.

He approached her, though cautiously. Trembling, she waited for him to near. When he was within a few feet, Mahina started to growl. She wanted him to know she wasn't happy that he'd followed her. Despite her anger, pleasure at his arrival made her insides warm and her muscles tingle. It was harder as a wolf to deny him. Her desire was too primitive to keep at bay for long.

So instead of succumbing to desire as he appeared to expect by the way he sniffed at her neck, Mahina nipped him with the tips of her sharp teeth. He jumped back. She growled again, warning him away, but Ren was stubborn. He came closer to her again, but this time his head dipped a little in submission.

Although she appreciated the gesture, she didn't want to be seduced by his advances. She turned and bounded back into the trees. She ran away just as she had earlier in the gym.

And like last time, Ren followed her.

Her escape quickly turned into a game of chase. Mahina was quick and agile, especially able to maneuver around trees and through thick underbrush. But Ren kept up to her. At one point, she knew he could've overrun her, but he chose to stay behind. Near enough that she was fully aware of his presence but far enough to respect her space.

Mahina found the gesture odd, especially from a wolf. As a man she might've expected it, but in animal form it was so much harder to keep their instincts at bay. The need to feed, to mate, constantly swirled in a lycan's gut. She found the primary urges difficult to ignore. How could Ren be so in control of himself?

After another circle through the trees and out again into the clearing, Mahina gave in to the needs pouring through her body. She'd gone too long without giving in to them, without loosening up, on so many levels. She'd not felt secure enough to let go. Until now.

Finding a clear spot in the grass, she nestled down onto her belly and shifted back to human form.

It was just as painful going back to human form as it was becoming a wolf. By the time she was finished, sweat soaked her skin and slick tendrils of hair stuck to her forehead. Sighing, she wiped at them just as Ren nestled in beside her and shifted back.

Fascinated, she watched him change. She'd seen others in her pack shift back and forth, but never had she been this close. Shifting took a lot of energy and strength and the lycan was at his or her most vulnerable. Anything could happen during a shift, and shifting lycans could do nothing to protect themselves. Ren had given Mahina the gift of ultimate trust.

When he was finished, he lay in the fetal position on his side. His long, lean form was slick with perspiration. Shivers racked his body. His short, dark hair stuck up at wild angles. Teeth chattering, Ren regarded her, a look of longing in his striking blue eyes.

She crouched next to him, her arms lying protectively around her legs, partially for security and partially for warmth. Clouds had rolled in since they'd been playing tag in the trees. The smell of rain was present in the cool air.

"Do you want to lie on me to get me warm?" He smiled.

"Suck it up. It's not that cold out here."

He set his hand onto her foot. "Then why are you shivering?"

She shrugged, but made no move to remove his hand from her foot. She actually liked his touch. It gave her a sense of comfort. Something she hadn't realized she needed.

"Why did you follow me?"

"Because you needed me to."

She eyed him, but had no retort. He was right. In a way she did need him. Right here. Right now. Where no one was looking. In a place just for the two of them. A place she didn't need to be

Captain Mahina Garner, the tough, jaded, no-nonsense lycan with nerves of steel. She could be just Mahina, a woman with needs and hungers.

And she hungered for Ren.

FOUR

Ren noticed the change in Mahina. It was subtle, but he sensed it. Her guard had dropped, allowing him in. And he was damn well going to take the opportunity she afforded him. He'd been waiting months for her to see him as a man, someone she could find solace with, and not as a fellow police officer, someone she just worked with.

Their kiss in the bar still haunted him. The memory plagued him at night with erotic dreams that went unfulfilled. He kicked himself for being such a coward. He supposed he feared her rejection.

Sitting up, he moved his hand up her leg, tracing his fingers over the hard muscles of her calf. She quivered under his touch. Her response created an intense heat inside his body, made him want to caress her more. He wanted to see the pleasure on her face as he touched her.

He covered her hand that was wrapped protectively over her knees and met her gaze.

"Did you mean what you said back in the gym? About wanting me?" she whispered.

"Yes," he replied, his breath coming out in puffs of steam. He squeezed her hand to make his point.

"Why? I'm not the most appealing woman."

He smiled then. It was just like Mahina to downplay her looks. She was so busy being the tough-as-nails woman in charge that she didn't realize she was extremely attractive. That men actually stopped in their tracks to look at her. She was always so focused on whatever she was doing that she never noticed their reactions. He knew she hadn't known about his attraction to her.

She had the most expressive eyes he'd ever seen. He could read every emotion in their golden depths. He especially enjoyed them when anger sparked there. He'd imagine what all that energy and spirit would be like in bed. He knew she'd be just as fierce at sex as she was with everything else she did.

Right now her eyes were dark with desire. He grew hard while he gazed at her, taking in every slope and rise of her sublime lithe body. A woman couldn't move the way Mahina did and not be exquisitely built.

"I knew you'd be beautiful naked."

She laughed. "You don't need to charm me. I've already decided to have sex with you."

"Well, that was easy." Smiling, he rubbed his thumb over the back of her hand.

Her eyes narrowed, and he heard a change in her breathing pattern. "Easy? I'm afraid that's not in my vocabulary."

She moved like lightning, and pinned him to the ground, her muscular legs straddling his stomach, her hands pushing on his shoulders.

He liked her on top. She looked like a warrior queen besting an enemy. Her wavy, lustrous hair flowed around her like a dark cloud, the ends lifting in the breeze. The expression on her face was one of predatory fierceness as she gazed down at him, her lips parted in desire.

He loved her dominant position because it also afforded him an amazing view of her beautiful body and allowed ample room to touch and caress her. Skimming his fingers up along her rib cage, Ren reveled in every quiver of her muscles, every catch of her breath. When he filled his palms with her firm breasts, he was rewarded with her moan of pleasure.

"Damn, you feel good." He flicked his thumbs over her taut nipples.

As her eyelids fluttered closed, she let her head fall back and pushed her breasts farther into his hands. While he continued to pluck her nipples, she ground her pelvis onto his. He could feel the warm moisture of her against his skin. She was ready for him and he was eager to take her. His iron-hard cock throbbed, fervently urging him to find bliss in her wet center.

"I want you so badly," he growled, finding it difficult to control himself when all he really wanted to do was plunge into her and ride her hard until the sun came up.

She fell forward, her hair becoming a dark curtain around her face. "Too much talking," she said, a quiver in her voice that told him she, too, was struggling to maintain restraint.

He moved one hand down, slowly brushing his fingers against her hard abs to her navel. With one finger he traced the outline of her belly button, then moved even lower still to the dark tuft of hair between her legs. Without pause, Ren slid his fingers into her moist center. She was hot and wet, like liquid silk in his hand.

He knew she'd be fierce during sex, raw and passionate and unbridled. He bit down on his lip to stop from digging his fingers into her hips and lifting her to settle her onto him. It was difficult to give her control of the situation, but he sensed that this was what she needed to get a sense of control back into her life. To help her forget that she'd almost died today.

Sex was the great celebrator. And he really wanted to celebrate. Now. Until the sun glowed over them both with its hot rays.

Sliding his fingers over her slick core, he found her sensitive nub and began to circle it with one tip. Ren gasped when she dug her nails into his shoulders and hung on as he took her up. He loved the look on her face while he manipulated her sensitive nerves. A combination of delirium and delicious agony. She alternated between grimacing and panting as he pressed harder.

With his other hand still on her breast, he pulled her down to him, running his tongue over one tight nipple and then the other, until finally he settled himself at one and suckled her hard. She let out a breathy moan, raking her nails over his shoulders and down his chest.

He winced as the pain surged through him, but it quickly turned to pleasure. He loved when a woman got aggressive. He reveled in it. Especially knowing that he'd heal in a matter of hours. The red marks across his body would be well worth it in the end when he was sated, slaking his hard, pulse-pounding desire for her.

Still suckling on her nipples, he increased his tempo on her nub, circling it faster, harder, sliding a finger down into her hot center, then back up. She rocked her body in time with his fingers, grinding down onto his hand. That urged him to stroke vigorously to give her the release she sought.

Her thigh muscles tightened around his waist. Mouth open, panting, she threw her head back. He knew she was close to coming.

Biting down on her flesh, Ren pinched her nub between his fingers. It was enough to push Mahina over the edge. And she came, hard.

With a deep groan, she threw herself forward, burying her face in his neck, her hands streaking over him to find a solid hold. Her fingers found the scabbed-over bullet wound, her nails tearing into the newly formed scab.

Pain exploded through him and he couldn't stop the gasp that burst from between his lips.

Wide-eyed, Mahina sat up and gazed down at him, her face blanched with worry. "What's the matter? Did I hurt you?"

Ren didn't want her to know about his injury. He didn't want her to worry or to blame herself. "I'm fine."

"You are not fine, Calder." Her gaze searched his face then fell to his shoulder. He knew what she was looking at. He could feel the warm trickle of fresh blood on his skin. "Damn it! You're injured."

"I'm okay, really."

She put one hand on his chin and turned his head. The other hand pressed on his shoulder as she leaned down to look at the wound over his lateral muscle. "When did you get this?"

"Doesn't matter."

Her eyes narrowed, and he could see the comprehension dawning in them. "The bullet grazed you when you took me to the ground."

He didn't say anything, but kept her gaze. He couldn't lie to her, but he also still couldn't admit it.

Shaking her head, she rolled off him, then pushed to her feet. "You should've told me."

Sighing, he sat up. "Why? So you could blame yourself?"

"Well, it *is* my fault." She glared down at him. "If I hadn't charged at him. If I'd only seen the damn gun."

Ren pushed to a stand. He wanted to touch her, soothe her somehow, but he knew she'd resent it. "Mahina, it's part of the job. We were in a volatile situation where anyone could've gotten shot."

"Yeah—it was because of my mistake that *you* got shot saving my butt."

"And I'd do it again without pause. This is nothing." He touched his injury to make his point. "Only trace amounts of silver entered my system. It'll heal in a few weeks. It's a small price to pay for your safety."

"Nobody should have to pay for my carelessness. Especially not you."

"Why not me?" He took a step toward her.

Her eyes narrowed, and he could see she was fighting the urge to flee.

"You know it's okay to admit you have feelings for me. There's no one around to hear you." He spread his arms out toward the empty night sky.

"We're done." She turned on her heel. "I'm going back to the car."

He watched as she stepped into the copse of trees situated between them and the main road. She was so stubborn it nearly drove him crazy. Actually, in fact, it did drive him mad. He just wanted to toss her over his shoulder and take her somewhere so they could finish dealing with the simmering passion between them. Having sex would either sate both of them and they could move on with their lives or it would change everything. Maybe that was what Mahina was afraid of—the everything part.

He didn't care. It was going to be taken care of one way or another tonight. He refused to go another day, or minute, thinking about what could be between them. He'd barely had a taste while he brought her to climax, and he wanted, no, demanded more.

Jaw clenched, Ren followed her into the trees, determined to claim her as his once and for all.

FIVE

Mahina was still vibrating from anger and pent-up desire when she heard Ren walking behind her, following her. Although she wanted to stop and let him gather her into his arms, she refused to turn around. A relationship between them was impractical. There were too many factors at play against them. When they worked together, she was his superior. They were both dominant lycans, both inside and outside the pack. That dynamic never worked out. And she couldn't have Ren risk his life again for her. She had no doubt he would in an instant.

Carefully she stepped over sharp rocks and broken branches. Her human feet weren't as tough as her wolf ones. But she refused to shift and run back to the car. It would just entice Ren to chase her again. She'd walk even if it meant cut soles and scratched calves.

She'd gotten about halfway to the road when she felt the first drops of moisture peppering her skin. It was cool yet refreshing and she shivered from the top of her head to the bottoms of her feet. There was something sensual, primal even, about being naked in the rain. It was then that Ren's masculine scent wafted to her nostrils on a puff of fresh air. It was as if he was teasing and taunting her.

Straightening her shoulders, she decided she would not be enticed any longer. Still, the feel of his fingers on her and in her pulsed over her skin. A violent quiver shook her body when she thought about what he had done to her, and what she had wanted him to do. Ren possessed a powerful form and she knew from one look at the length of him, he would be a passionate and tireless lover.

She shook her head clear of the erotic images staking claim on her mind. Only a few more yards to go before she could get dressed, jump into her car and drive home, safely, with her life intact. She feared making love with Ren would open a well of emotions, feelings she didn't want to deal with, ever. It was easier to keep them tightly locked inside her head and heart. Releasing them would only complicate her life.

She'd gone this long without the complications a serious relationship would bring. Because she knew getting involved with Ren could be nothing but serious. He was that type of man—he made her body flare and her heart flutter; she knew it could never be simple with him. It could never just be sex between consenting adults. It would definitely end up being so much more than that. And she wasn't sure if she was ready for what that meant.

As Mahina edged closer to the road, the woods thinned and the rain came down harder and faster. She could see the road through the last remaining trees. No longer protected by the canopy of leaves, she felt the cool fat drops of liquid soak her hair.

While she walked out from beneath the trees and into the ditch along the side of the road, she had to wipe away the wet strands of hair sticking to her forehead and cheeks. A few feet from her car, she thought maybe she could actually get out of here. But she could still feel Ren's presence behind her. She was curious why he hadn't said or done anything thus far. Maybe he'd given up.

Curiosity got the better of her and she turned just as she reached her car. He was right there behind her, invading her space. She could feel the warmth of his body, and he hadn't even touched her. His gaze was fierce. Desire radiated up and down her inner thighs.

"I can't let you go, Mahina."

She was powerless to move. He'd only have to touch her and she'd be lost to him. Relief surged over her that he wouldn't let her go. She'd been afraid that he would. That the feelings she thought he had for her weren't really that strong. She thanked God she'd been wrong.

Before she could speak, he yanked her to him, pressing her body to his and capturing her mouth. The kiss was hot and fierce, unquenchable even by the rain that cascaded in rivulets over their touching bodies. She lost all reason as Ren dipped and swept his tongue over her lips and into her mouth, making love to her with his kiss.

A growl sounded deep in his throat as she streaked her hands over his chest, down his sides to cup the rock-hard cheeks of his buttocks. She pulled him closer, reveling in the way his erection dug into her belly. She wanted him inside her, deep and penetrating.

Pressing kisses to her chin and neck, Ren edged her onto the car. The backs of her knees hit the front fender. There was nowhere to go but onto her back.

He licked the rain from her neck just below her ear. "You're mine, Mahina. No one will ever claim you like I will."

Wrapping her hand in his wet hair, she turned his head to hers. "Yeah, yeah, yeah. Again you talk way too much." She crushed her mouth to his and possessed him completely.

Frantic for her, Ren pressed her down onto the hood of her car and traveled her body with his mouth. He latched on to one breast, teasing the nipple with his tongue and teeth. Moaning, she pulled on his hair, wanting him to take more of her. He couldn't fill her fast enough.

She should've been cold with the chilly rain battering her skin and the cool metal at her back, but somehow she didn't feel anything but the inner furnace of her own body pulsing with desire and Ren's heat blanketing her.

"Hurry," she said, unsure, never having begged before. Never wanting to with any man before. It was both humbling and exhilarating at the same time.

Ren heeded her words. Still suckling at her breasts, he let his hands travel down her legs. When he reached her calves, he gripped them and, standing, spread her legs wide, positioning himself between them.

He looked like a wild man hovering above her with the rain slicking his black hair onto his forehead and making his golden skin sparkle from the pearls of water rolling down his chest. Growling low in his throat again, he slid her down the hood of the car, pulling her sex to his. Bending her legs back, he positioned himself at her opening and with one sudden thrust, he buried himself inside her quivering flesh.

She cried out as he entered her. He filled her utterly and she had to catch her breath as he started to move inside. Gripping her legs tightly, he slid out slowly then thrust back in, gaining in rhythm. After a few more controlled thrusts, he was slamming into her wildly, beads of sweat mingling with the droplets of rain.

Feeling her grip slipping, Mahina reached up and covered his hands on her legs. She needed to touch him even if it was just on his fingers. Every plunge inside her drove her near the edge of delirium. An intense, brutal orgasm was building inside. She could already feel its explosive power deep within her belly, swirling, boiling, waiting to erupt and send her spiraling out of control.

No man had pushed her this far. No man had ever made her feel like crying while making love to her. Emotions she could no longer contain erupted inside her heart. It split open like a ripe tomato, passionate and messy, but it allowed Ren in.

As if sensing the shift, he relinquished his hold on her legs and covered her body with his. Once he was settled on top of her, she wrapped her arms around him, digging her nails into his back, and held him tight as the first flutters of climax rippled through her.

As surges of pleasure cascaded over her, Ren nuzzled at her neck. Still sliding in and out of her, he wrapped his arms around her head and bit down on the skin between her neck and shoulder, right in the same place he'd been shot earlier. It was a lycan thing to do, a way of marking one's mate so that all other male lycans would know.

Mahina was so lost in the moment, she didn't care. To her, at this moment, she was his. Completely. Utterly. She'd deal with the future later. Because right now, all she could feel was pleasure, all she desired was him. She'd never been in a more perfect place than she was right now with Ren buried deep inside her, his lips tasting her skin.

One, two, three more quick thrusts and Ren was moaning in her ear, lost in his release. Squeezing him tight, and closing her eyes, she followed him down, falling, plunging into the pool of pure bliss. In that one minute, all she could do was hold on as explosions of sensory stimuli bombarded her mercilessly.

As her body quieted, Mahina slowly let her arms slide away from Ren and splayed them out onto the car's hood. She stared up at the sky. The rain had stopped, and the moon peered out between gray rolls of clouds. The storm had ended.

She sighed happily. She felt like molten gold—as if her bones had melted, she was so relaxed. The man certainly knew how to love her. She smiled to herself.

He stirred on top of her, pressing his lips to her neck, up to her cheek and then to brush across her lips. "You look very satisfied."

"Completely."

Chuckling, he kissed her again, thoroughly, so she felt it all the way down to her toes, then rolled onto his back and stared up at the sky, their shoulders and fingers touching.

They stayed like that for a bit, silent, soaking up the beauty of the night. Mahina loved the calm after a good rainstorm. Everything had been cleansed. Including her. And she felt refreshed and invigorated. Or it could've been all because of Ren.

He cleared his throat. "I want more than just this night, Mahina."

"I know."

He turned his head to look at her. "Are you going to be able to handle that?"

Turning her head, she smiled. "Are you?"

"I'm willing even if it kills me."

Laughing, Mahina rolled off the hood onto her feet, feeling the urgent need to run. Except not *from* him. She wanted to run *with* him, side by side through the trees and grass.

"It just might." She nodded toward the woods. "Let's go."

"Running? Again?"

"Yeah. If you want to be my man, you have to learn to keep up."

He slid down the hood to stand beside her. "I'm ready when you are."

Crouching, Mahina shifted. It was still a painful process but it felt good, especially when the man she thought she could love in time was shifting at her side going through the same thing.

When she was done, she waited until Ren finished. The beautiful black wolf turned toward her and huffed through his nostrils, blowing on her neck in affection. She returned the gesture and together they ran into the trees to start a new chase.

* * * * *

BROKEN SOULS

Bonnie Vanak

For my beloved Frank, who taught me
to believe in second chances.

BONNIE VANAK

fell in love with romance novels during childhood. She lives in Florida with her husband and two dogs, and she loves to hear from readers. Visit her Web site at www.bonnievanak.com, or e-mail her at bonnievanak@aol.com.

Dear Reader,

When I created the Draicon, my race of werewolves, I wanted them to have destined mates. Yet I wondered what happened to Draicon who lost their destined mates. Did they get a second chance at love?

This is why I wrote "Broken Souls." Baylor and Katia are two lost, broken souls whose destined mates were killed during an attack by Morphs, former Draicon who have turned evil. They are on the verge of committing to each other, but Katia is torn between Baylor and loyalty to her missing father. If he is still alive, she must return to his pack.

In desperation, Katia performs a dangerous and forbidden candle spell using her own blood to call forth her father. But what form will her father assume? Has he turned evil, and is she walking straight into a trap?

Against all odds, Baylor is determined to protect Katia and win her love. He will risk not only his carefully guarded heart, but his very life when he sees the true nature of the being she has summoned.

Baylor and Katia are sorely tested in "Broken Souls." Yet in the end, they discover that they can find true happiness, even though they are not destined mates. Because nothing, not even the forces of evil, can separate those determined to make their own destiny and share their lives and their hearts.

I hope you enjoy Baylor and Katia's story of loyalty, love and second chances.

Happy reading,

Bonnie Vanak

ONE

I must not do this.

Katia Howard studied the candle stubs in her bedroom. Colored wax dripped off the table like miniature stalactites. Each taper represented a spell to aid a particular Draicon werewolf.

Damian, their pack leader, had forbidden the blood-to-blood spell. It was too dangerous and might call forth a relative who'd turned evil. If someone found out she was performing one, she'd be severely punished.

I have no choice.

Outside, a howling wind made the pine tree branches sway and dip. Autumn in New Mexico had turned the air cold. Shadows danced along the wall from the nearby lamp, casting eerie light over a picture of Elvis.

Baylor always teased about the King, even though he was the one who'd purchased the poster for her on eBay. Baylor. Her best friend. His warm, wet kisses intoxicated her, made all good sense flee. Katia felt open and yearning at the thought of his hard, muscled body finally claiming hers.

He'd put her in this predicament. She stared at the white candle, its phallic shape a reminder of why she was here. Baylor's ultimatum. Mate and bond with him for life, or he'd find another.

I have to do this.

It was her last chance to find her father and discover what happened to her family. Until she did, Katia had resolved to never settle down.

She was a Taneam, a Draicon enchantress whose candle spells coaxed out a person's best abilities. The Morphs, former Draicon who turned evil by killing a relative, feared Taneams. It was said Taneams could use a white light spell to find a spark of goodness hiding inside a Morph, a faint trace of his Draicon self, and make it burn. Such a feat might reverse the evil and the Morph would not have to be destroyed, or at the very least weaken the Morph so it could no longer kill Draicon.

The problem was the spell became a treacherous double-edged sword. The user became too confident she could change the Morph and closed her eyes to the truth of a Morph's power.

Katia knew all about a Morph's power.

Her aunts and uncles walking out the door, then their screams. Finding nothing, but scenting the lingering stench of Morph. Her mother chanting the white light spell, and the horror of realizing it hadn't worked when Katia's destined mate left the house and never returned.

After that, everything became a blurred memory. Her mother and sisters had vanished. She vividly remembered sitting with her father, watching the front door, the taste of fear in her mouth like metal shavings…a scream buried in her throat as a stream of cockroaches writhed beneath the rags they'd stuffed beneath the door to keep them out….

Immobilized by terror as the Morphs then shifted into their true selves. Fangs yawning open, talons clawing her arms and body, burning pain mingling with the sick scent of her own blood. She'd shape-shifted to defend herself. Then they turned on her father, a sea of bodies attacking him and he yelled an order for her to…

What?

All she knew was it involved a promise she'd made. Did she break that promise or keep it?

She could only recall bolting out the back door. Running until the day Baylor found her and took her home to his pack four years ago.

Though Damian and Baylor had searched for him, her father had never been found. She believed he still lived. Family loyalty came above all else. Even this pack, that had adopted and loved her.

Maybe even Baylor, the one Draicon who meant the most to her.

"I have to do this," she whispered. "Oh, Papa, where are you? Come to me."

To protect the pack from evil forces, she set out sage and other herbs in a ring around another tall white candle and then lit it. Katia uttered a powerful protection spell. Peace settled in the air.

She picked up the small paring knife. Gritting her teeth, Katia sliced her palm. Crimson welled up. She held her hand over the candle, letting her life's blood coat the wax.

When it was covered from tip to end, Katia let her cut heal. A match flared to life as she struck it, the orange flame quivering in her shaking fingers.

It was so still she could hear the sounds of her own breath rasping.

She lit the candle.

Dark, forbidden words filled the air as she waved her hands, coaxing the flame toward her. She finished chanting, watched the flame burn.

Suddenly it flared, and turned black. Then just as quickly, it shifted back to orange.

Katia shivered.

Baylor Devereux was working out in the basement gym.

Clad only in navy sweatpants, he danced barefoot about the floor. His knuckles wrapped in white tape, he took jabs at a heavy punching bag. It shuddered and swung from the force of his blows.

Katia hung back, staring. Sweat glistened on the muscles of his arms, and droplets dotted the dark covering of hair on his heavy chest. She studied his long, athletic limbs and broad shoulders, his curly brown hair tousled, his jaw square and chiseled. Her gaze dropped to his mouth, pursed in full concentration. Full and sensual, she knew the pleasure of his long, slow kisses.

He was equally concentrated in kissing as much as he was in fighting. She sensed he'd be equally passionate in bed if she finally surrendered.

Since the death of her destined mate, she'd had other lovers. But Baylor was different than the others because she cared so much about him. Being his lover meant forging a lasting emotional tie. How could she do so when her father might be alive and, thanks to the spell she'd performed twelve hours earlier, he might return and she'd have to leave Baylor behind? Her first duty was to her family.

Muscles and sinew stretched beneath his tanned skin as he flexed his broad shoulders. Katia breathed in his scent—musk, spice and male. Baylor stopped, sidestepping the punching bag. He wiped sweat off his brow with the back of one hand. Then he whipped his head around, his nostrils flaring.

He'd scented her.

"Katia?"

She stepped out from the shadows. "I like watching you work out," she confessed.

His boyish grin tugged at her heart. "I like knowing you like watching." He picked up a towel, dried off and then slung it around his shoulders as he paced over.

"Are you ready to give me your answer yet, Katia?"

"I still have until Damian's return," she reminded him. "I came to ask if you wanted to join me for dinner tonight on my balcony. Your favorite, rare lamb. The moon's out tonight."

His eyes lit up and then the gleam faded. "Can't. I have to patrol. Nicolas wants us to ensure the territory is Morph-free."

Pack leader Damian was in New Orleans, hunting down Jamie, his mate who'd run away after infecting him with a lethal disease. Nicolas, Baylor's former nemesis and the pack beta who had healed Damian, was temporarily in charge. Days after Damian had killed Kane, the self-appointed Morph leader, little threat existed. But obviously Nicolas wanted to ensure the safety of their people.

A horrible premonition seized her as she remembered others she'd cared about who left and never returned. Something terrible might happen....

"Don't go out tonight. Tell Nicolas you have to stay in. Protect us at home instead."

"What is it, Katie?"

"I don't think it's safe out there."

Baylor cupped her face and kissed her forehead. "I have to show Nicolas I'm as loyal as the next male, and that I'm willing to obey."

Katia tugged at his hand. "Come with me."

He glanced at the clock on the wall. "I have time only for a shower and then I have to get Ryan. We're patrolling the northern boundary, the most vulnerable."

"Then come to my room after you shower. It will take only a minute."

Baylor gave her a heavy-lidded look. "Only a minute? Sweetheart, not with me."

He chuckled at her blush and escorted her upstairs.

Half an hour later, he came to her room, his dark curls damp, his face freshly shaved. The neatly pressed gray trousers and black cable-knit sweater made him look polished and urbane. His thick, dark curls were clipped short. He could have been an ad for *GQ* magazine.

Breath caught in Katia's throat as he gave her a long, lingering kiss. Katia slid her arms about his neck, kissing him back, reluctant to break away.

Finally she did.

Baylor heaved a frustrated sigh. "I don't know how much more of this I can take," he muttered, resting his forehead against hers.

Neither do I.

He paced to the window and braced his palms on the sill, staring into the darkness.

"What is it, Baylor? You look worried."

His gaze darted away to the Elvis poster. "I am. I'm thinking you believe he's still alive and was abducted by aliens," he drawled.

Katia burst into laughter. "You're one to talk. You like Alan Jackson."

"It's five o'clock somewhere."

"And mambo! You're French and you like Cuban music!"

Baylor did a quick, elegant shuffle of his tasseled loafers. "Good for dancing, senorita."

A boyish grin touched his mouth as he switched off the player. "I like a lot of music, but all you play is Elvis."

Her cheery mood evaporated. Katia bit her lip. "I guess because my mother liked his music so much. It must remind me of home and those innocent times."

"Sweetheart," he murmured, pulling her into his arms.

She buried her head against his chest, inhaling his masculine scent. "Sometimes, I just miss them all so much," she whispered.

Wordlessly, he held her, stroking her hair. Katia closed her eyes, feeling the comfort he provided. He was her best friend, but he wanted more.

She wanted to give him more, but couldn't. Not yet.

Katia pulled out of his embrace. "Your turn. Tell me what's bothering you."

"My biggest concern is you."

"Baylor," she chided. "Truth between us always, remember?"

He ran a hand through his curls. "Truth always. I wish I could show Nicolas I am loyal to the pack." He was silent a moment. "I owe him my loyalty."

"You wouldn't have said that before," she pointed out.

Baylor glanced away, looking slightly shamefaced. "You know how I pushed all his buttons, saying things I didn't mean just to rile him about Maggie. I never fully trusted him. And then Nicolas proved his own loyalty to our pack and Damian. I misjudged him and I was wrong." He looked troubled. "It's the second big mistake I've made in this pack. The first was far worse."

"Why do you feel so compelled to prove you're loyal, Baylor? Nicolas isn't one to hold a grudge."

His expression became guarded. "Long ago, I exercised poor judgment and it cost the pack. I'll never do that again. The pack comes first, always. I thought Nicolas would be a danger to us because he was a powerful male and an outsider, and I was wrong. If it weren't for Nicolas healing him, Damian would have died. I apologized to Nicolas, but I don't want to give him any reason to doubt my loyalty."

Apologizing to Nicolas took a great deal of courage for someone as proud as Baylor. Katia looked at the thick, dark brows over his piercing gray eyes, his sensual mouth and aristocratic features. Of all their people, he most closely bore the stamp of kinship with Damian.

She picked up a tall white candle.

"I was going to light one of these for my Draicaron the night he went out to patrol our territory. We'd just become lovers. I wanted to protect him, but he refused."

Her lower lip wobbled. "I waited. He never came home to me. H-his was the only body we found. I don't want anything happening to you, Baylor. Can't you stay here with us?"

"Sweetheart, I can't," he said gently, touching her cheek. "I'll be fine."

He felt compelled to prove himself. Fine. She'd coax his loyalty to the surface, and he wouldn't feel the need to do so.

"Let me light a candle for you," she urged.

"If it makes you feel better."

Baylor watched as she lit the candle, and chanted in a low voice. The flame burned brightly, casting his face in eerie light. When she finished, he drew her into his arms. She nestled against his broad chest.

"Katia, I've waited so long for you."

"I know you've been patient. You're so good to me, Baylor, and I care so much for you, but I have to find my father first."

Katia drew back, feeling him tense.

"Your father is gone. You must accept this."

"Accept that I lost my entire family?"

"I lost my whole family as well," he said quietly. "But Damian's pack is our family now. Your father is dead."

"Damian is your cousin. I have no one," she whispered.

"You have all of us. We're your family now. You take care of the pack."

"But it's not the same. If I could find my father…"

"It's not just that, Katia. Why do you really want to find him?"

To beg his forgiveness for my cowardice.

"Please, let's drop it."

Baylor sniffed the air, his look turning to one of anticipation. "I have to go," he said absently. "Time to patrol."

"You should eat first to replenish your magick. And I thought you had to wait for Ryan."

"No time for dinner. Ryan will catch up with me."

He kissed her hard, and then raced off. She heard him run down the hallway.

Had the spell she cast been too powerful? It was obvious Baylor was eager to flush out any enemy. But what if he proved himself by acting reckless?

Katia fled to the French doors, flung them open and stepped onto her balcony. A silver wash of moonlight spilled over the open field below. She saw Baylor run out of the lodge, waving his hands and making his clothing vanish.

A strong wolf stood where the man had.

"Come back to me," she whispered, watching him run off with the night. "Please. Don't be like my family and never return. Don't you dare die on me."

TWO

The scent of fresh blood tinged the night air. The metallic aroma mingling with a faint stench of rotting decay made his nostrils flare. Wolf senses kicked into high alert. Somewhere close by, a Morph made a kill.

Baylor's ears pricked forward as his sharpened gaze scanned his surroundings. Marcel pack territory covered miles of land in northern New Mexico's Pinyon Valley, and their enemies had long scattered. Then why was he picking up the trail of a Morph so close to home?

In wolf form, he put his muzzle to the ground, sniffing out the strange smells. Wind ruffled his gray fur. Grayish moonlight slanted through the thick firs and oaks. The air was cool with a hint of snow, but an oppressive heaviness lingered. No sounds of life echoed around him. No owls hooting softly from overhead branches or even a small animal rustling in the undergrowth.

Danger lurked in these peaceful woods. It was his job to flush it out and dispatch it.

He was patrolling the northern boundaries, searching for Morphs and doubting he'd find any. Morphs could shape-shift into any animal form. They thirsted for Draicon blood, for killing and ingesting the victim's fear gave them powers to continually shift and clone themselves.

The Morph scent faded, leaving only the faint odor of blood and something slightly sweet. Baylor trotted forward, tensing his muscles. He itched for a good battle, to take out his frustrations on a lone Morph. Fighting took his mind off Katia.

Katia, with her winsome smile, corn-silk blond hair and soft lips kissing him senseless. Katia, who comforted him when he needed it, coaxing him to talk when he'd surely bottle up his feelings. Katia's trusting belief in him made Baylor feel like he could conquer the world. There was something deep and lasting between them. But she refused to become lovers and kept stalling when he'd asked her to bond with him for life.

Finally, he told her he needed an answer by Damian's return or he'd have to find another female.

He did not tell her what he'd already decided. If Katia refused him, he'd leave the pack. How could he remain, her scent always in his nostrils, her gentle smile engraved in his mind?

Baylor had cared for her from the moment he'd found her, naked and bloodied, in an abandoned cabin on the pack's territory. Shivering, she'd then shifted into wolf, but didn't snarl. Instead she'd crawled into a corner away from him. When he'd advanced, holding out a hand and crooning in a soft voice, she shifted back into human form.

And then he'd raced back to the lodge with her in his arms.

Katia hadn't trusted him until he'd promised to always tell her the truth. "I'll never hurt you, you can trust that. Truth between us always, okay?"

She'd nodded in mute acceptance. It took her a full week to speak. When she finally did, her story shocked even the normally unflappable Damian.

Baylor understood her longing to find her father. But he also knew the danger of how love for a relative could override common sense. Most of his immediate family had died after

Morphs attacked their stronghold when he was twenty. Only Baylor and his twin brother, Simon, had survived, killing the enemy and then fleeing. They became separated while trying to cross a flooded river.

When Damian found Baylor and invited him to join his newly formed pack, Baylor had hope Simon still lived. He finally found his twin. Then he made the biggest mistake of his life.

He'd argued with Damian to take in Simon, telling Damian his brother was not Morph, and made excuses for Simon's odd behavior. Baylor doubted his twin was evil.

Knowing Damian needed his strength and fighting skills, Baylor had gambled. He told Damian if Simon could not join the pack, he would not join as well. Simon joined Damian's pack, and shortly afterward, showed his true face and killed two pack females. Baylor had been forced to terminate his own twin's life. Damian told him his action proved Baylor's loyalty to the pack, but Baylor felt compelled to prove himself always.

He never forgave himself for insisting on finding his twin and blackmailing Damian into letting Simon join the pack, and for the two lives lost to Simon's darkness.

Katia didn't know his dark past. He couldn't risk telling her. Katia stressed loyalty to family above all else. She might reject him. And now Baylor would do anything to prevent Katia from making that same dreadful decision to kill a loved one.

He and Katia were a good match. Both of them had lost their destined mates. His Draicara had been killed in childhood. But she refused to mate until she found proof of her father's death.

More than four years of searching failed to produce Katia's father.

Don't do this to yourself, Katia. Stay blissfully ignorant. I only want to make you happy, my darling.

The powerful scent of blood wafted on the wind. Picking up the trail again, Baylor growled low in his throat. He headed east, eager to kill the enemy.

He entered a clearing and saw the blood source. A deer, its sightless eyes staring at the moon, its throat torn out. Baylor scented nothing but deer blood and something else, something familiar that had a rotting smell. A screech above sent his blood racing. Burning pain screamed along his nerve endings as the raptor bit his ear. He howled as sharp talons raked along his hind-quarters and a knifelike beak pecked at his head, trying to get to his eyes. Snarling, he turned, leaped up and snapped his powerful jaws at a wing, hearing the ensuing crunch of hollow bones. Screams echoed in the air and acid Morph blood splashed over his muzzle, burning his nose and fur.

One down, how many more to take out?

He shook his head, running, leaping over the deer carcass, trying to fight off the winged predators swooping down and attacking him. Baylor dove into a small copse of thick brush and tried to ease the pain, concentrated on directing healing energy to his injuries. As magick flowed through him, he went emotionless to analyze his attackers. Peering out from his cover, he watched and judged. Only one Morph, and it had cloned itself. Soon its energy would diminish.

Come and get me, he said silently, watching for the next attack. The thought of a Morph this close to their territory chilled him. The deer had been bait for a hungry, unaware Draicon in wolf form. He thought about this Morph getting into the lodge, buzzing through Katia's window as a fly and then shifting into a cougar and tearing out her throat like it had to the deer....

Anger roared through him, adrenaline pumped. When the Morph shifted again, he was ready. Baylor charged out of the bushes. And ground to a dead halt.

He faced a dozen porcupines. Quills bristling, they ambled toward him. Those sharp spines in his muzzle, his eyes, would make him go down and they would shift again for the kill.

Not so fast. Baylor shifted back into human form. Two steel daggers appeared in his palms as he waved his hands. He tossed the knives at the advancing creatures, who howled and writhed. Not dead, but incapacitated. Baylor summoned two more daggers, threw them. The tactic worked, for the Morph realized its disadvantage. The enemy abandoned its injured clones and shifted again into a wolf. The clones evaporated into gray ash.

One wolf, less energy for the Morph to maintain. Baylor flashed a dangerous smile and shifted back into his wolf form. The odds were his now.

Snarling, he charged, head low, jaws open, smacking into the Morph-wolf with a powerful thud of his muscled body. As the Morph sank its teeth into his backside, Baylor seized the advantage and, from the underside, went for its throat. Acid blood poured over him as his jaws sank down. The Morph howled in pain, flopped over and Baylor released it.

He drew away, shifted back into human form. The dagger in his hands was thrown with sure, steady aim. Straight into the heart, the only way to kill his enemy.

The Morph lay still. In a minute, it dissolved into gray ash.

Spent, he trembled, exhausted from the depletion of energy and magick. For a moment he sagged against a tree, knifelike pain screeching through his veins. He closed his eyes, and centered himself to resist collapsing onto the cold forest ground. Katia's sweet smile, her wide ice-blue eyes and her gentleness flashed into his mind. Shivering, he held the image, calling her name softly to avoid surrendering to unconsciousness. Then he waved his hands in the air, using his precious reserve of magick to destroy the carcass so no other animal would devour it and die.

Baylor willed himself to walk. If he shifted to wolf again, he'd use up what little energy he had left. Had to make it on foot. Couldn't even summon enough energy to clothe himself or he'd risk never making it home. A violent shiver racked him as cold wind slapped against his flesh.

As he left the clearing, the hair on his nape rose. Overhead he heard the distant flap of wings, as if an owl suddenly took off from a tree limb. A shudder went through him as a horrid suspicion surfaced.

Why was the Morph prowling near their territory when all others had been driven away? What drew him here? Who was he, a rogue loner?

Or worse?

THREE

Baylor wasn't home yet.

Katia gave a desultory stir to the buttercream frosting as she waited for the cake to rise and the last Draicon to come home. Most of the pack had already retired. The few patrols Nicolas sent out had returned. All but Baylor. The Draicon dearest to her must be in trouble.

In a corner, a small brown Shih Tzu slept on a fluffy pillow. Misha, Maggie's beloved dog, loved the kitchen as much as Katia did. Since she'd arrived, she'd transformed the kitchen, and now checked curtains hung at the windows and the oak cabinets, while gleaming granite countertops and jars of spices in red canisters gave it a homey air.

But it felt empty without Baylor. What if something had happened to Baylor?

"Are you trying to wake everyone? It smells terrific in here."

A small shriek fled from her mouth. Nicolas stood in the doorway, yawning. Surprise filled his dark eyes.

"Sorry, didn't mean to startle you. Why are you up, Katia?"

"I had insomnia. Baking makes me feel better."

He sniffed. "Double-layer chocolate fudge. Baylor's favorite."

Nicolas's grin faded as he studied her downturned mouth.

"Hey, don't worry. He can take care of himself. And I told him to take Ryan. Ryan is a skilled fighter."

Katia went to the oven, slid her hands into two blue mitts. She opened the door and put the cake on the range and slammed the door shut. After removing the gloves, she reached for a small ceramic jar holding toothpicks.

"He's loyal and will never let you down. Mate him, Katia. You've been looking after everyone else in the pack too long."

Nicolas crossed the room, studied the scented candles on the counter. Baylor, a successful Internet investment counselor, encouraged her to open her own store on a Web site. Katia's Creations sold her homemade candles, sachets and soaps, earning her a very comfortable living. Baylor's belief in her talents fed her confidence.

"Damian will want you to mate with Baylor," Nicolas pressed. "When he returns with Jamie, he'll want to breed as soon as possible and encourage the pack to do the same."

And that was why Baylor had issued his deadline, she realized. Damian must have said something to him before he left for New Orleans. And once their leader returned with his own mate, he'd urge the pack to pair off and begin leading normal lives once more.

Katia turned off the oven. "My first duty is to my blood. If there is a chance any of them are alive, especially my father…"

"We're your family now. Your father died fighting the Morphs."

"He could still be alive. How can I commit if he is? My loyalty lies with my family."

Nicolas gave her a level look. "Wouldn't your father want you settled with Baylor? We all know how you feel about him."

How could she give herself, body and soul, to Baylor when the chance existed that her father still lived? Her first loyalty was to her people. Damian's pack had adopted her. The blood ties weren't the same.

What do I want? Forgiveness? Absolution for running away?

"What's going on?"

Maggie's sleepy voice whipped Katia's attention to the doorway. Nicolas went to her, kissed her cheek.

"Katia's worried about Baylor. So she's baking."

More footsteps sounded on the stairs. Katia removed the cake, set it on a tray and dumped the glass baking pan into the sink. A cluster of males drifted into the wide, open kitchen.

"I woke up," admitted Owen, an older Draicon and the pack's dentist. "Something's wrong. I feel it. So did Margie, but I told her to go back to sleep."

The others nodded. Nicolas told them Baylor wasn't back yet. They were a tightly knit group who worried when one of their own hadn't made it home yet. Enough of them had been lost in the past to Morph attacks.

Ryan, a broad-shouldered male with dark hair, entered the kitchen wearing only jeans. At his side was Patty, a redhead clad in an oversize man's shirt. Ryan yawned and scratched his muscular chest. "We heard all the talk. What's up?"

Katia's heart raced with panic. If Ryan was here, then Baylor was alone.

Nicolas studied the love bite on Patty's neck and then glared at Ryan. "What the hell? How could you disobey a direct order? You left Baylor on his own. If anything happens to him, I'll kick your ass."

"What order? I wasn't told anything."

"I told Baylor to take you with him to patrol the northern territory." Nicolas's expression shifted. "He didn't tell you, did he?"

The bristling tension fled Ryan's shoulders. "Damn. You think I let him go it alone on that turf, where the Morphs once had a stronghold? No way. That's suicidal."

Tension filled the air, despite Nicolas's assurances of Baylor's fighting skills. The testosterone level, already heightened, soared as Ryan began arguing and other males joined in.

Katia lit one of her special herbal candles and murmured a

quick spell. A soothing scent filled the air. Ryan and the males calmed and talk switched to a vigorous discussion of sports. Maggie heaved a relieved sigh.

"Thank you, Katia." Maggie, the pack's empath, touched her arm. "You have such a special gift, and you're so important to us. What would we do without you?"

Emotion clogged her throat. They had been her substitute family. Leaving would be difficult, but she had to do what she must.

Katia iced the cake as Maggie helped with dishes. Soon everyone was eating. Minutes later, more footsteps on the stairs and most of the pack females joined them.

Where was he?

The front door slammed. She followed the others, who were streaming into the living room. Her bare feet skidded on the polished wood.

Baylor slumped against the staircase. Soft golden light from the living room revealed bloodied gashes and burns across his square, handsome face. He shivered, his leanly muscled, naked body covered with a colorful assortment of bruises, blood and deep gouges. Blood dripped from his right ear. Katia cried out.

She raced to his side, hooked an arm about him as his legs started to give way. Katia's Draicon strength kicked in. She lifted Baylor as if his six-foot, one-hundred-seventy-pound, muscled frame weighed no more than a bag of sugar.

A faint protest followed. "I'm all right. It's nothing."

Impatient, she pushed through the crowd exclaiming over him, and gently laid him on the sofa. "It's not nothing, stop being such a…a…male," she snapped.

Maggie came over. "Easy, sweetie, I'll heal him."

Anxious, Katia watched the pack's empath gently lay her hands on Baylor, taking on his injuries. After a minute he sagged back in relief. Bruises and lacerations left his body and appeared on Maggie's. Nicolas helped his mate to a chair. Pale-faced, she leaned back.

"Give me a minute. He was badly hurt. More than he let on." Maggie closed her eyes.

As the injuries began fading from Maggie, Katia fetched a thick handwoven wool blanket and laid it over Baylor, tucking it around him. She lingered, her trembling hand brushing back his silky, dark curls.

"Why did you have to go it alone? What if you died, Baylor? What would I do then?" she whispered, her throat squeezing tight with emotion.

Aurelia, another member of the pack, returned from the kitchen with raw steak to replenish Baylor's lost energy. As he ate, Katia curled up next to him, needing the contact. When Baylor finished and pushed the plate away with a sigh of relief, Nicolas sat on the coffee table before him.

"What happened?" Nicolas asked.

"Morph, northern boundary. Killed a deer as bait. It flushed me out, attacked. I got it."

Nicolas frowned and folded his arms across his chest. "What the hell was it doing on our land? We got the last of Kane's people."

Baylor said nothing, but his gaze flicked to Katia.

Shouldering his way through the crowd, Ryan approached the sofa. He stared down at Baylor, his jaw clenched. "Dammit, why didn't you tell me? I've seen roadkill look more alive than you did."

"Screw you," Baylor shot back cheerfully.

"No, thanks, you're not my type." Ryan ran a hand over his jaw. "You did good, Baylor. If anyone could survive that turf, it was you."

A rueful smile touched Baylor's mouth.

"Enough of the congratulations on not getting killed. I ordered you to take Ryan. Why did you disobey, Baylor?" Nicolas demanded.

Silence draped the air. Finally, he spoke. "I wanted to show you how devoted I am to protecting the pack. If something happened…you'd lose only one of us."

"You did this to prove yourself? What kind of fool idea is this?"

"I don't know..." Baylor frowned. "I had this overwhelming compulsion to do it. Like I was being controlled by an outside force, as if..."

Katia's stomach pitched as she thought of the candle stub upstairs.

"Someone put a spell on me," he finished.

The entire pack's gaze riveted to Katia. Baylor tucked the blanket about himself like a toga, and stood. His penetrating gray gaze locked with hers.

"We need to talk, Katia."

His deep voice was firm, brooked no refusal. Her jaw dropped as she stared at the square, powerful hand thrust before her.

"I think you should rest," she began.

His strong fingers curled around her small palm, enfolding it like a flower. A violent flush filled her cheeks as he steered her up the stairs.

Baylor overrode her protests as he opened her bedroom door. When she was inside, he closed it. "It wasn't a protection spell, but a loyalty spell."

"I only wanted to help," she countered.

His look softened. He beckoned to her. "Come here."

Baylor held out his arms. She went into them with a sigh, burying her head against his chest. Katia looked up, unable to guard her emotions. "When I saw you...bloodied and standing at the staircase..." Her voice broke.

"Hey, hey," he said softly, tipping up her chin. "Nothing can keep me down. Especially not a Morph."

She nodded, a little relieved. "When you didn't come home, it brought back all these memories of when my family didn't, either. I don't know...if I could take it again."

"I'm back now and as long as I have you in my life, I'll make damn certain to return to you. Kiss me, Katia," he told her in a deep, sensual voice that rippled across her skin like dark silk.

Katia crumbled under the intense look in his eyes. His mouth was warm and firm. Her head tilted back as he deepened the kiss and fisted a hand in her long hair. The sensual deliberateness of his tongue's slow strokes inside her mouth made the space between her legs throb. His other hand skimmed down her body, then pressed her close against his erection.

She broke free, and went to the closed French doors leading to her balcony. Pale moonlight shone through the doors, spilling onto the hardwood floor. Katia stared at the silvery light splashing over the fields and the woods beyond.

"Katia, why do you keep putting me off? I know you want me," he blurted.

Silence greeted him. Katia turned and saw the stark anguish in his deep gray eyes.

"You're like quicksand, Baylor. Every time I draw near you, I sink deeper and it's more of a struggle to release myself. And yet I can't help but be close to you. You make me feel alive and happy, but it's frightening. If we make love, I'm afraid I'll sink down for good. It means too much to me."

She heard his intake of breath across the room. "I'd never hurt you. No matter how far you sank or deep you went. I'm with you all the way."

"I feel so adrift, so broken." Her voice dropped as she rubbed a knuckle against the glass.

"I'll be your anchor, sweetheart. Let me."

Katia wanted a life with Baylor. But life stood still until she found her father.

Still Baylor deserved the whole truth.

"Baylor, there's more to why I have to find my father."

She gulped down a quivering breath as he joined her. "I need his forgiveness. I made a promise to him years ago and I can't remember what it was. That's the reason I need to find him if he's alive. He was fighting the Morphs and I ran away, like a coward."

"Oh, Katia," he said softly. "You did what you had to."

"Papa yelled that promise at me, and then I ran. If only I could remember what it was! Everything is a blur and that's why I can't remember what happened to our pack. They just...disappeared."

"Trauma does that sometimes. And you suffered plenty," he said gently.

"But it's no excuse for my actions. I should have stayed. I could have done something."

"And be killed? Do you truly think your father would want that?"

"If I could just talk to him, one last time, hear from his lips what he asked..." Her voice trailed off. How could she perform magick spells that helped others when she couldn't even help herself?

"Why couldn't you tell me before?"

"I was too ashamed. I was afraid of what you'd think of me."

"That you're strong and courageous? Filled with the desire to live and love again?" He brushed back her hair. "Listen to me, Katia. If you find him, and he's Draicon, you wouldn't have to leave for any pack he's formed. You could stay with us. We need you."

"He's my father. I'd have to go with him." Torn, she stared at him. "He's my family, but I wouldn't want to leave you."

Baylor sighed. "We could make it work out. Maybe I'd go with you as your mate if your father will have me in his pack. It's something to think about so you won't have to choose between us."

"But how can you leave here?"

"It would be damn hard, but losing you would be worse." Baylor cupped her face and kissed each of her cheeks. "It would kill me inside."

Wild joy beat inside her. She hugged him, feeling his solid body, his warmth. Arousal spiked, shoving aside reason, leaving behind only the fierce desire to join with him. Mirrored in his eyes was the same driving passion, twined with deep tenderness and adoration. Katia's heart turned over.

"Be mine, Katia. Say yes," he said softly.

"Yes," she whispered. Tonight's events had taught her how much Baylor meant to her, and she couldn't resist him any longer.

The blanket fell to the floor. She stared at his hard body, and the steely erection jutting out from his groin. A shiver of anticipation raced through her as she undressed.

Baylor led her to the bed. Katia drew in a breath sharp with desire as his heated gaze raked over her in admiration. He drew close and pressed his face against her neck, nuzzling her.

"You're so hot and ready for me. I can scent you. It's driving me mad," he whispered, inhaling her fragrance.

His hands, capable of ripping the enemy in half, were gentle and reverent on her body. Baylor cupped her breasts, flicking his thumbs over her nipples, making them harden beneath his slow strokes. Moisture pooled between her legs as she quivered with the fierceness of wanting him. His hand cupped the back of her head, tunneling through the long fall of her hair. His mouth, oh, it felt warm and smooth moving over hers, the slight pressure of his tongue licking her lips. She moaned as he pulled her closer, teasing her with his delicious taste. Lazily his tongue flicked over hers, then his teeth nipped playfully.

His skin was hot to the touch as she traced the lean lines of his body. A groan rumbled from his deep chest as she undulated her hips against his. The sound awoke her inner wolf, urging her to stoke the banked flames inside him.

Abandoning all caution, she sucked at his tongue, her hands gliding down to squeeze his ass. Enough playtime. Baylor broke the kiss.

Emotion smoldered in his eyes, turning them to dark stone gray. "I don't know if I can control myself with you."

She sensed the wild wolf inside him, the tearing, clawing need for him to mate with her at last. Katia reached down and lightly scraped her nails over the muscles of his bare back.

"Then don't."

The smoldering look in Baylor's eyes warned she'd unleashed the beast. It made her breath hitch with anticipation as he lifted her into his arms and placed her on the bed's edge.

She clung to his wide shoulders as he nibbled the hollow of her throat, chased each hot, possessive kiss with a delicate flick of his tongue. Katia writhed, hooking her hands about his neck as if she were drowning. He nuzzled her neck, then bit down, sucking hard. Marking her as his own in the primitive way of their race.

Warmth spread through her body as his lips trailed over the curve of one breast and then closed tightly over the taut nipple. His tongue rasped over the turgid peak, flicking and swirling. Then his teeth lightly clasped down as he suckled.

She wasn't drowning, she was dying. Baylor raised his head, passion darkening his eyes to stone-gray as he drew her legs wide apart. Then he dropped to his knees.

"My beautiful Katia, you're so wet for me."

Breath escaped her in a hissing gasp as he put his mouth on her. His tongue stroked, demanding and coaxing, as she clutched his hair and arched upward in shameless need. A scream ripped out of her throat as she convulsed in a shattering climax.

Katia watched, her limbs languid and heavy as Baylor then mounted her. His lean fingers laced through hers as she snaked her arms around the strong muscles of his neck, urging him closer. She inhaled his musky, masculine scent and opened her legs wider, moving her hips upward in a natural response.

The need to mate overrode all else, even her feelings of fear and vulnerability to this strong male taking not only her body, but also her heart.

He looked down at her with fierce concentration and took her in a single, hard thrust intended to dominate and claim.

Sinew and muscles bunched and coiled in his arms. Sweat dampened his dark curls. Inside her, she felt his penis twitch and thicken even more.

"You're mine now, Katia," he said with a possessive growl. "Only mine."

Katia gasped as he held her thighs open and began to drive in to her. His cock was hard and thick, filling her completely. Intimately joined, she felt whole and alive in this bonding of flesh as her emotions raced to the surface.

Her hands gripped the taut muscles of his ass and she raised her hips, eager to meet his hard thrusts. Baylor's hard flesh slapped against hers, his ragged panting growing with each pounding drive of his hips. Katia gasped, her back arching as her body tightened around him. She dug her fingers into his shoulders. So close, almost there…

Baylor looked down at her. A bead of sweat rolled off his temple, splashed onto her cheek like a tear. "Look at me, Katia," he demanded.

The orgasm forced a scream from her throat as her core squeezed him tight. Corded muscles in his neck stood out in stark relief as he threw his head back and groaned, calling her name. He collapsed atop her, his head resting on the pillow beside hers, his labored breathing echoing in her ear as she tenderly stroked his back.

Baylor slowly separated them, and rolled off. He lay on his back, panting, his gaze tender upon her. Katia ran a hand through his sweat-dampened curls, and skimmed down his body, testing the quivering muscles.

After a minute, she raised her head and studied his groin. A proud smile touched his mouth.

"Already?" she teased.

He held out his arms as she climbed atop him. Slowly she sank down, biting her lip at the fullness. The delicious thickness was almost too much to bear. Baylor grasped her hips, raising her as she began to ride him, her head tossed back.

They came together, she crying out his name, Baylor shouting hers.

After, they lay, trembling and spent, in each other's arms. Finally the cadence of her heart slowed to a normal rhythm and her breathing no longer rasped hard. Katia kissed his shoulder as he buried his face into her hair. Cool air dried the sweat on their bodies.

"If I had a lifetime with you, it might be enough," he murmured, running a hand gently down the small of her back, arousing her all over again.

She toyed with the damp hair on his chest. "Would you really leave for me and live in my father's pack?"

He looked troubled. "It's a decision I hope I'd not have to make. I'd rather have you stay here. And I'd have to make damn certain first that he's still one of us."

Cold suspicion filled her as she pulled away from him. "What do you mean, one of us?"

Tenderness faded from his expression, replaced by the protective male, his gaze hard in the moonlight. "A Draicon. Because if he isn't, all bets are off."

Her heart dropped at his next words.

"I'll have to destroy him."

FOUR

Morning broke in a wash of bright sunshine. Baylor blinked, awakened to the incredible joy of Katia lying in his arms. She gave a soft sigh and nestled closer, her silken flesh arousing him. He dropped a kiss on her forehead, loving the healthy flush to her cheeks, the slight smile she'd displayed as she slept.

She looked happy and content. Why couldn't she understand he desired nothing less than to keep her that way? He never wanted her to experience the horrors he'd endured.

"Wake up, Katie darling," he whispered.

Sleepy blue eyes opened, and her smile widened. "Good morning."

She shifted, one long, slender leg entangled with his. Her full breasts pressed against his body. Baylor felt his cock harden. He wanted her so much. To retire with her each night, waken her with tender kisses and spend their days together.

He nuzzled her neck with a lingering caress, but she pulled away.

"I'm sure you're hungry after last night. I'll make you sausage and eggs after I shower." She stretched, the movement lifting her breasts as the sheet spilled to her waist. "I made you a cake last night, but the pack decimated it."

He didn't want breakfast. He wanted her. He'd eat cardboard if only Katia would mate him for life. And what if she discovered Baylor killed his own twin? His chest constricted at the thought of the horror in Katia's eyes.

She slid out of bed, and went into the bathroom. He donned a robe and went to his own room. After he showered, he returned. Katia stood at her mirror, running a comb through her long hair.

Baylor felt his blood stir as he gazed at her tall, voluptuous body. Blond hair cascaded down her back. Her round face, satin skin and gentle smile were the same as if she were eighteen. Like all Draicon, Katia aged very slowly.

How he loved burying his head into her hair, inhaling her scent, curling his body against hers as they shared each other's heat. Watching in pride as her eyes darkened, and wringing a cry from her throat as she surrendered to passion.

An urgent desperation drove him. Baylor picked up her hand.

"Katia, mate me, now. Nicolas can perform the ceremony. I want you by my side for the rest of our lives. I love you, and no one will ever love you more than me."

He poured all his feelings into the words. Anxiety churned in his stomach as he waited for her answer.

Katia removed her hand from his, not before he caught the slight trembling in her fingers. She set the comb down on the dresser.

"I need more time. Why are you so impatient?"

He ran a hand through his damp curls. "I need a mate, Katia. I need you. Why are you putting me off?"

"Baylor, I want those things. You're only sixty and we have plenty of time," she said softly. "If my father survived, then it's my duty to find him. My family comes first."

The last thread of his temper snapped. "How long, Katia? How long will you wait? When life passes you by and you sit there, letting everything before you slip through your fingers that you could have now?"

"As long as it takes. It won't be long now. I'll know for certain soon."

"And how can you, after four years? Do you think he'll magically appear…?"

The guarded look in her eyes told him everything. Baylor went to her candle table, plucked several candles free, examining each one. His candle, the ones she'd lit for Maggie and Nicolas, for Damian…

It would be a white candle smeared with her blood. No white candles.

Relief flooded him. Of course she wouldn't be so foolish, or desperate.

A lump beneath a scarf on her dresser caught his eye. Baylor's heart raced as he went and picked up the silk covering.

The stub of a white candle was covered in a rust stain. He inhaled and closed his eyes, smelling her. A sharp, horrid memory surfaced.

Like all Draicon, Katia had a special scent marker unique to her original pack. Each pack member shared it, passed through their DNA.

He recognized this scent, the faint scent he'd picked up in the woods last night after tracking down… The Morph.

Baylor turned, watching her chin jut out in mutiny.

"I had to do it. How can you understand?"

Anguish knotted his guts at the despair in her eyes. "I understand wanting something so bad you'd do anything, almost anything. More than you know. But this endangers you. It endangers us."

"I did a protection spell. The pack's not endangered. He's alive, I know it, and he's going to come to me." She glanced at the wall clock. "By tonight, the second night of the full moon."

"As what, Katia?" Baylor threw the candle stub across the room. "In what form? Will you endanger the pack by bringing him here?"

"He's my father and blood." Katia tensed and turned her back. "You'd better leave, Baylor. Before I say something I'll regret."

He left, giving her one last look. "If he comes here, Katia, I'm dealing with him first." *Before you do, and your emotions cloud your judgment, like they did when I saw Simon.*

As the full moon made its appearance over the horizon, the downstairs bell rang. Baylor froze. The lodge seldom got visitors.

He raced downstairs and barreled into the living room, barring Aurelia from answering the door. His gaze swung to Nicolas, who looked wary.

"Gather the males and come with me." Baylor was ready to defend his pack.

Nicolas wasted no time. In a minute, the pack males stood at the foyer.

"What's outside may not be friendly to us, and especially not to Katia," Baylor told Nicolas.

"Then it's my duty as leader to intercept the danger and protect her."

"Not any longer. It's my duty right now, since last night," Baylor countered, giving all the males a meaningful look.

Nicolas's eyes widened, then he nodded. "Well, then." He stared at the heavy oak door protecting them from the outside world.

"Answer it, Baylor."

Baylor opened the door.

FIVE

A tall male, his graying blond hair tossed by the wind, stood outside. Dressed in worn jeans, a blue chambray work shirt and a sheepskin jacket, he had ice-blue eyes.

Blue eyes like Katia's.

"I'm James Howard. I've come for my daughter, Katia."

Every muscle tensed in Baylor's body. A low growl rumbled deep in his chest. He scented the familiar smell from the woods.

Nicolas motioned to the other males, who walked outside with him. Ryan, the last male, closed the door and folded his arms across his chest. The low growl rumbling from Ryan's throat echoed Baylor's hostility.

"Strange how you suddenly show up now," Baylor said slowly, circling Katia's father.

James studied him with a wary look. Baylor sniffed, his rage growing by the minute.

"We have a request of any visitor here before granting entry. Blink," Baylor told him.

Katia's father merely looked away. "I have to see her now." The older male looked upward and yelled, "Katia! It's Papa!"

"Blink before I rip your throat out," Baylor snarled.

The door flung open and Katia ran outside. She held out her arms. "Oh, Papa!"

Her happy cry turned to outraged shock as Baylor leaped forward and slammed the male against the outside wall.

"You bastard," he snarled, one hand pinning the taller male's throat. "You have the *cojones* to dare to invade our territory? I'll show you a real welcome."

Nicolas quickly pulled Katia away.

"Baylor, are you insane? This is my father!"

"Baylor, what's going on?" Nicolas sounded calm.

"It's him, the Morph from the woods who attacked me. He's learned to mask most of his true scent somehow." Baylor turned back to James, who did not struggle, or even look at him. The male's sole focus was on Katia.

"Are you insane? This is my father!" Katia struggled in Nicolas's grip.

Baylor held the male's chin in a steely grip. "Blink. Show me your true self."

James did not blink. Finally he did, so quickly Baylor almost missed it.

His eyes were without pupils. Black, soulless. Morph.

"Proof enough," Baylor muttered. He lifted Katia's father by his neck and threw him away from the lodge, away from her.

The male landed with a grunt. Katia screamed, the sound piercing Baylor like a thousand needles, but he kept his concentration. Baylor gave a flying leap, landing on the male, who struggled beneath him in his human form.

With one hand on his throat, Baylor growled. "Now I'll finish you off."

"No, oh, please, stop!" Katia cried out.

Startled, he turned, loosening his grip enough for the Morph to twist out from under him. The creature snarled and ran off.

Katia's tormented sobs gave him a measure of reason. Not in front of her. Time enough later to kill. He howled his frustration.

But his cries were not half as anguished as that of the one he loved.

Katia remained in her room. To ensure she wouldn't stray from the lodge, Nicolas ordered the other females to accompany her at all times. Nicolas believed Baylor's assertions that Katia's father was a Morph.

He was not pleased when Baylor informed him about the illegal candle spell. However, he agreed to delay Katia's punishment until Baylor talked with her.

With a heavy heart, Baylor mounted the stairs to her room. The light of the full moon spilled through the opened French doors. Cold air washed over him. He went to close the doors.

"Don't," she said dully. "Leave them open to the night. I like the full moon."

He joined her on the bed. She did not move away.

"Sweetheart, I'm so worried about you." Baylor touched her silky hair, wanting to comfort her, pull her into his arms. But she sat as still as a statue.

"You wanted to hurt him. My father," she said softly. "How can you think he's evil?"

Baylor gathered her hands in his. "Katia, what I have to tell you isn't easy to hear, but the truth between us. Always."

Dammit, this was so hard. He hated hurting her, but he had to tell her.

"He isn't Draicon, sweetheart. He's the same one I tangled with that nearly killed me. He's Morph, Katia."

She tried wrenching her hands from his, but he held her fast. "He's turned evil."

"He can't be a Morph. He vowed he would die before turning. He promised us. You're wrong, Baylor."

"I wish I was," he said grimly. "I detected a trace of his original scent and the markers are like yours."

Doubt and wild hope raced across her face. "Then he isn't fully Morph. He's still Draicon deep inside, Baylor."

"There is no such thing. You can't change him." *How well I know this. I thought I could change my twin.*

"I'm a Taneam. I can coax out his goodness."

Baylor's heart sank at the stubborn tilt of her chin. She refused to see reason.

"He's still my father. There's still some goodness inside him. I can call it out. I know I can."

"No, you can't, Katia. And if I see him again on our land, his ass is mine."

"You would kill my father?" she whispered.

"He's no longer the father you knew, Katia. He's dead to you, to the whole Draicon race. He's pure evil."

"I can try the white light spell." A frown twisted her lovely mouth. "I remember most of it. I think my mother chanted the spell, but it didn't work. Maybe because she didn't have enough moonlight to empower the words."

Baylor hedged. He'd heard of the spell's tremendous strength. It might not work, but it could lessen the Morph's power. But only if it posed no threat.

"Can you tell me in all honesty it will not endanger you or the pack?"

Katia met his gaze evenly. "Not to the pack, but to me, if I don't implement a safeguard first." She removed her hands.

At her table, she took a long white taper and lit it, coaxing the flame toward her as she chanted, her eyes closed.

"That was it?"

"No. That spell was to protect me. This is the white light spell."

Katia took another white taper, set it in a silver pool of moonlight and lit it. "Light needs light, and the full moon provides the strongest." She lifted her arms and began to chant.

Respectful awe washed over him. Damn, she was so lovely, the fall of blond hair glinting in the moonlight, long gold lashes sweeping over her cheeks as her lilting voice filled the air.

The delicate orange flame turned white, and widened. White light began filling the room. Transfixed, he watched, feeling his spirit and his heart opening wide. Love, tenderness and all his emotions for her poured to the surface. He felt as if nothing evil could penetrate the room, only goodness and Katia's white light, her pure, loving spirit…

A black flame suddenly surged from the taper. It grew, blotting out the white light. Baylor yelled and grabbed Katia away as it crested upward.

Then the flame settled down and became an ordinary orange. It sputtered once and died. Baylor sighed and ran a hand around her neck, gently squeezing her in comfort.

"It won't work, sweetheart. It turned black."

"But there was white light inside the black. I saw it. Please, try to understand. My father needs my magick, and I owe my loyalty to my family, just as you would if your family had lived before you joined with Damian. Wouldn't you have done anything to save them?"

Baylor dropped his hand, his guts churning. Now was the time to confess. He clenched his hands. Dammit, he didn't want to, but had to, to save her from making the same terrible choice and facing the same pain he had, he would do it. Her welfare came first.

"I did," he said quietly. "My twin brother, Simon. After Damian and I found each other, I realized Simon could be alive as well. I found him and insisted Damian let him join the pack, even though deep inside, I knew something was wrong with Simon."

He told her the details, his chest squeezing so tightly it felt hard to breathe. When he dared to raise his gaze, he tensed at the stricken look in her eyes.

"You killed him. Your own twin?"

"I had to save the pack. Family loyalty blinded me to the truth, Katia. Please, don't let it blind you."

"It's not the same. It can't be. My father made a promise never to turn to evil. I believed him."

"I never thought my brother would, but he did. It can happen, sweetheart."

A low, eerie howl drifted through the window. The hairs on the back of his nape saluted the air. He knew that howl. What was out there was no Draicon.

Katia's expression shifted to eager anticipation.

"My spell worked! I recognize his call. It's my papa!"

"Katia, stop it. Wait, and I'll check things out first."

"Like you did when you attacked him? You think he's the enemy, just like you did with Nicolas. You have a hard time trusting outsiders, so why should I trust you?"

"You're not going anywhere," he ordered, wounded by the acute truth of her words.

Anger flashed in her eyes. "Stop giving me orders."

She waved her hands, dispensing of her clothing. Katia shifted into wolf, bound through the door and sprang easily over the second-floor balcony, landing on the ground below.

"Dammit!" Baylor ran to the lodge's intercom used only in emergencies, and pressed the button. "Katia's in the woods after the Morph. I need help, *now*."

Then he shifted and raced after her. He caught a whiff of a faint scent. Sweet, faint, like cologne, like flowers. But no flowers bloomed this time of year.

Morphs did.

He knew what drove her, the desperate, nearly insane longing to find out if someone you loved was still alive. Hot breath heaving from his nostrils fogged the cool night air as he ran, closing the distance between them. Baylor bolted forward, cutting her off. He growled low in his throat, nudged her backward, toward the lodge.

Katia sidestepped him, trotting deeper into the woods.

Baylor raced after her, and leaped. He pinned her to the ground with his muscled weight. Forcing her into a submissive position, he gently clamped down on the back of her neck. Not enough to hurt, but enough pressure to get his point across.

Tail lowered, Katia whined softly. He climbed off, nudged her again toward the lodge. When she resisted, trying to dodge him, he nipped her flank.

Each time she tried to pass, he did the same. Suddenly a group of muscled, aggressive wolves raced into the clearing.

The pack males.

Nicolas, the largest, regarded the scene, clearly assessing the situation. He went to the nearest oak and sniffed, and issued a growl low in his throat.

Then he raced off into the woods, the other males following.

Baylor went to the oak. The strong scent of Morph flooded his nostrils. Male possessiveness twined with the need to protect his own. Snarling, he lifted his leg and erased the scent by covering it.

Try getting to her, you bastard, and I'll rip your throat out. She's mine.

He herded Katia back to the lodge. At the back door, they both shifted back and entered, grabbing terry-cloth robes from a bin near the entrance. Katia climbed the steps as he followed. Inside her room, she shot him an icy glare.

"What the hell were you thinking?" Baylor fisted his hands. "Dammit, Katia, that was a fool thing to do."

"You condemn me for doing what you once did when you went after your own twin?"

He closed his eyes. "No. I just want to prevent you from making the same mistake I did. Your father is not what you think."

"And if I could reverse the evil inside him, would you trust him enough to go with us?"

A heavy weight compressed his chest. "You know I could not. I'd have to stay here."

Katia fell silent as Baylor paced her room. Finally, Nicolas entered, his jaw tensed.

"We captured him and locked him up in the old shed in silver chains. The one where we found you." He looked directly at Katia. "He's still in wolf form and weakened."

The wild hope flaring on her face deeply troubled Baylor. "If he's weakened, it's from the white light spell. It wasn't strong enough, but the full spell is."

"I'm giving you one day before I let Baylor at him to finish him off, only because he's your father."

"He can change. I can find the good inside him," Katia cried out.

"And I'm the Good Fairy," Nicolas growled. "One day, Katia."

The door slammed behind him. Katia went to the French doors. Baylor raced there first, closed them. "You're staying here."

"You'll have to chain me up to stop me from going to him."

"Fine."

Baylor tugged off the belt fastening his robe. He tied one end to the bedpost in a knot and chanted magick words in a low voice. Understanding dawned in her eyes, and she tried to bolt, but he easily caught her, and looped the other end around her wrist.

His knot was secure, leaving enough slack as to not cut off her circulation.

When he returned, wearing the thick glove and the bracelet Nicolas had given him, she still sat on the bed. Baylor untied her. "I'm sorry, sweetheart, but I have to do this," he said quietly. The sterling silver bracelet clicked onto her slim wrist like a manacle.

A soft cry fled her lips as she tugged at it. Baylor pulled his glove off, his heart twisting at the panic squeezing her face.

"You told Nicolas about the blood spell… Please, Baylor, get it off!"

"I can't. You know Damian's rules. You have to wear it for the next two weeks, no matter what. You're free to go wherever you want, but the bracelet stays on."

He brushed his lips against her temple, but she jerked away. The stamp of deep hurt in her eyes sliced him like a hot knife across his flesh.

She turned away. "Get out of here. I don't even want to look at you."

Emotion squeezed his throat. Baylor fisted his hands. "Katia, this is to keep you safe, not just as punishment. I'd never hurt you. Ever."

As he went to close the door behind him, he heard her soft reply.

"But you already have."

SIX

"I want to return to my family's home in the Colorado mountains."

Katia's heart pounded as she faced Nicolas and Baylor in the living room. They said her father was a Morph. She owed them her loyalty, but didn't she owe it to her father more? If she could find the secret spell her mother had hidden away, the one too powerful to use except in the most extreme circumstances…she might even reverse her father's evil. But then what? Didn't family come first?

But how could she leave Baylor? Even though his shocking confession had deeply troubled and saddened her, she knew that leaving him would be the most difficult choice of all. Because, in spite of his words, Baylor would never join with her father. Katia felt a lump clog her throat.

"Why?" Nicolas asked.

"I need my mother's journal."

Baylor sat near the pine coffee table, his thighs splayed open, his arms dangling over the chair's sides. "Katia, we searched your home when you came to us. Thoroughly."

"She hid it to prevent Morphs from finding it. It had a mixture of powerful spells in it. I wasn't strong enough back then to go with you. But I need to go now."

His steely gaze locked with hers. "Truth between us always, Katia. What's in the journal?"

She dragged in a breath. "The full white light spell. The one I did wasn't strong enough. This one is. And my mother's journal can tell me what really happened to my family, why they vanished."

A hollow ache settled in her chest. "It might even tell me the promise I made to my father."

Nicolas's mouth compressed. "I gave you one day. Your father is still locked up, so it's safe. But the bracelet stays on so you'll need an escort." He turned to Baylor. "You'll need something other than that pricey-ass import of yours. Take my truck."

"Your truck can't wheeze its way up an anthill. Ryan's SUV has a better ride. I'll leave him my Jag," Baylor replied.

"You act like you have a claim on me." Katia glared at Baylor.

He sat beside her, cupping her chin and forcing it up to meet his stone-gray gaze. "I do. And I'm not willing to relinquish that claim."

Silence hung between them during the drive to Silverton. Trees stripped of their leaves and frost-covered fields of rust-colored grass passed by their windows. His thick cable-knit sweater, wool trousers and leather jacket failed to keep out the icy cold piercing his body at the thought of the answers Katia might find. Baylor clutched the steering wheel with white-knuckled intensity as he drove north on the two-lane highway.

Dressed in a heavy blue sweater, jeans and sneakers, Katia stared at the passing scenery. Baylor cleared his throat and forced out the words.

"Katia, all I ever cared about is your happiness. I can't even begin to think of what you're going through right now. I wish things could be different for you. But there can be no change."

His heart lurched again at her frozen tone. "So your answer is to kill him. My own father."

A light snow frosted the ground as they drove past the town of Silverton and into the mountains. Baylor became pressingly aware of the isolation. Shadows lengthened and deepened. Theirs was the sole vehicle on the road.

After a while he reached the turnoff and hooked a left, climbing up a steep drive. In the clearing he saw a single-story house. The paint was faded, and the house looked abandoned and was in a state of disrepair. Baylor parked, shut off the ignition and glanced at her.

"Stay here until I come out."

No birds sung in the overhead trees. Only the cold wind whispered against the leafless limbs. A lingering air of evil clung to the house's exterior.

Baylor approached the front door and jiggled the knob. Unlocked. He went inside, investigating each room, and climbed down to the basement. It appeared welcoming and cozy with the murals of mountains painted on the concrete walls, comfortable couches and chairs by the fireplace.

Near an old-fashioned stereo there was a stack of albums. Baylor shifted through them, smiling a little as he came upon a fat Elvis album that bulged oddly. He peeked inside and saw not one, but a couple of vinyl records inside. A smile touched his face. He'd done the same, lost album covers and stuffed other records inside. Baylor brought the musty cover to his nose, inhaling it. Katia's scent still lingered.

He closed his eyes, grief engulfing him as the house's enormous sorrow squeezed him.

Baylor picked up the Elvis album. Maybe it would cheer her. Katia didn't look at him as he placed it in the SUV.

Those lovely ice-blue eyes were sad as they regarded him, "Baylor, I need to do this alone, to make peace, and try to jog my memory."

Reluctantly, he agreed. Baylor kept guard outside, sitting on the stone bench by the long-dead garden. Finally she came out and sat next to him.

"I found nothing and remembered nothing." Her lush, melodious voice was as quiet as the cold air brushing over the mountains.

Baylor cupped her face. "Are you okay?"

"Fine." She pulled free. "Sometimes we hid very important documents in the shed. It's out back."

"I'll check it out first."

Everything appeared normal. He scented nothing, his wolf senses not alerting him to danger. Still, he couldn't shake off an uneasy feeling as he sat on the stone bench, waiting for Katia to return.

His cell rang. Baylor checked caller ID. Home. "What's up?"

"Where's Katia?"

The low urgency in Nicolas's voice made Baylor's skin crawl. "She's here, with me. We're just about to leave."

"Do it, now. Ryan went to check the shed and James is gone. Katia's spell must have worn off and James regained strength. We don't know when he escaped."

Baylor thumbed off the phone. As a Morph, James could shift into a bird, track them and fly straight to Katia.

He raced toward the shed, his mouth dry, his heart pounding with panic. As he rounded the corner, he heard her scream.

Baylor pumped his legs faster, praying he was not too late.

The man standing before her wore a chambray work shirt, jeans and worn boots. He looked like her father.

But he had literally appeared out of the sky. As she'd left the shed, Katia heard a flap of wings overhead. When the owl landed, it shifted.

Into the man who had raised her, burped her as a baby, who screamed at her as Morphs engulfed him with their sharp talons...

"Papa," she whispered.

He was a Morph and the truth slammed into her like a solid punch. Only Morphs could shape-shift into other animal forms.

"Hello, Katia. At last we found each other."

"Why did you follow me here?"

"I had to. The blood spell is too powerful, and it called me, your last living male blood relative, to your side. You called me out of hiding. I could not fight the spell. So here I am."

Baylor had never lied to her. She trusted him. She no longer trusted her father.

Instinct and emotion warred. "Why, Papa? Why didn't you ever look for me before?"

"You're light and goodness. And we know what happens when light meets darkness. Light pushes it aside." He stepped closer. "And so you found me."

The bright smile faded. Yellow fangs grew in his mouth. His features shifted, as he began to shrivel, his voice deepening to a raspy hollow.

"I'm hungry and desperate. And I need you," it rasped.

Terror lashed her as her mouth went dry. Katia stumbled backward. Her father changed, the thick hair turning wispy and greasy, the handsome face elongating and growing gaunt. His eyes, pitch-black. Soulless.

"No," she cried out. "I chanted a spell to bring out the goodness, there has to be some spark left in you."

"I didn't think you were alive. And then you broke through and found me and called me to your side. But I need your energy, Katia. The energy from your death."

Bent over, his hunched figure was a nightmare from the primordial ooze of her darkest fears. Talons erupted from his fingertips.

She screamed.

"Leave her alone!"

Baylor's voice echoed over the mountain. He waved his hands as he ran, shape-shifting into a wolf. Just as quickly, James shifted. The two wolves collided, biting and snarling.

Katia waved her hands, but nothing happened. The bracelet, the damn bracelet. It prohibited her from doing magick. Baylor, the stronger gray wolf, tore at her father's flank. James retreated, blood streaming from his fur. Baylor bared his fangs, growling, slowly approaching him.

Baylor would kill him.

Suddenly James shifted into his human form, clad in work shirt and jeans. He held out his hands to Katia. "Help me. I can change back into Draicon, only you can turn me from the evil I am. Don't let him hurt me."

"Papa."

"Don't listen to him, Katia. He'll kill you, absorb your fear and grow stronger." Baylor had shifted back to his clothed human form, two silver daggers in his palms.

"Baylor, please, wait."

Baylor turned, saw her expression. He hesitated. It proved his undoing.

James leaped up, bursting into a cloud of stinging insects, swarming at Baylor. Baylor swatted at them and cursed, but then they flew overhead to the rocky mountain slope above them. Horrified, Katia watched as James shifted again into her father.

A cruel smile touched his mouth as he threw a man-sized boulder at her. Baylor shouted and pushed Katia aside.

The rock fell on his legs, pinning him. Baylor writhed, trying to lift it, but then her father turned into a bird and flew down. James landed, and shifted into his human self. Hatred twisted his face as he stalked toward Baylor.

He was going to kill him and feed on his dying fear.

Her father was family. But he had turned evil and was Morph.

The full impact of the spell she'd performed earlier hit her like a splash of icy water. Finally, she understood and accepted the truth of Baylor's words.

You can't change him. But you can save Baylor.

With a shriek, she charged. Power and purpose filled her as she grabbed one of Baylor's dropped daggers and barreled into her father. As James tumbled onto his back, she jumped atop his chest and lifted the knife.

Katia hesitated and stared down at his face. Tormented eyes, blue as her own, stared back.

"Why?" she asked brokenly.

"I'm sorry, Peanut. Do it. Now. Please."

Peanut. He'd never called her Peanut before. Confusion washed over her. Someone else had, but who? Grief-stricken, she stared down at him. Then she dimly heard him whisper. *Release me*.

The blade sank deep into his heart. Acid blood spurted, splashed over her clothing. With a shudder, James lay still and died.

She climbed off, watching as if from a great distance as he dissolved into ash. "Papa," she whispered.

Baylor freed himself, pushing the boulder off his legs as she ran to him. He struggled to his feet, grimacing as he limped. "Katia, I'm so sorry," he said thickly.

"I killed my own father. What does that make me, Baylor? A murderer."

"It makes you a survivor, with a broken heart." Anguish flashed in his eyes. "Damn, I wish I could have saved you from this."

"It had to be me, so I could finally let him go." Her vision blurred as warmth trickled down her cheeks. "The spell I did as a safeguard finally worked on me. It was a truth spell, so I would not be blinded by emotion. He was Morph. And he was going to kill the one I love."

She turned away, letting the wind dry her tears as Baylor slid his arms around her.

SEVEN

Baylor felt his bones knit back together as Katia drove them back to the lodge. Any attempts he'd made at cajoling Katia into conversation were met with dead silence. The one he loved was hurting bad and he couldn't comfort her.

When she pulled in front of the lodge, parked and switched off the ignition, he placed a hand over hers. "Katia, talk to me. Tell me what you're feeling."

For a few minutes she said nothing. When she spoke, the grief in her voice laced him.

"My family is really gone now. I feel so broken."

Baylor tenderly cupped her cheek. "You're a broken soul, just as I am. Our destined mates are gone, and our families. But we have each other."

"It was meant to be. He needed me to release him. He looked peaceful, at the end."

He held her close. Giving her all his strength, as she had been strong for him and saved him. Her smile was sad as he kissed her. Baylor let her go into the house.

After a debriefing by Nicolas, Baylor showered and shaved, racking his brain for ways he could make her smile again, and to laugh. First she needed healing. She had lost something very precious to her all over.

Baylor suddenly remembered the album he'd left in the SUV. He brought it into the living room. Maybe Elvis would make her feel better.

He slid out the three records and placed them on the table. But the album still bulged oddly. Baylor opened the album sleeve wide and shook it. A slim notebook spilled onto the floor. His pulse raced.

Her mother's journal.

Baylor hesitated and then opened it and read. Overwhelming joy filled his heart. "I know how to make you laugh again, Katie," he said aloud.

He dialed the number in the journal. Baylor talked a few minutes to the male Draicon on the phone, and then he was put on the phone with a woman whose voice was as soft and gentle as Katia's.

They talked for a few minutes, but her next words made his blood pressure plummet. Baylor squeezed the phone so tight, his knuckles whitened. He closed his eyes, leaning against the kitchen counter. How could he do this? Let her go?

Finally, he spoke, his heart so heavy it felt like a steel lump inside his chest.

After he hung up, he went upstairs to Katia's room, clutching her mother's journal.

Katia was cleaning the candles off her table. Baylor fingered bits of melted wax.

"Katia, that spell you did, it was a blood spell to call any male relative to your side."

She gave him a puzzled look. "Yes. Why do you ask?"

"Did your father ever call you 'Peanut'?"

She frowned. "It's odd. He never did. And yet he did just before I…" Her voice trailed off as she stared into the distance as if recalling a memory. "Papa always called me his princess. My cousin Gerry called me 'Peanut' because I was the youngest."

"It wasn't your father you killed, sweetheart, but your cousin Gerry. He must have duplicated your father's human form to fool you into thinking your father was alive so you would trust him."

She took the journal he held out.

"Your mother wrote that Gerry turned Morph by killing his parents. He buried the bodies and convinced your cousins to turn. Your mother chanted the white light spell, and your Draicaron insisted on finding Gerry to see if it worked."

Blood drained from her face as the impact of his words sank in. "I remember now. Gerry killed him. I heard his screams, and Mama destroyed the written spell. She refused to let anyone else make that mistake."

He gently cupped her cheek, holding her like a frail glass bottle as if she'd shatter. "Your candle spells protected everyone inside. But when your aunts and uncles left the house to search for their children…"

Katia's lower lip wobbled precariously. "They refused to believe their own children would murder them to turn Morph. They said I wasn't telling the truth about Gerry. I kept pleading with them not to leave, they were walking to their deaths."

"Your father insisted on defending his home. And your mother and sisters were determined to stay with him. So were you, because your candle magick was powerful."

"It wasn't powerful enough," she whispered. "I couldn't save any of them."

"Yes, you did, sweetheart. It was you who saved your mother and sisters."

She stared at him with a mixture of joy and incredulity. "What do you mean?"

"Because your magick was the strongest, you promised that you would stay and protect your father. Your promise convinced your mothers and sisters to flee to a friend's pack in Alaska. Your father let you remain only because you made a promise to run if your cousins managed to break into the house. James knew you would want to fight, but you had to survive. That was the promise you made."

He kissed the tears off her cheeks. "You remembered how important the journal was because your mother told you she'd write in there the phone number to where they are staying. I called and spoke to her. She had sent people from the pack to look for you, but the Morphs had destroyed all your scent markers so you couldn't be traced. She's now waiting for your call."

The journal fell to the floor as Katia squeezed him hard. "That's why I played those Elvis songs. I burned the memory into my brain to help me find her journal."

"It wasn't the music. There is hope for you yet. What a relief," he said dryly.

She burst into laughter. He grinned.

He'd made her laugh again, and relished the joyful sound. Her family was alive after all. *And what if she decides to return with them? Leaving you behind*?

Baylor ignored the hollow ache in his chest as he held her in his arms.

A week later, Katia's mother and sisters were due to arrive. When the bell rang, Baylor opened the door without hesitation. Four blond female Draicon came inside, escorted by ten grim-faced, burly males. Katia sprang to her feet as Baylor ushered them inside.

"Someone's here for you, sweetheart," he told her tenderly.

"Mama," she whispered. "Janice, Detra, Cindy!"

Love engulfed her as they embraced. Her mother's voice sounded just as soothing as it had years ago.

"Honey, we looked and never found you. We thought you were dead."

"I'm here, Mama." Choked with emotion, she couldn't stop hugging them. Katia's heart felt full to bursting as they talked, laughed, and caught up.

The males from Ronin's pack went to the room's far side. They kept glaring at Baylor, lounging against a window.

"We'll take you back. You belong with your family, Katia." Her mother patted her hand.

Katia glanced over her shoulder at Baylor, standing near the window, who gazed at her so tenderly that her breath hitched. How many females were as lucky as her to be loved this much? She glanced back at her mother.

"Mama, why didn't you keep looking for me? Why did you give up?"

"Oh, honey, I didn't want to give up. But Ronin sent his best trackers, and they could not pick up your scent. He said you probably had been destroyed by Morphs like they had killed your father."

Her mother looked away, her lips trembling. "I just couldn't face coming back here, knowing your father was dead. I kept hoping you'd find the journal so you had a way back to me. I never imagined you'd become so traumatized you'd forget everything I told you, even where I hid it. I love you so much, Katia. If I could do it over again, I'd leave everything to find you." Tears brimmed in her eyes. "But now you're with us, and we'll never be separated again."

She hugged her mother again. "Never again, Mama. And I have news. I'm taking a special someone with me, Mama. Baylor."

Silence hung between them. Then her mother spoke, her eyes stricken. "It's not possible, honey. Ronin's pack, one reason we were accepted was because they have so few females. They won't allow an outside male."

Katia's heart lurched. "He's a valiant fighter, a loyal one. I love him, how can I tell him?"

"He already knows. I told him when he called. He told me that the decision was yours. He would not stand in the way of your choice. He only wants to make you happy."

Her mother sighed. "And if he wants you to be happy, he'll

understand your decision to leave here. We're your family, Katia, all you have left. Family comes above all else, remember?"

Katia studied Baylor across the room. How could she choose between her beloved mother and sisters and the male she loved?

Emotion clogged her throat. "I have to go think, Mama." She went outside to ruminate over the hardest decision of all.

Two hours later, Katia found Baylor still in the living room by the window, looking sad.

His face went expressionless as he glanced at her. "Have you made your decision, Katia? Are you ready to commit?"

She slid her arms around his waist. "Yes, I have. I'm making the only commitment I can make. Here, with you and our pack."

"Katia," he said thickly, embracing her. Baylor rested his cheek against the top of her head. "Are you certain? They're your blood, your family."

"And you're my missing half. Not of my soul as a destined mate is, but my heart. We're two broken pieces made whole. How can I leave my heart behind?"

He said nothing, but took her mouth in a hard kiss, a possessive one that sent fire singing through her veins. Baylor pulled back, giving her a tender look.

For a moment she rested against him, feeling peace settle over her heart. "I told my mother, and I think she understands. I can visit them, but I'm staying here with you. I love you, Baylor. I've always loved you. In my heart, my soul, my mind. I love my mother and sisters as well, but you come first. I thought about how you found me four years ago, broken and defeated, and you made me whole. And I realized if I were lost from you, you would never stop looking for me," she whispered.

He stroked her hair. "I would always search for you. Long ago you made a promise to your father. I'm making one to you now. I promise to try to make you happy. Because I love you so much, it's all I ever wanted, for you to be happy."

They went upstairs to her room, stripped off their clothing and fell onto her bed. As he stroked her, murmuring endearments, she hooked her arms about his neck.

Slowly, he parted her legs and entered her. His thrusts were gentle as he stared down at her intently.

Katia let all her love for him shine in her eyes. Emotions rushed to the surface and she did not suppress them. They made tender love and when she climaxed, her gaze focused on Baylor as he regarded her tenderly.

He held her in his arms after as she rested her head on his shoulder.

"I want Nicolas to mate us in a formal ceremony," she said, stroking the hard muscles of his chest. "Let's do it today."

"Impatient, aren't we," he teased.

"I need you. I love you so much, Baylor."

"Katie, darling, don't worry. You have me for a lifetime."

"Maybe long enough, as long as we're together," she replied, kissing him.

* * * * *

Choose the romance that suits your reading mood

Suspense and Paranormal

Harlequin Intrigue®
Breathtaking romantic suspense.
Crime stories that will keep you
on the edge of your seat.

Silhouette® Romantic Suspense
Heart-racing sensuality and the
promise of a sweeping romance
set against the backdrop of
suspense.

Silhouette® Nocturne™
Dark and sensual paranormal
romance reads that stretch
the boundaries of conflict and
desire, life and death.

Look for these and many other Harlequin and Silhouette romance books wherever books are sold, including most bookstores, supermarkets, drugstores and discount stores.

SMP60SUSPENSERI

Choose the romance that suits your reading mood

Passion

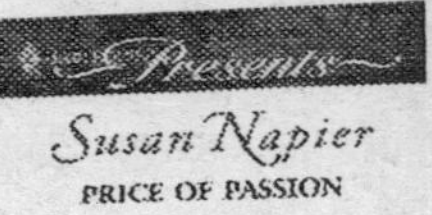

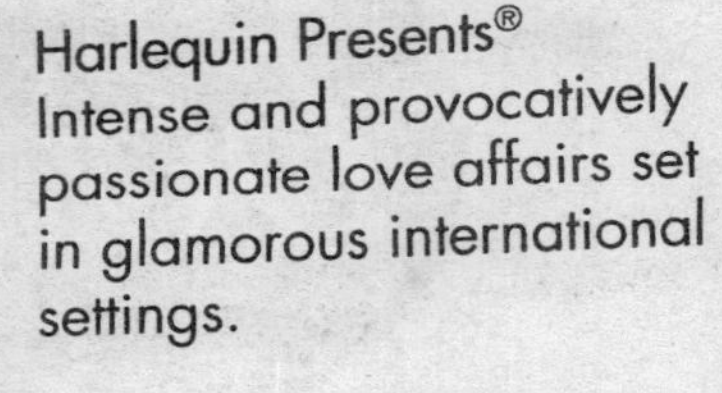

Harlequin Presents®
Intense and provocatively passionate love affairs set in glamorous international settings.

Silhouette Desire®
Rich, powerful heroes and scandalous family sagas.

Harlequin® Blaze™
Fun, flirtatious and steamy books that tell it like it is, inside and outside the bedroom.

Look for these and many other Harlequin and Silhouette romance books wherever books are sold, including most bookstores, supermarkets, drugstores and discount stores.

SMP60PASSIONR